THE HOME TEAM

Written from Dave's deep knowledge of tactical operations and martial arts, and with a Northwest flair mixed in, *The Home Team* grabs you from the start and surprises you at the end. As Dave's former pastor, it was thrilling to read a story of authentic faith lived out in gripping circumstances. A great read that is both tightly written and timely.

Rev. Brian Wiele
www.bluespigot.org

The Home Team is a wonderful story that weaves Dave Pratt's life experience as a Tae Kwan Do master, Christian, and retired army officer. It is a reminder that God's will, love, and guidance are everywhere. Dave brings together his military experience, lifelong journey in martial arts, and his commitment to God and blends it into an action-packed, compelling story of human nature, conflict, faith, and self-discovery. It has the power to touch the heart and to awaken consciousness. It is a story well-worth reading and contains a message we can all relate to.

Grand Master Richard Na
Master Na's Black Belt Academy

Dave's rich personal experience as a martial arts master, military officer, and Christian brings *The Home Team* to life and gives it an amazing sense of reality. The action is tight and real, and Dave places you right there in the middle of the lives and actions of the Home Team. The locations come alive, and the characters are rich with real life and faith challenges. Dave is a wonderful storyteller who draws you into this exciting adventure and baffling mystery. What a joy to read a fantastic, high-quality, action adventure of people living out their faith in very difficult circumstances. It challenges us to grow and live out our faith in what may seem to us as challenging circumstances. *The Home Team* is a great read that is hard to put down. It is a book with character that anyone in the family can read and enjoy.

Robert Samuelson

Retired Pastor and Dave's brother in Christ

THE HOME TEAM

DAVE PRATT

AMBASSADOR INTERNATIONAL
GREENVILLE, SOUTH CAROLINA & BELFAST, NORTHERN IRELAND

www.ambassador-international.com

THE HOME TEAM

ISBN: 978-1-64960-401-9
eISBN: 978-1-64960-450-7
Library of Congress Control Number: 2022947554

Cover Design by Hannah Linder Designs
Interior Typesetting by Dentelle Design
Edited by Martin Wiles

AMBASSADOR INTERNATIONAL
Emerald House
411 University Ridge, Suite B14
Greenville, SC 29601
United States
www.ambassador-international.com

AMBASSADOR BOOKS
The Mount
2 Woodstock Link
Belfast, BT6 8DD
Northern Ireland, United Kingdom
www.ambassadormedia.co.uk

The colophon is a trademark of Ambassador, a Christian publishing company.

This book is dedicated to Jesus Christ for His unwavering forgiveness, mercy, and grace and for not giving up on me or the people I served with when any of us were placed in harm's way.

And to my beloved wife, Rafaela, who provided me with my own special Home Team.

Special thanks also go to my readers, Sharon and Robert, for their keen eye, faith, and biblical knowledge, the Ambassador International team for their faith in the story, and Martin Wiles for his insightful editorial guidance.

CHAPTER 1

Through the binoculars, Major Sam Anthem carefully scanned the small adobe shack, squatting in the middle of the clearing. Through the two open, pane-less windows that he could see from his position, he methodically cataloged the silhouettes of three men facing away from him on the near side of the building's interior and two more leaning against the far wall. All held some sort of rifle. All but one looked quite young, perhaps in their teens. And they must have been rank amateurs since they allowed someone on the outside to profile them.

Sam squatted just inside a thick canopy of pine trees that towered over him. The lush green plant growth surrounding him would have been beautiful on a travel brochure, but in the oppressing midday Mexican heat on this humid morning, all he could smell was decaying vegetation and his own sweat.

He brushed the thumb-sized beetle that perched on the toe of his soft-soled tactical boots. "Sorry, little guy," he muttered. "I'm not on your menu today."

Still scanning the building's interior, he noticed one silhouette that stood out from the others. A female—and possibly the person identified in the morning's mission brief he and the other three members of his team had been provided before they had infiltrated this portion of the Mexican countryside.

A click sounded over the cochlear implant behind his left ear. Much like the implants used to aid the deaf, the implants he and his team used provided secure message radio reception. A button on the smartwatches they wore allowed them to change frequencies for the implants as well as provided a convenient microphone for transmitting.

"Home Team . . . status?" The voice sounded like the speaker stood right next to him, but it was transmitted from a small, nondescript office building in northern Florida, home base for the Extreme Operations Group.

"Overwatch, this is Mike Tango. Status is one and holding," Sam replied, using his call sign and the number one to indicate he'd arrived at his assigned checkpoint.

"Foxtrot X-ray, one and standing by," Allen Farrell added. A tall, lean twenty-nine-year-old with long, blond hair, fair skin, and eyes so blue they stopped everyone in their tracks, Allen was point for the mission. A skilled operator known as Fox to the members of the Home Team, Allen held multiple master-level certificates in Okinawan Karate, American Kenpo, and Brazilian Ju-Jitsu and functioned as the team's expert in all things explosive.

"Romeo Mike, also status one and ready," Leah McCarthy, one of the two female members of his team, replied. Dubbed Romeo by the team, Leah was the team's armorer and sniper. At five-one, twenty-eight years old and with thick, sunset bronze hair and wide, dark eyes, she was often mistaken as the diminutive, soft woman she appeared to be. It was a judgment people made only once about the strong, driven woman with whipcord muscles. She hated the

"Romeo" moniker the team assigned her, insisting it should be used for a male team member, but it only encouraged her teammates to use the nickname more.

The final member of the team, Jessica Falcone, was the last to respond. "This is Charlie Papa. Status is one and ready." She was a tall, elegant thirty-year-old with thick hair the color of darkest night, bronze skin, and piercing brown eyes. Dubbed by the team as Cap, Jessica possessed the brain of Einstein, the trim of a professional athlete, and the fighting skills of a mixed martial arts champion—which she was. In addition to holding her own in just about any scrape, Cap guided the team through the myriad political and technological issues that confronted them as they carried out their unique sorts of missions that the Extreme Operations Group required.

Sam considered the adobe hut before him as Overwatch reached out to him once more. "Mike Tango? What's the hold?"

Sam sighed. He'd been looking forward to his team's latest mission. But more than once in recent months, he'd been diverted from the team's primary mission to clean up some secondary mess, such as rescuing yet another civilian who'd gotten lost in the jungle or kidnapped by bandits.

"I need a vacation," he whispered, then felt guilty at the thought. When it came right down to it, he had little to complain about. Working for the U.S. State Department's Extreme Operations Group was what he'd trained for all his adult life. Rescuing this woman was a priority mission for his team, and today, it would be his job to complete that mission.

The group's director had briefed the team about a special Non-Governmental Organization (NGO) staff member missing in the area:

Consuelo Zamora, a popular Christian missionary and medical aid worker known throughout Mexico as Paloma Blanca. She'd disappeared two days before. They suspected kidnapping for ransom, but no ransom demand had yet materialized. The director designated her rescue as a high priority for the team, should the opportunity arise . . . and it had.

On his final scan of the tiny adobe hut, Sam caught a good look at the face of the woman as she leaned away from the building's shadowed back wall and into the light. She was beautiful. Slender build, dark eyes, raven-colored hair, and mocha skin. He could swear their eyes met when he paused to examine her face through his field glasses. He called up her photo on the small tablet computer strapped to his left forearm and compared it with the woman in the adobe. There could be no doubt. It was Consuelo.

With the identity confirmed, Sam whispered into his wrist mic, "This is Mike Tango. I have eyes on the secondary objective. She's captive in a small adobe thirty feet north of my location. I see five tangos with the subject, which seems like a lot of guards for a single hostage. Tangos are armed."

Overwatch waited several beats before replying. "Understood. There's no way they could know we would be looking for her today, so I'm uncertain why the numbers should be so high. Can you handle the rescue solo, Empty, or do you need assistance?"

That Overwatch dispensed with radio protocol and called him by his team nickname spoke volumes, suggesting the staff at headquarters might share his frustration at one of their operatives being diverted from the team's primary mission. Today's op-plan marked a major departure in how the group and its boss, the U.S. Secretary of State, dealt with drug cartels south of the Mexican border.

A lot rested on the mission's first-time approach to addressing the constant drug flow into the United States and turning that around.

"Looks like amateur hour at this end, Overwatch," Sam replied. "I'm good solo on this one."

"Roger, Mike Tango. Moving Empty to the secondary frequency," Overwatch replied. "Fox, Cap, and Romeo, you are go for the primary mission on the current frequency."

"Good luck, guys," Sam whispered.

"No luck needed, Empty. A simple paintball game at our end," Fox replied with a laugh. "What I want to know is how you always get to rescue the girl?"

"Short straw again, Fox." Sam chuckled, although his heart wasn't in it.

"Radio discipline, people," Overwatch reminded them.

Sam heard a soft click as Overwatch moved him to the secondary frequency and then said, "You are go for the secondary target, Mike Tango."

"I am status two for the secondary target," Sam replied, using the number that indicated his readiness to engage his target. "Let me know how they do."

"Roger that," came Overwatch's soft reply.

Sam slipped his small rucksack from his back and eased it to the forest floor atop his carbine, hiding both just inside the thick growth. For what he had to do, the short-barreled tactical rifle would be in the way. He ran a hand across his tactical vest, once again giving thanks for recent improvements that kept its body armor thin, flexible, and light yet still able to stop anything short of a .50 round. He checked the Sig Sauer 226 in its thigh holster again. He considered leaving it behind with the vest but relented in favor of the group's policy to always be armed.

He eased himself into the clearing surrounding the small building. The sun hit him like a hammer as he left the forest's shade and scrambled forward a few steps at a time, pausing for a beat and then moving again as he watched for anyone looking out the adobe's windows and for the venomous snakes that populated the area. Halfway to the building, he dropped and crawled the remainder of the way. With the one window facing him and the apparent absence of anyone on guard, staying out of sight was simple. He neither heard nor saw any response to his approach.

He assumed the door was on the opposite side of the building and considered edging around the perimeter of the building and entering there but discarded the thought. Too far to go and too much risk moving through the dry brush surrounding the building and being heard or seen. The window nearest him was nothing more than a square hole in the adobe wall, not more than three feet above the ground but large enough for him to vault through.

Sam pulled a small directional mirror from his cargo pants pocket, extending the mirror's handle and easing it up to just above the windowsill. As he expected. Five tangos and the woman. Four of the tangos stood around the perimeter of the room. One boy stood just inside and to the left of the window. Two more leaned against the opposite west wall on either side of the adobe's single open door. Another leaned against the north wall to the right of Sam's position.

The fifth tango's position caused Sam to pause. Not more than twelve or thirteen years old, the boy held an aged M16 rifle with a rusted barrel and stood in front of the Zamora woman, feet wide and braced as though guarding her rather than holding her captive.

Sam adjusted the mirror to examine the woman's face, looking for bruises, cuts, or any sign of injury that might hamper her rescue and their subsequent escape. He saw none, but instead found the deepest brown, most expressive eyes he had ever seen staring right back at him. Set in an oval, tanned face with a small but strong chin, full lips, and a straight, strong nose, her stare took away his breath.

"Steady, boy," he whispered to himself.

"Say again?" came Overwatch's reply, Sam again forgetting his mic remained open.

"Status is three," Sam replied, ignoring the question and confirming he was ready to move inside.

As Sam watched, the woman dropped her eyes to the boy squatting in front of her and moved her head slowly left and then right. *Okay,* Sam thought. The fifth tango would get the benefit of the doubt for now. But if he raised that rifle at all, it would be the end of his short career as a cartel soldier.

"You are go for engagement. God speed," Overwatch replied.

With the last word barely out of Overwatch's mouth, Sam placed his right hand on the windowsill and vaulted through the opening. As his feet struck ground, he lashed out a left knife-hand strike. The hard, calloused edge of his hand struck the boy to the left of the window on the temple, dropping him, his AK rattling to the ground beside him.

Sam took two rapid sliding steps across the room and faced the two guards on either side of the door, noting that they, too, were young and also armed with M16s. Both appeared to come out of a dazed slumber as he simultaneously jabbed a lights-out punch to the jaw of the boy on the right and delivered a side kick to the head of the one on the left. They both dropped, their weapons clattering to the floor beside them.

Sam moved like a blur across the small room to the fourth guard standing at the north wall. The young man managed to raise his rifle before Sam dropped low and side-stepped under the rifle's barrel. Sam heard the click of the rifle's safety coming off as he reached the boy. He jerked the rifle away with his left hand and landed a straight-fingered punch with his right hand to the boy's sternum. The boy gasped as the air left his lungs. Sam cast the rifle aside and chopped the meaty edges of both hands to opposite sides of the boy's neck. The simultaneous strikes compressed critical arteries, cutting off the flow of oxygen to the brain. The boy's eyes rolled up as he joined the other guards on the floor, unconscious.

The entire engagement lasted less than a minute. Sam let out a long breath and turned to find the woman and her guard standing before him, the boy's eyes defiant. No more than five feet separated them, and Sam noticed that the boy's finger was on the trigger guard, not the trigger.

Consuelo placed a hand on the boy's shoulder and said in rapid Spanish, "Coloca tu rifle en el suelo. Este hombre not te hara dano."

Despite her words, the barrel of the boy's rifle did not move.

Sam chuckled, although there was little humor in his tone. "Ma'am, I did not understand your words, but if he keeps that rifle pointed at me, I will have to hurt him."

The woman eased the M16's barrel down until it pointed to the ground. The boy kept the barrel pointed as she directed but retained his guarding stance between Sam and the woman.

The threat past, Sam keyed his wrist mic. "Overwatch, Mike Tango. Secondary objective is secure. Two for exfiltration at the rendezvous point in twenty mikes."

Interrupted by a light touch of a hand on his shoulder, Sam turned to meet those dark eyes once again. "The boy goes with us," she said.

"Ma'am, my job is to get you to a haven," Sam countered. "I have no orders about taking this budding drug-runner with us."

"The cartel killed his family," she said. "He was forced into this. I have known his grandparents for years and have seen dozens of boys like him forced into the cartels. He is a good boy. He goes with us, or I will not go with you."

"Ma'am," Sam started.

The look she gave him, one of deep concern and even deeper resolution, settled the issue.

Sam waved a hand around the room and found it hard to keep the sarcasm from his words. "What about the rest of these young men? You want to bring them, too?"

"They're not dead?"

Sam shook his head. "No, ma'am. They will wake up sore but will live to a ripe, old age if the cartel lets them."

"Thank you for that," she replied. "But Antonio comes with us."

Sam gave her one last pleading glance, then shrugged, keyed his mic, and said, "Overwatch, make that three for exfil."

CHAPTER 2

Just over a mile away, Cartel boss Carlos Estevez enjoyed the midday meal with his only daughter and two grandchildren in the first-floor dining room of his massive hacienda, escaping the oppressive heat and ever-present taste of dust in the air. Sitting in the center of a large, rectangular compound surrounded by high, barbed wire-topped adobe walls with guard towers at each corner and the gates, the compound stood as a testament to the old drug lord's prominence in Mexico's growing illegal drug trade.

Sunlight winked through the dining room's tall, multi-paned stained-glass windows as he and his small family enjoyed a meal of carne asada, tortillas, and fresh fruit—gathered from the hillsides beyond the thick woods that surrounded the Estevez compound. With the aroma of fresh-made tortillas in the air, his thoughts wandered back to a time when there were many more people at this table and his two sons' laughter echoed through the house. But that was years ago before the Mexican and United States governments had joined forces against him and his peers. So many of his people had died during that time, with many interdicted shipments and burned poppy fields laid to waste.

The detestable U.S. agents appeared and disappeared like ghosts, untouchable by his men no matter how they prepared and no matter how many he hired to scour the countryside. He smiled grimly. Perhaps the next time would be different. For the first time, he had information he might be able to use against the Americans.

His thoughts were interrupted as a window shattered, sending down shards of glass along with droplets of thick red fluid.

"Quickly!" he called in rapid Spanish to his daughter. "Take the children to the safe room."

More glass shattered as his daughter hurried the children from the room. His brother, who managed the compound's guard security force, dashed into the room. "We are under attack!"

"Tell me something I don't know," Estevez called back as he retrieved his .45 caliber revolver from his desk across the room.

The two dashed through the hacienda's wide entry area to the front door, the staccato sound of weapons' fire rattling across the compound's dusty yard. Leaning into the opening to see what was happening outside, Estevez's brother was shoved back as bullets pounded his chest.

"I'm hit," he called as a deep red stain spread across his loose, white shirt and his knees buckled, dropping him to the floor. "Wait," he said in the next moment. "What is this? I'm not bleeding. These are not real bullets. They are fake and filled with red paint."

As the man spoke, a paint bullet struck him in the forehead and slammed him to his back. He struggled to his feet, rubbing a large red welt on his forehead. "They hurt, but they don't kill."

Estevez squatted down and peered around the base of the door frame, watching as a half dozen of his men dodged from the long bunkhouse on the opposite side of the compound to the tall, squat warehouse where he stored his finished product. One by one, they were knocked off their feet as they fired their weapons high over the compound's walls toward the dense tree line surrounding the compound.

As he watched, a man in the guard tower next to the front gate took several shots to his torso, spun, and tumbled from his perch—striking the dusty ground at the tower's base with a thud. The man staggered to his feet and limped away, cradling one arm. Estevez saw dark red blossoms color his chest.

All across the compound, red paint covered everything: his men, the two new pickup trucks, and his buildings. As the firing diminished, he noted that the people shooting the paint bullets focused the last of their crimson shots on the buildings in the compound, painting the warehouse's front door, one side of the long bunkhouse, and the front of the hacienda.

Finally, the firing stopped, and an oppressive silence replaced the terror and excitement of the past five minutes. Estevez stepped outside and was met by his other brother, who ran the cartel's information technology program.

"This is a mess," Estevez said. "But did you at least get some information we can use from your end?"

"Sorry, Jefe," the man replied. "The ghosts took out the compound's cameras at the beginning of the attack. I think it must be the sniper who is always with them. We have nothing."

"What about the little snare we set up with that religious medical worker?" Estevez asked.

"There, I have some good news," his brother replied. "Our sources were correct about the U.S. operatives not being able to resist freeing the woman we used as bait. We captured several clear video images of the operative sent to free her."

"A religious woman," Estevez murmured. "I was never sure we should have taken that one hostage. As you say, our informants suggested her to be a bait the Americans could not resist, but . . ."

Estevez's brother handed him a photo of Sam leading the woman and one of her guards away from the adobe hut after he had freed them. "But it worked, and we now have these photos. We overheard this man called 'Empty' by his handlers during the radio transmissions we intercepted."

"Empty?" Estevez rolled the word around on his tongue and hefted the photos in one hand as though they carried significant weight. "Now we know that our attackers are not ghosts but are men just like us. Pass the pictures around to our men so they can recognize this man if they see him again. Our sources in the U.S. may not have gotten the day of this attack right, but at least we got this."

"Yes, Jefe," his brother replied, "but why the red paint when they could have used real bullets and killed many of us?"

Estevez smiled grimly and settled his arm across his brother's shoulders. "It was a message, Hermano, a very important message."

CHAPTER 3

The next day, Consuelo Zamora stepped out of her hotel in downtown Aguascalientes, Mexico, punching numbers into her cell phone as she headed for a quick lunch on the city's broad, cobblestone plaza. She emerged from a tree-shrouded side street and into the wide, long plaza, inhaling the fragrant aroma of the abundant blooming flowers lining the walk.

Amazing, she thought, as she walked with the cell phone held to her ear, *that one day ago I was a prisoner in the backwoods of Mexico; and just twelve months ago, this plaza was deserted because of the Covid-19 pandemic.* Now, freed by her mysterious rescuer and with several vaccines available and distributed around the world, she and the people of this magnificent city were returning to their favorite places as though nothing had ever happened. Such a crazy world!

"Connie? Tell me you are safe, please," said the worried, female voice on the other end of the line.

Lucinda Meyers was a dedicated, passionate woman in her mid-forties. She was also the executive director of Christian Medical Outreach for Mexico, a nonprofit, nongovernmental organization that paid Consuelo's salary. Lucinda loved Consuelo like a sister, and Consuelo shared her feelings, as well as the commitment to the NGO's mission to serve the people of the Mexican frontier and spread the message of Jesus Christ.

"I am fine, Lucy," Consuelo replied. "I arrived late last evening after being rescued from the cartel—at least, I think it was the cartel."

"You're not hurt? You're not injured? Did they harm you in any way?" Lucy continued.

"I am fine, Hermana," Consuelo replied, using the Spanish word for sister.

Both Lucy and Consuelo were first-generation Mexican Americans with a deep love for both their native land and their adopted home. Both moved to the U.S. early in life. Lucy started the faith-based non-profit on a shoestring budget intending to help her native country toward a better future and a closer relationship with Christ. Consuelo joined Lucy at the Christian nonprofit a decade later to put her nursing skills and her faith to work serving God.

"Thank God," Lucy said. "I am not sending you out alone into that cartel-infested countryside again without bodyguards—ever!"

"I am fine, and you needn't make any promises about things you can't control. Besides, what do you always say about faith being our armor and Jesus Christ being the strong Shield that protects us?"

She heard Lucy sigh. "Don't you go putting words in my mouth, even if I do say them."

"I am fine, Lucy. God had my back, as always. He was my Shield and my Armor."

"You're right, of course, but when you went offline and I couldn't reach you, I thought I was going to have a stroke," Lucy said.

Consuelo continued her walk across the plaza as they talked. As the midday sun peaked in a crystal-clear, blue sky, she passed the massive Cathedral Basilica de Nuestra Senora de la Asuncion on her left with its towering bell towers, yellow stone walls, and wrap-around, wrought iron fence. Over her right shoulder stood the long, two-story building of the historic Palacio de Gobierno where Mexico's constitution was crafted. Mexico's rich history adorned every interior wall. Ahead of her stood the beautiful gardens where the city held concerts and other special events. She paused and spun on her heel, taking in a deep breath and admiring the downtown scenery. This was one of her favorite places in all of Mexico, and she relished the chance for another visit.

Gathering herself, she picked up her pace, her steps long and strong for a person of her diminutive size but conditioned by four years of working in environments that required a certain amount of fortitude. She wondered at all those years in some of the most dangerous but needy areas of the country. They had been good years in many ways with all the help she and her mission teams provided to the many small villages on the Mexican frontier. But they had also been difficult years. Kidnapped twice, she remained a realist about the danger of her work and considered that it might be time for a change.

"Connie? You still there?" Lucy asked.

Just ahead, Consuelo could see the green and beige patio umbrellas of the open-air cantina, which spread across the left side of the plaza, just beyond the ancient basilica.

"Sorry, Lucy. Lost in thought," Consuelo replied.

"I know you have been through a lot in the last few days—" Lucy started.

"I think we need to talk about that," Consuelo said before Lucy could finish.

She approached the maître de at the reception podium for the outdoor cantina. Twenty small, round tables surrounded by a velvet rope and silver posts demarked the cantina's boundaries. Each table boasted a green or beige umbrella opened and angled to protect patrons from the growing spring heat. It was the perfect setting for a relaxing interlude or a cool afternoon cerveza—exactly what she needed.

The maître de, an overweight, kind-faced man with a receding hairline recognized her from the many times she had frequented the cantina in the past and greeted her by name. "Paloma Blanca, I am so honored to see you again."

She returned his smile but waved off the profusion of words that might have followed. She recognized she was well known in this part of Mexico but did not relish the attention it brought. She did what she did for God and for those she served, not for the notoriety.

Still beaming but disappointed that he was unable to recite the speech he had in mind, the maître de nodded and led the way to a table located near two men and two women who relaxed over dessert. She absently scanned the faces of the people at that table but stopped when she reached the man sitting at the far side of the café's table. It was Mike Tango.

In the next second, her attention was drawn back to her phone as Lucy yelled, "What do you mean, Connie? What do we need to talk about? I don't like the tone of that . . ."

"I'm going to have to get back to you on that, Luce," Consuelo said, ending the call.

She ignored the maître de's wave toward her table and strode over to the four Americans. She stopped a step away from their table and smiled at Mike Tango. Only a day ago, he had rescued her from her captives, but at another level, it felt like ages.

"Mike Tango?" she asked, a broad smile crossing her face. She'd been told her eyes twinkled when she smiled like this, and she hoped they did now.

Cleaned up, Mike Tango appeared even more handsome than he had in the jungle. He had medium-length black hair and a physique that bordered on slender but with shoulder and chest muscles that strained his light, open-collar aloha shirt. His long face supported a small nose that appeared to have been broken multiple times. She noted the surprise in his wide, brown-eyed expression as he recognized her.

All four stood as soon as she spoke, although Mike knocked over his chair and a glass in the process.

The other man at the table, who now stood close to her, offered a smile she knew had been used on many a female. In size and physique, he matched Mike, but the similarities ended there. He had long, dirty blond hair, fair skin with a deep, fresh sunburn, and startling blue eyes.

The two women at the table could not have been more different. One was as tall as Mike and had ebony hair, a naturally tanned complexion that spoke of Mexican heritage, and intelligent, dark eyes. She was beautiful in her form-fitting jeans and a pale-blue, open-collared, sleeveless blouse that hung loosely at her waist, making Consuelo wonder if her appearance was sufficient.

The other woman was tiny, closer to Consuelo's height at five feet, one inch. She wore a thick braid of red-bronze hair that draped down one shoulder and hung to her hips. Her eyes flashed in the bright sunlight, dark as coal on her pixie-like face. Her skin glowed with a golden bronze that took no sun to bring out its color. Like the first woman, she wore form-fitting jeans and a sleeveless blouse that hung to her hips. Consuelo could not have known but would not have been surprised to learn that the team's loose-fitting shirts and blouses concealed pistols holstered at their backs.

"Busted, and his actual name is Sam," the blond man nearest her said. "You must be the woman Sam met yesterday."

Consuelo turned to the man speaking and caught that smile again. This one is dangerous, she decided. Good-looking and dangerous and just not in terms related to adventures in the jungle.

He lifted a tanned, long-fingered hand toward the man she now knew as Sam and let out a low, soft laugh. "You've been made, buddy."

She followed his hand back to where Sam stood. Sam nodded and said, "Folks, please let me introduce Senorita Consuelo Zamora."

The tiny woman cast Sam a sly grin. "I guess you did pull the short straw yesterday."

Sam gave the smaller woman a withering look as his cheeks turned an attractive shade of pink under his tan. "Would you like to join us, Miss Zamora?" he asked.

Consuelo felt an odd warmth run through her when he said her name, every syllable pronounced with perfect Mexican inflection. She found herself feeling awkward and uncertain, and it took her a second to gather herself before she replied. "Thank you, no. I have some calls to make during lunch, but I did want to thank you again for your timely rescue."

"All part of the job, ma'am," Sam replied. "How is Antonio doing? Is he well?"

His follow-up question brought that same warmth flooding through her again. That he would ask after. . . What had he called Antonio before? A budding drug-runner? It seemed so thoughtful.

"Antonio is fine, thank you. He can't stop talking about the ride you gave him in the Blackhawk helicopter. In fact, he's the subject of one of the calls I need to make. If all goes well, I'm going to take him home with me to the U.S."

Sam frowned. "You're headed to the U.S.?"

"I am," she replied. "That was my home before I started my missionary work here in Mexico, and I am now headed to the Pacific Northwest. Washington State. Once we get there, I hope to adopt Antonio. I have you to thank for much of that."

Sam raised his eyebrows. "I'm glad it is working out for you."

"I thank God for the opportunity. I knew Antonio's grandparents when I worked in the area where they lived. They and the rest of his family are all gone now, killed by the cartel."

The tall woman with black hair offered an understanding smile. "That is an amazing thing. Not many people would go so far for a kid like him."

"I agree," added the tiny woman.

Consuelo blushed at their compliment. "I just do what I can. Now, I will leave you all to your day. Thank you again for everything you have done for me and, I expect, countless others."

As she turned and stepped over to her table, she heard a man at the American's table say, "You got to rescue *her*?" He put great emphasis on the last word. "It's just not fair. Why don't I get any of those assignments?"

She heard the tiny woman add with a laugh, "Did you see Sam's reaction when she came up to the table? I have never seen him turn so red."

The taller woman added, with a laugh in her tone, "I think he's smitten."

Consuelo's smiled at the words but was glad she faced away from their table when she did. A handsome man like that smitten? That was a nice thought. Then again, she would not likely see him again.

"You guys can stop any time," she heard Sam reply as she took her seat and retrieved her cell phone. Time to call Lucy and break the bad news.

CHAPTER 4

A day later Director Paul Samuelson examined the M4A1 and the Sig Sauer 226 lying in the center of his leather desk blotter. They smelled of fresh gun oil and felt cool to the touch. He hated what he would have to say about them to Sam in a few short minutes.

The small, nondescript office sat in an unremarkable, single-story cinder block building in a small town in northern Florida. His large, gray, metal desk hugged the back wall of the room whose walls were painted a drab gun-metal gray. Two metal chairs lined the opposite wall with cracked, gray, vinyl seat cushions. A single window high on the left wall let in a sliver of brilliant sunlight from yet another gorgeous Florida morning. A few blocks away, the Atlantic Ocean rippled its waves against gold sand beaches flanked by waving palm trees, but here in the headquarters of the Extreme Operations Group, all was gray drab, a throwback to the seventies when the government had gotten a good deal on gray paint and gray metal furniture.

Samuelson rubbed a tanned, wrinkled hand over his short-cropped salt-and-pepper hair. And now he had to deal with this.

A knock at the door was followed by the face of his young second in command, a newly transferred Army Ranger, who aspired to greater things. Talented beyond reason, Phil Connelly's eager eyes always made Paul smile, even as he tried to hide his reaction whenever the young man was nearby. He waved a hand, and the trim, six-feet, athletic soldier entered the office with perfect posture and military poise.

Phil's job as Samuelson's deputy and assistant had begun a few months before and would have a brief tenure. The twenty-four-year-old showed too much talent to waste in an office. Without the aspiring Army Ranger's knowledge, Samuelson had already arranged a grueling six-month training course for the young man at the CIA's training facility in a remote area in Washington State. Navy Seals would lead the training, ensuring that Phil moved one step closer to qualifying for membership on one of the group's teams. And he needed talent in the field right now, Samuelson reflected, with the losses the group had encountered of late.

"Major Anthem is here to see you, sir," Phil announced from his position of attention before Paul's desk.

Samuelson held up a hand, drawing Phil's eyes. "We don't use rank in this office, Phil. You must remember that. Please let him in."

Phil nodded and spun on his heel, pulling open the office door. Sam stepped through on cue and, without a word, eased himself into one of the gray, metal chairs across from his boss.

Samuelson dismissed Phil and let the silence in the room linger a moment as he examined one of his best operators: Samuel Emerson Anthem. An inch under six feet tall, Sam possessed a quick mind and the physical presence of an Olympic-level athlete decathlete. The group physician mentioned something about his heart and lungs being larger than normal and pumping more oxygen to his body than the average person.

Paul rarely called in one of his operators for a private meeting and figured the tension that Sam was showing came from that.

"Do you understand why you're here?"

"Not sure." Sam's expression was a mixture of concern and confusion. "Did I do something wrong on that last mission?"

"No," Paul replied. "You redirected as ordered and exfiltrated the Zamora woman. By all accounts, you performed as expected." Shifting in his chair so that Sam could see the two weapons on his desk, he continued. "These are yours."

Sam's eyebrows furrowed. He had visited his equipment cage in the warehouse just before this meeting and saw no evidence of anyone entering it, although he had not opened the locked cabinet containing his pistol and the M4A1 carbine.

"Is there a problem with them, sir?" Sam asked.

"No," Paul replied. "They have been well maintained as best I can see."

"Then why are they in your office?

Leaning forward in his chair, Paul said, "I continue to hear rumors that you hesitate to use them when it might help your team. I need to know if that's true or not. You hold the group record for marksmanship with every weapon in our arsenal, from that ancient Sig 226 of yours to the M4A1, MP5s, knives—and rocks, for all I know. There is no one better in the group at empty-hand fighting than you, but I need to know you are prepared to use whatever tools are necessary when the need arises."

Sam dropped his eyes from his boss' face to his hands, still folded in his lap. His tone was flat when he responded. "I got the woman out safely. Mission complete."

Paul pulled his chair across the room near to where Sam sat. "Is this about the little girl in Guatemala? That was an accident. You were trapped and landed in a room with four tangos after that thatch roof gave in and dropped you into their laps. Those men were armed to the teeth. You had no choice but to fight your way out. You didn't know that little girl was hiding in that shack."

"She was only four," Sam replied, eyes still downcast.

"We don't even know if it was your bullet that killed her. More likely, it was a ricochet."

When Sam didn't respond, Paul continued. "You saw the group shrink?"

"I did. She signed off on my return to duty," Sam replied.

Paul leaned back in his chair. "Yes, she did, and I am inclined to give you the benefit of the doubt. But do not forget that when things get rugged out there, everyone is counting on you to do your job with whatever tools you have, including these," Paul said, tapping the pistol and carbine with a pointed finger.

Paul let out a long breath. "I have another mission for you, but I need your assurance that you will use all the tools in your arsenal. If you can't do that, I can have you transferred back to the regular army, where you can serve out the rest of your career."

Sam's eyes snapped up. "No, sir. I mean, I don't want to go back to regular service. I love my job. Home Team is my family."

"Good enough. I'm sending Home Team back to Mexico. You'll be leaving later this morning, and I want you to lead. The mission two days ago appears to have been a success. Cap, Romeo, and Fox painted the cartel's compound a rainbow of colors with the new paintball bullets while you were busy rescuing Ms. Zamora. Our intel from the area suggests that the cartel boss got the message that we can get to him and his operation anytime we desire. I hope this next effort will put him on track to adopt our recommendations for changing his ways."

The director pulled a thick manila envelope from a drawer in his desk and handed it to Sam, who tucked the Sig behind his belt, set the carbine on the chair, and accepted the envelope.

"It's a complicated mission," Paul said. "But I know you're the right person to lead it. You will be taking Team Two along as backup. It is imperative that we turn the cartel boss and that he signs up for the secretary's drugs-to-ag program. It's all outlined in the operations package in the envelope."

"Are you sure you want me to do this, given your concerns," Sam asked. "Any of the other three on my team would do a great job as team leader."

Paul shook his head. "Nope. I want you to lead. While I am concerned about your reticence to use all your weapons, the other members of Home Team have backed you up as having done what you needed for the success of your team's missions. You have a college degree in agriculture. When you read the mission brief in the envelope, you will understand why I selected you. And on the way out, stop by the dispensary in the logistics building. There's another Covid-19 vaccine out, and I need your team to get the latest dose."

Sam rubbed at his shoulder as he remembered the last time they'd all been vaccinated. "We had four shots last time we went out."

Paul smiled. "True, but until the powers that be settle on a final Covid-19 vaccine, if they ever do, you are going to get every version that comes out. But not to worry. This one, you snort."

Sam blew out the long breath. "I am sure it will be a great experience, sir."

The director stood from his chair, a tacit announcement that the meeting was over. Sam turned to the door, then paused and turned to lock eyes with his boss. "Thanks for the confidence in me, sir. We'll get the job done."

"I know, son. Never a doubt in my mind."

Sam nodded and stepped out of the office. As he passed into the reception area where Phil was sure to hear his next words, Sam called back, "Have you told Phil about his training coming up, sir?"

Paul heard Phil's startled response and knew Sam was smiling as he exited the front door. He shook his head but was smiling as he moaned his next words, "The most secure operational force in the country, and I can't keep a secret around this place."

A second later, Phil stood in Paul's office. "Sir? What about that training?"

CHAPTER 5

The sound of the CH-47D Chinook's heavy engines and thumping rotors beat a steady rhythm through Sam's insulated earphones. The air in the passenger compartment smelled of aviation fuel and sweaty bodies as he and the seven other operators on the mission struggled to get comfortable. The army's fifty-year-old helicopter was not configured for the comfort of passengers, but it more than met the need for two teams of operators, their equipment, and the vehicles infiltrating the jungles of Mexico.

Sam triggered his mic to reach the helicopter's crew. "Time to demark?"

"Five miles," the co-pilot replied. "Coming in low. Rotors moving to flutter mode now. Radar is clear of tangos."

"Good news, Papa Two," Sam replied, using the co-pilot's call sign. "Home Team status?"

Jessica would be Sam's second-in-command for this operation and sat next to him on the hard bench seat, checking her gear. She gave him a simple thumbs-up in reply and said, "Cap is go."

Allen was the next to chime in. "Fox is go."

"Romeo is go," Leah, the final member of Home Team, replied.

"Team Two?" Sam said. "Status?"

The Team Two leader, call sign Alpha Delta and shortened to Dog for this mission, didn't miss a beat. "Team Two geared up and ready to rock."

"All go," Sam concluded. "Final kit checks. Team Two on Humvee One. Home Team will take Humvee Two. Each team proceeds on their alternate routes. Primary routes are to be avoided."

"Wait, Empty," Dog replied. "When did that news come down?"

"Overwatch messaged me a few minutes ago. One of the teams in another area of operations was compromised this morning. In case of a mission leak, Overwatch advised caution, so it's my choice. We go to the secondary routes."

"Roger, Home Team leader," Dog replied.

"Wheels down in thirty seconds," Papa Two announced over the headsets.

The eight operators unbuckled from the seat harnesses, stood in unison, removed their headsets, and slung their rucks on their backs. All wore deep green, battle dress camo uniforms and skull helmets with forward-rear cameras. Seven carried the group's standard Remington M4A1 carbine rifles and held six loaded magazines in their tactical vest pockets. The remaining men from Team Two hefted a suppressed .50 caliber M107 semi-automatic, long-range sniper rifle capable of delivering accurate rapid fire on targets at two thousand meters. All carried the side arms of their choice. For Sam, it was his old but trusty Sig Sauer 226 .40 caliber pistol with one round in the chamber and ten in the clip.

Sam strapped his M4A1 across the back of his ruck and swung the pack into position on his back, drawing an odd look from the Team Two operators. Fox saw the look and triggered his mic. "No worries, boys. Empty will stand his ground. He just isn't fond of that M4A1." Fox pounded one fist into the palm of his other hand. "He likes working with his hands."

The comment drew knowing nods and more than a few chuckles from the two teams.

They braced themselves as the chopper crunched down and the tail ramp lowered. All four operators moved to either side of the two Humvees and released the clamps that secured the vehicles in flight. A minute later, both vehicles were loaded and down the ramp, seconds before the CH47 lifted off, its dual rotors pounding down the grass and low trees surrounding the small clearing.

"Mike Tango," Sam whispered into his wrist mic, announcing himself. "Radio silence to checkpoint one."

The two Humvees headed out of the clearing and then shifted direction, rolling down two separate paths, barely visible through the thick forest growth.

Thirty minutes later, the two Humvees drew together, nose to tail, at the junction of two narrow dirt roads. Both carried branches and long grass on their hoods and sides from the thick growth.

The Home Team Humvee pulled to the lead position. Sam climbed out, joined a second later by Dog. The remaining operators spread out behind and ahead of the vehicles, providing cover.

Sam selected a secure channel where he would communicate privately with Overwatch and whispered into his wrist mic, "Overwatch, this is Mike Tango. Status one at checkpoint one."

"Empty, this is Overwatch," came the reply, although it was not the usual intelligence analyst at the other end of the call. This voice sounded older, a little raspy. Sam decided that it had to be Director

Samuelson. "Move to the open channel, Empty. I want everyone there to hear what I have to say."

"Yes, sir. Moving to tack two," Sam said, changing the channel selection on his tactical wristwatch.

"Mike Tango and team, standing by," Sam said as he circled a hand over his head, signaling for the rest of the team to monitor the communication.

"This is Director Samuelson, everyone, so listen up. Home Team is leading this mission today for one important reason. They were at the same location last week, and they know the ground. Estevez is one of the leading cartel bosses in Mexico and is responsible for almost a third of the illegal drugs entering the U.S. each year. It has been rumored that he's grown tired of his trade because of the constant danger to his fighting. He lost his wife to Covid and a son and a brother to the fighting with us and the other cartels. His remaining family includes a daughter and two grandchildren. If—and I say, *if*—this turns out to be true, we plan to offer Estevez a way out. If it is not true, then we plan to bring him down in partnership with the Mexican government. Last week, Home Team entered the compound and shot the place up with paintball slugs, so Estevez knows he is exposed."

Still standing beside Sam, Dog silently mouthed the question, "Paintball?"

Sam nodded and whispered, "True."

Alpha Dog frowned. "You've got to be kidding."

"Get your head into this, Alpha Dog," Director Samuelson said and then continued. "The red paintball slugs that Romeo, Fox, and Cap painted the Estevez compound and men with were our first calling card. Today, you will step up our approach. Half of the ammo each of you carries is non-lethal rounds. I want you to spread them liberally across Estevez's team once you enter the compound. They are a high-velocity polymer, and our tests suggest they will knock your target down and render them unable to continue the fight. They can kill if you hit your target in the head, neck, or other vital spots on the body. Your goal is to knock as many of Estevez's men out of the action as possible without killing them."

Alpha Dog snorted. "Non-lethal rounds? You're putting our teams at risk going this route. We'll have to go in harder and hotter to be sure we get the jump on the tangos and not get our tails blown off."

"Noted, Team Two leader," Samuelson replied, "but this is the plan. If you aren't up to the task, you can remain in position until the rest of your team completes the mission with Home Team."

"No, I'm in. It's dumb, but I'm in," Alpha Dog replied.

"Good," Samuelson said. "Team Two's sniper will shoot paintball rounds like Home Team used last week. The sniper's goal is to paint Estevez or his two brothers, Marcos and Ricardo, who are also Estevez's bodyguards. Given the velocity of the sniper rounds, when he hits his targets, they will go down and also be painted with a nasty red paint intended as a reminder of the earlier mission.

"Once you have neutralized Estevez's soldiers, Empty and Fox will approach Estevez. Empty will explain one of the most unique offers the U.S. has ever made to a cartel boss. Empty has the script for this operation, so follow his lead. But once Empty and Fox enter the building where Estevez and his family are located, swap your non-lethal rounds for your standard rounds in case things do not go as planned. At that point, the rules of engagement are as normal on any other mission. This approach should work, but if anyone on that compound chooses to engage you, do what you need to stay safe and return home in one piece. Is everyone clear on the plan?" Samuelson concluded.

Sam heard seven clicks of the team's mics, indicating compliance, and then said "Roger, Overwatch. Home Team and Team Two are status two and standing by."

"Home Team and Team Two, you are status three. Move on the target and Godspeed."

The teams remounted the Humvees and drove the remaining two miles through the thick woods to the Estevez compound with Sam's Humvee leading.

Their entry into the compound would be direct and fast through the front gate—its two nine-feet wooden doors affixed to two tall adobe spires. The spires resembled church bell towers and joined with the thick white, nine-feet brick and adobe wall that encircled the two-acre compound.

Guard towers stood atop the gate spires and at each corner of the rectangular compound. Inside the walls was Estevez's main house where they would most likely find him and his family, a bunkhouse for the dozen men he employed on the grounds, and a large warehouse where he kept most of his illicit drug stock. Outside the compound walls were twenty yards of clear ground between the compound walls and the thick jungle.

The first order of business was setting up the sniper in the right position in the tall trees that lined the open space. The sniper would knock down and paint the gate guards. Once that was done, the rest of the two teams would crash the front gate.

They dropped the sniper twenty yards before they paused at the edge of the forest to ensure he was in position. A few minutes later, Sam heard, "Rascal, status two and standing by." The sniper was in position.

"Overwatch, this is Empty. All teams are status two and ready."

Overwatch responded in less than a second. "You are cleared for engagement."

"Roger Overwatch. We are status three," Sam replied.

Sam waited until he heard the distinctive spit of the sniper rifle and saw the gate tower guards slump out of commission.

"Gate guard non-op," came Rascal's voice across Sam's cochlear.

"Roger, Rascal. Stand by," Sam replied.

Sam pumped his fist, and Romeo hit the gas for the Home Team Humvee. The two vehicles shot forward, Home Team in the lead with Team Two's vehicle following bumper-to-bumper. The tall, wooden gate rose before them as they cleared the trees at thirty miles per hour over a bumpy, dirt track.

"Eyes open, boys and girls," Sam called. "Here we go!"

Team Two's Humvee took the lead and crashed through the ancient gate, flinging the tall, wooden gates wide open. Sam dove through the Humvee's open door as Romeo jerked the vehicle right and slammed on the brakes. He tucked, rolled, and regained his feet in a moment, a move he could not have done if he had his carbine strapped to his back like the rest of his team. Strapped to his front, it was an easy matter to curl around the weapon as he rolled.

Fox jumped from the right rear door with his M4A1 up and already firing. Romeo and Cap emerged from the opposite side of the Humvee as several of Estevez's men brandished weapons and signaled the alarm.

Sam saw the two Estevez men aim their Heckler & Kocheach MP5Ks in his direction. He dashed the corner of the main house as they opened fire, noting that the K version of the MP5 was an experimental light machine gun. Few outside the special operations community even knew the MP5K existed.

The two men stitched the ground around the corner of the house with a thick barrage of high-velocity rounds as Sam crouched. Fox took off at a run and made the corner of the warehouse fifteen yards to Sam's left. He lifted a hand in Sam's direction. They both smiled as they heard the crack of the two rounds fired by Romeo and Cap and saw the two Estevez men with the MP5Ks go down.

"Team Two, take the warehouse as planned. Romeo and Cap, take the bunkhouse. Hold no one. Knock everyone you see down with the non-lethal rounds. We want them hurting and unable to respond before we leave this place," Sam ordered.

"Yee-haw!" came Dog's response over the radio. "Team Two, status three."

Team Two opened up in unison with their M4A1s on semi-automatic as the three operators left the cover of their Humvee and approached the warehouse. The staccato crack, crack, crack of their weapons echoed across the compound to Sam's right as they charged the warehouse, knocking down three Estevez soldiers and then taking cover just outside the warehouse's wide front door.

In the same second, Sam saw Jessica and Leah race across the compound's open yard toward the long, low bunkhouse on his left as he and Fox provided cover. Sam drew his Sig pistol down on an Estevez guard as he emerged from the bunkhouse still pulling on his boots, but Fox was quicker, knocking the man off his feet with a single shot.

"Thanks, Fox-man," came Romeo's call as she and Cap entered the low adobe building through a wide double door. A short burst of rifle fire sounded from inside, followed by one scream and some words in rapid Spanish that Sam could not have understood. Those words were followed by another short, semi-automatic burst of gunfire and then silence.

Glancing back to his right, Sam saw Dog line up to kick down the warehouse door. His first kick had no effect. A shoulder blow against the door staggered Dog as the operator bounced back from the heavy door.

Sam suppressed a grin. He knew what was coming next.

"Going volatile," Dog announced, and Sam watched as Dog placed a small charge at each of the warehouse door's two hinges, then ducked as rifle fire crackled through the air, just missing Dog's head. Dog and his two teammates returned fire toward two men who'd emerged from the main house, knocking both men down.

As Dog's men fired, Sam and Fox both stepped from cover and raced for the main house's front door. As they moved, three more men emerged from the house, each carrying the new MP5.

Trouble, Sam thought, raising his Sig in a two-handed grip. A second later, he felt and heard the hiss of three rounds from the sniper's rifle buzz by and thump into the three men's chests seconds apart, flipping the men onto their backs and painting their shirt fronts red.

"Nice shooting, Rascal," Sam offered over his wrist mic.

"De nada, sir," the sniper replied through the cochlear speaker behind Sam's ear.

Sam and Fox crouched by the main house's front door in time to hear two loud explosions as Dog lifted the warehouse door off its hinges with the C4 chargers. Sam watched as Dog's teammates kicked the door the rest of the way open and sprinted into the building. Sam heard the staccato sound of all three weapons on automatic fire as Team Two spayed rubber bullets throughout the building. Seconds later, the firing stopped.

Sam did some mental math. They had accounted for at least ten guards. There had to be more of Estevez's soldiers in the area. The original estimate of twelve soldiers at the compound was only that: an estimate. But the current lack of gunfire suggested anyone remaining upright was in the main house. If this was his place, he'd position at least two men at the front and back doors of the house with good visibility out the windows Sam saw at the front and knew to exist at the back of the house. In addition to those, Estevez had his two brothers who were his bodyguards, along with his daughter and her children.

He and the rest of Home Team would enter the house but would need to be quiet and careful.

"Dog, this is Empty. Sitrep."

"All quiet in the warehouse, but you should see the pile of heroin, pot, and who knows what else is in this place. There must be a fortune in drugs here!" Dog replied.

"And the guards?" Sam asked.

"All down, hurting, unconscious, and out of commission for the time being," Dog reported.

"Dog, you and your team move to the yard near the gate. You are cover and backup while Home Team moves into the house. Keep the Humvees ready to roll on a moment's notice."

"Roger, Empty. Moving into position now," Dog replied.

"Rascal, you full op?" Sam called to the sniper.

"Roger, Empty. I have a clear shot through the front of the house, including all the windows."

"Roger, Rascal. Romeo and Cap. Sitrep?" Sam asked, requesting their status in the bunkhouse.

"All secure in the bunkhouse. Same report as from Dog," Jessica replied.

"Roger, Cap," Sam said. "You and Romeo take the back of the house. Enter on my signal. I would expect two or three tangos by the back door, but I can't be sure. Fox and I will enter the front of the house, expecting the same."

"Roger," Romeo replied for both she and Cap.

Sam crouched on the right side of the main house's front door and glanced over at Fox who stood to his left. He held up a finger and counted off, one . . . two . . . three. "Home team, status three," Sam said into his wrist mic.

"Cap and Romeo moving inside," came the reply from Jessica.

Fox swung around and kicked in the front door. Sam dove, rolled, and came up in a crouch on a marble floor in an entryway with his Sig held out before him. Rich, dark wood paneling covered the walls with art scattered around the room that appeared old and valuable. Overhead, a crystal chandelier twinkled light across the room, and the half dozen vases filled with fresh flowers that decorated the entry.

Fox followed on Sam's heels, keeping his feet and scanning the room, the barrel of his M4A1 leading the way. They paused a half-beat as three men emerged, two from a side door and one from a long, wide stairway leading up to the second floor. All had MP5s in their hands. The one on the stairs opened fire. Fox crouched, spun on his heels, and snapped off a shot that flung the man back onto the stairs.

Sam dropped and dove low for the two men at the door leading into the entryway. Reaching the first man as he raised his submachine gun his way, Sam gathered his feet and came up just in front of the gun's barrel, dropping his Sig pistol and joining his hands at the thumbs in a "V" and shooting them up under the MP5 at the same time the man pulled the trigger. On full-automatic, bullets ripped up the wall next to the front door, stitching holes up and across part of the ceiling.

When the gun stopped spitting bullets, Sam pulled it and the man off balance toward him with his left hand, retrieved his pistol with his right, and clubbed the man in the temple with the pistol grip.

The third man had taken several steps across the floor toward Allen but turned in response to the struggle between Sam and his compatriot. He leveled his MP5 and put a single shot into Sam's right side at less than five feet. The tactical vest took the brunt of the impact, but the bullet felt like a sledgehammer crashing into Sam's body. Before Sam could recover, Allen brought his carbine around and put three rubber slugs in the man's chest. The man rocked back from the impact of the hard rubber bullets and fell toward Sam, who punched the man in the temple for good measure and in frustration for letting the cartel thug get the drop on him. Unconscious, the cartel guard lay full-length on the marble floor, eyes rolled up into his head.

Fox gave Sam a dour look. "Nice move with the pistol, but someday, you are going to shoot that thing. You could have taken both of them out from a distance."

"I suppose," Sam replied as three shots echoed from the back of the house.

"Romeo. Cap. Report," Sam called into his wrist mic.

"All secure here, Boss," Cap replied. "That was almost too easy."

"One of you stay where you are to guard the back. The other come forward to cover the front door. Dog, you continue to hold position. Fox and I will head upstairs to make contact with Estevez."

"Roger," Romeo replied a breath later. "Cap will come forward."

"Roger," Dog repeated.

Sam glanced at the clock displayed on his arm-tablet. All told, the operation had taken four minutes. They were on schedule.

"Overwatch, Fox and I are headed to meet Estevez."

"Roger, Empty. Good luck."

Sam waved to Fox, who followed Sam up the wide, ornately carved staircase that curved around the right side of the entryway. Their soft jungle boots padded softly up the glossy wooden stairs of what looked like teak and mahogany. Allen carried his M7A1 at the ready, barrel covering their left side away from the wall. Sam carried the Sig loosely in his right hand and rubbed his sore ribs with his left as they climbed. Nothing felt broken, but he'd have a good-sized bruise by the end of the day.

"Nice digs," Allen murmured. "Maybe crime does pay."

"Not funny," Sam replied.

They found two men waiting at the top of the stairs, neither of which was Don Estevez. Ricardo and Marcos, Sam concluded by the way they stood, feet spread wide, a pistol in each man's right hand and pointed at Sam and Allen. Although one stood at least six-feet-two and the other much less than that, the family resemblance with

Don Estevez was obvious: ebony hair, dark eyes, ruddy complexions, stocky, and built like tanks.

The tall one called out as Sam and Fox continued up the stairs. "You gringos. Come no farther."

"Fox?" Sam said as he climbed the last few steps, holstered his pistol, and placed his forefingers in his ears.

Fox stepped around Sam and fired a single shot from the hip, not missing a stride as he climbed the last two steps. The bodyguard on the left fell, clutching his chest.

A more elderly man hurried from a door and crossed to the remaining bodyguard. "Hold, Marcos. Do not fire your weapon. All of our men are down, except for you and me. We have been fairly taken, and I do not want any further harm to come to our men, Marie, or the niños pequeños."

"Hola, Don Estevez," Sam offered, choosing the man's honorific title to set the tone for the meeting to come as he and Allen halted at the top of the stairs. He did not have to look to know that Fox had both men covered.

Sam guessed Estevez was in his sixties. He wore gray slacks made of some sort of silky material and an embroidered, white, open-collared shirt that hung outside his slacks in the current Mexican style. About Sam's height and trim for a man his age, he appeared in good shape but with the start of a small paunch. His face was creased and deeply tanned, and a sharp, Aztec blade of a nose split the distance between wide, dark eyes. His hair was thick and white and coiffed back severely from his forehead.

"Won't you both please come into my office," Estevez offered in lightly accented English. "My daughter and grandchildren are there, as I am sure you already know. Do you have a message to relay to me from your government?" The old man paused and shrugged. "Or do you plan to eliminate us all?"

Estevez turned and led the way into a large room that hosted thick Egyptian rugs stretched over dark, hardwood floors and silk and leather furnishings. Ornate artwork graced the room's walls. The office was expansive with a large, oak desk at the far end and two conversation areas carved out by leather wingback chairs and sofas. A long, rosewood pool table with red felt finishes stood near the door where the visitors entered. A beautiful, young woman, perhaps thirty years old, and two small children sat on a couch beneath a tall, stained-glass window. Estevez's daughter and his two grandchildren.

"Thank you, sir," Sam replied, raising a hand to point to where the daughter and grandchildren sat. "Please take a seat with your daughter and her children, if you will."

Estevez nodded and eased down onto the wide leather next to his daughter. The youngest of the grandchildren, perhaps four years old, climbed into the man's lap. When Marcos, the remaining conscious brother and bodyguard, attempted to join Estevez, Sam waved him off. "We need to keep you where we can see you. Go stand by that window to the other side of Señor Estevez."

Marcos glanced at Estevez before walking the few steps to the window and pausing there.

"Now, Rascal," Sam murmured into his mic.

"Status three," the sniper replied.

A small piece of the window behind Marcos shattered and blew inward. The big bodyguard staggered and turned to face the window. As he did, a second shot took him in the chest and flung him to the floor. Red paint covered his side and his shirt front as his eyes rolled back into his head.

"Ah," Estevez offered, glancing at his unconscious brother on the floor next to his chair. "More of your paintball weapons. I take it you are making a point."

"That is correct, sir," Sam replied. He dragged a chair across the room and placed it in front of Estevez and straddled it. Fox remained by the door, covering the room with his carbine.

"My job is to convey a joint offer to you from the Mexican and U.S. governments. If you agree to their terms, they will subsidize you with two million dollars per year for five years, give you sufficient weapons to defend yourself from the other cartels in the area, and leave you and your people alone."

Estevez leaned forward in his chair, thick eyebrows rising. "You have my attention. Please explain the terms that you speak of."

"No later than one month from today, you will begin the process of plowing up and destroying your poppy and marijuana fields and dismantling your drug production factories. We know where they are located and will be watching to ensure your compliance. You will convert those fields to general agriculture of your choice. Within six months, all of your drug production facilities and fields must be converted to general agriculture, producing crops for local markets and export. Both countries will make the necessary equipment available to you to get this job done in the time required. If you meet the terms of this agreement and maintain operations as prescribed, you will be given a full pardon by both the United States and Mexican governments. You will be granted exclusive contracts for the export of your products to the United States and markets throughout Mexico and Central America. You will receive subsidies of no less than one million dollars per year during the first five years of operations to ensure your ongoing viability and success, in addition to the two million that is intended for your discretionary use."

Estevez leaned back in his chair, smiled, and folded his hands in his lap. "And if I choose not to accept this offer?"

"None of your men have been seriously hurt during this operation or the one several days ago. As we speak, my team is changing all of its ammunition from non-lethal rounds to high-velocity, hollow-point ammunition. If you do not accept this offer, we will destroy your operation and all the people associated with it."

Sam slid a meaningful glance over to where Estevez's daughter and grandchildren sat but did not say another word.

Estevez followed Sam's gaze and frowned. "I believe that you give me no choice. Do I have any time to consider this?"

Sam did not reply but lifted his wrist mic to his lips and said, "Rascal, take the shot."

A third bullet whizzed through the window and punched a hole through the forehead of a man depicted in a tall painting on the far side of the room.

Estevez raised his hands in submission, then returned them to the shoulders of his grandson sitting in his lap. "Please tell those for whom you work that I accept the terms of your offer. As I am sure you already know, this will not sit well with the other cartel bosses in the area."

"In addition to the arms we will provide to you and your men, I am authorized to provide special operations teams to stay on-site as you make the transition from drugs to general agriculture," Sam said. "That should help with the other cartels."

Estevez sighed, again. "Yes, I suppose that should do. As I am sure you already know, I have grown weary of all the death surrounding me from the fighting and the Covid-19 pandemic. I have been considering a change for some time."

Sam nodded.

"Then this will just push the transition ahead a little faster than anticipated," Estevez said.

"I have seen the studies of the thousands of hectares that you own and the test results from the soil and the irrigation prospects," Sam replied. "If you apply yourself to this transition, I believe your current wealth will be protected and enhanced."

Estevez nodded and rose from his chair. "I think that maybe you are more than hired muscle."

Sam nodded. "We are all more and less than we seem, señor."

Estevez nodded again. "So true. Then it is agreed if your government can provide me with one more thing in exchange for my cooperation."

Sam frowned and drew his Sig from its thigh holster to emphasize his next words. He let his eyes roam across the faces in the room. "I would think that the continued safety of you and those who you care about would be enough."

"I can see your point," Estevez said, eyeing the gun. "But there is something even more dire than any punishment you might threaten us with."

"And that is?" Sam asked, glancing at the tablet computer strapped to his arm. They needed to exfiltrate soon before word traveled beyond the compound walls and alerted the other cartels in the area.

"The vaccine for the Covid-19 virus," Estevez replied. "In your country, everyone has gotten at least a first dose. For obvious reasons, the government of Mexico is reluctant to offer me, my family, and my employees with the same consideration."

"You want us to provide you with the vaccine?"

Estevez nodded. "Very much so."

Overwatch's voice sounded in Sam's ear. "We heard the request. We will comply."

Sam nodded and returned his pistol to its holster. "We will honor your request."

Sam held up a hand to forestall any more discussion as Overwatch explained the details of the vaccine delivery, then said, "A person from the U.S. Department of State and the Mexican Secretary of Agriculture's office will be here in a few days to sign the necessary paperwork to cement today's agreement. That person will bring the vaccine for you, your family, and your men at that time. It will be up to you to have it administered. They will provide sufficient doses that the villages nearest your compound can also be assured of immunization."

"Thank you," Estevez replied. He nodded toward his daughter and grandchildren. "I will do this for their sake if for no other reason."

Sam stepped forward and extended his hand. "Thank you, Señor Estevez. My men and I will leave immediately."

Estevez shook Sam's hand, his grip dry and firm. "And thank you as well, Mike Tango."

Sam's eyes narrowed as Estevez continued. "Yes, I know who you are. I am not so familiar with your friend by the door who goes by the call sign of Foxtrot X-ray or the other members of your team, but I am well aware of the man called 'Empty.' I also know that you and your team do not take a life when you have another alternative.

Your reputation precedes you, and you are well-respected, even if considered a deadly adversary by most."

Sam glanced at Fox, who gestured toward the tablet computer strapped to his right arm. Time to go.

Without another word, Sam spun on his heels and headed for the door. "Rally at the victors," he said, referring to the Humvees. "Time to leave."

As Sam and Allen descended the staircase and headed toward the front door, Sam keyed the mic on his smartwatch. "Overwatch, target has accepted the deal."

Samuelson's reply was immediate. "We monitored the conversation. Good news. Exfiltrate to checkpoint three. Your ride awaits."

"Roger, Overwatch, but there is one problem," Sam replied.

"Go ahead, Mike Tango."

"I've been made."

"We heard that, too," Director Samuelson dryly replied. "Come home, and we'll work through it."

CHAPTER 6

Allen, Jessica, Leah, and Sam sat at a gray, metal conference table in a small room just off the reception area of the Extreme Operations Group headquarters, wrapping up the mission debrief with the director. Jess and Allen sat on one side of the table with Leah and Sam on the other. Director Samuelson sat at the head of the table with Phil at the other end.

Team Two was not present, having served a supporting role on the mission being discussed. The room smelled of stale, cold coffee as Sam finished his summary of the teams' performances on the mission.

"All in all, every mission objective was achieved," Sam said. "Team performance was the deciding factor with Home Team and Team Two performing well both individually and in sync."

Paul Samuelson wiped a bead of sweat from his brow with a paper towel and jotted a note on the yellow legal tablet. "We'll let the cartel boss stew in his juice for a few weeks, and then we'll approach him again, just to be sure he is still committed to the agreement. In the meantime, we will run a disinformation program in his area, encouraging his competitors to pressure him. If we're lucky, we can have this nailed down in a few months and Estevez well along the way for converting his fields. It will mean a lot to Mexico's revitalization program and may well serve as a model for future operations."

"It is a unique approach, sir," Jessica replied. Sam knew the novel approach to turning cartels into legitimate trade and reclaiming Mexico's agricultural promise appealed to her.

Leah nodded, but Allen rolled his eyes. "I'll believe it when I see it. The greed factor plays a big role in the cartels. I doubt they will go down so easily."

Paul clapped his hands together and stood from his chair. "That is yet to be seen. For now, I believe we are done here. Sam, please stay with me for a moment. The rest of you are free to leave. I appreciate the op-tempo we've been living under for the last bunch of months, so Leah, Allen, and Jessica are on admin leave until recalled."

"Yes, sir," the three operators barked in unison, a wry grin on their faces, appreciating the opportunity for some rest and relaxation.

Paul waved Sam over to the chair next to him and sat back down.

"Sir?" Sam said, by way of question.

Paul dragged his chair around so that he faced Sam. "As much as I appreciate your team's efforts, I remain concerned about your reluctance to pull a trigger. You didn't mention it in your report, but the logistics data from the mission shows you did not fire your pistol or carbine once during the mission while the rest of the team chewed up a good portion of their ammunition load."

"I didn't need to," Sam replied. "The mission was successful, and I carried my weight. You can ask any member of the team."

"I did ask them. They all said you led the effort well and that you carried out the mission in the best manner possible."

Before Sam could respond, Paul cut him off with a raised hand. "The mission went fine, as they always do with you and Home Team.

But I am worried about your state of mind. That four-year-old girl who died was about the same age as your sister when she died—"

Sam cut Paul off, rose from his chair, and stepped toward the door. "I don't think that played a role in any of this. If you think I'm some sort of coward because of something that happened over five years ago . . ."

Paul stood and held up a hand to cut off Sam's next words. "I would never infer that. Your courage and dedication to the group's mission are not in question. However, it is my job to worry about each of my teams. You are not yet aware of this, but two other teams were out on missions while you were in Mexico. Both teams were ambushed well before they reached their objectives. One was hit in an airport just after landing. They didn't even get off the plane. Three dead and one wounded. The other team was five miles out from a site in Venezuela and was hit by drone fire. When they attempted to take down the drone, their ammunition proved to be defective. We got them out with the help of a Ranger platoon that happened to be in the area. I can't explain these two mission failures, but with all this happening, I need all hands on deck when my teams go out. I cannot worry about your willingness to do what must be done when times get tough."

Sam's shoulders sagged. He ran a hand through his hair and breathed out a long sigh. "I don't understand," he said.

Paul stepped over to his desk and retrieved a small card. "I want you to take a couple of months off."

Sam started to protest, but Paul stopped him with a glare. "This is non-negotiable. You are on two weeks of administrative leave now, like the rest of your team. Additionally, I expect you to take two months of vacation time to think things through. You have the leave time accumulated, and what you are going through is not uncommon with people in our profession. It does not mean you are any less or any better than anyone, but it does mean that you need to figure a few things out."

"I need to continue my work," Sam said, looking at his hands.

"I know how you feel, but we tend to see a lot of the dark side of life in our business. Our mission to deal with that dark side lets the rest of the country sleep easier at night, but it can add up for a person. Jessica, Leah, and Allen all have things that they do and people they interact with when they are not on an assignment. Jessica is a computer nerd and a churchgoer with many friends in both those worlds. Leah is a social butterfly and high-level performer in martial arts competitions. Allen has his sailboat and his nieces and nephews and a girlfriend in Vermont. Each has something else to engage them, besides this job."

Paul paused and then said, "What do you have in your life besides your work? Maybe that's what you need to figure out more than anything else. An operator with a well-rounded life is a better operative. If you had something in your life besides the work, maybe you'd relax more, and I could worry about you less."

Sam's silence was the only answer required, so Paul let him sit in that silence for a moment.

"What do you do when you're not on the job?" Sam finally asked.

Paul smiled and leaned back in his chair. "That's a fair question. I don't have a lot of hobbies or free time, but when I do, my family and my faith round out my life."

"You mean like your kids and God?" Sam asked.

Paul chuckled. "That is exactly what I mean: the wife, kids, and God. Don't get me wrong. I'm not trying to convert you. That would violate a long list of workplace rules, but on more occasions than I can count, my family and my faith got me through. Some of the best warriors I've worked with have held a deep faith. For me, it's the Christian faith. Others may go in a different direction, but all the good ones seem to believe in a Higher Power that directs and protects us. Even Leah attends church, although I am not sure that's true for Allen."

Sam nodded. "They never mentioned it."

Paul nodded. "When you're kicking butt and the bullets are flying, it's not a normal conversation piece. Church or not, I hope you'll give some thought to the topic of rounding out your life a bit. I believe it will make you a better operator and may help you through whatever it is that is bothering you right now."

Paul handed a business card to Sam. "This is the name and number of one of the best operators and friends I've ever known. I owe him my life a dozen times over. He's retired now and lives in Olympia, Washington, where I suggest you head for your vacation. I'd like you to look him up. He went through a lot of what you are dealing with right now and may be able to relate to your situation."

Sam turned the card over in his hand to read the few lines of typed print: the name Jim Carson, a phone number, and an address in Olympia.

"We served together in the CIA's tactical operations branch for ten years. He was a door-kicker while I was a mission specialist. I laid the operations plans, and then he and I and other operators went in and did the heavy lifting. We put a lot of miles under our belts and did a lot of good work together until he retired twelve years ago."

"Sounds like an interesting guy. Maybe I will look him up."

"I've let him know you might be stopping by. Head up there tomorrow. Spend a few weeks in the area. I think you might like it more than you can imagine."

Sam stuffed the card in his jean pocket. "I'll do that, sir."

Paul stuck out his hand, an unusual gesture for the man who generally avoided such things. "Have a good trip, Sam, and give my best to my old friend."

"It has been so long since I took a vacation that I probably won't know what to do with myself. If a mission comes up, please call me."

"We'll see," Paul said, leading the way out of the conference room.

CHAPTER 7

Hands stuck deep in his sweatpants' pockets, Sam strolled along the wide wooden promenade that skirted the port and marina in Olympia, Washington. The sky was clear, and the smell of diesel fuel, shellfish, and saltwater hung in the air. Powerboats and sailboats of all sizes, colors, and decades lined the endless rows of the docks below.

He'd arrived in Olympia two days ago a man with nothing but time on his hands. Once he'd checked into a hotel near the marina, Sam had called and connected with the man Director Samuelson had suggested. What Sam had not been prepared for was to find out that Jim Carson was a pastor working out of a small church in a suburb west and north of the city.

The two had agreed to meet at a coffee shop located near the local Home Depot superstore. When Sam arrived, Carson was waiting for him with a cup of coffee for himself in one hand and a steaming mocha in the other for Sam.

The coffee shop was large with the usual barista stationed at a peninsula in the center of a large room and a long bakery cabinet running off to one side. The walls were paneled in dark wood, lined with rough-cut timbers, and decorated in a nautical theme. Ten small tables and several couches were scattered throughout the area.

A floor-to-ceiling rock fireplace stood at one end of the place that served the room, and outside, on the patio, the rich aroma of freshly ground coffee hung invitingly in the air.

Pastor Carson was a tall, African American man with broad shoulders and a small pot pushing at his belt. The man's dark face was deeply lined from an excess of outdoor living. He wore faded jeans and a royal blue Seattle Seahawks football jersey with the number twelve on it. The jersey hung over shoulders that strained the seams of the garment. As big as he was, Carson moved smoothly as he negotiated around the tables, scattered around the coffee shop, to greet Sam. *Like a big cat,* Sam thought, and that said something special about a man four inches taller than Sam's own five foot ten. It was Sam's business to notice such things about the people he met, and Carson sized up as a formidable person.

Sam accepted the mocha as they settled at a small table in a relatively dark corner of the coffee shop and raised the mocha in salute. "Thanks for this. I see that Director Samuelson has preceded me. He told you what I drink."

"Yes, he did." Carson smiled. "He told me you like mochas. He also told me a little bit about why he wanted me to talk with you."

"Okay, I guess," Sam replied, unsure of where to go next with the conversation. He hadn't prepared himself to bare his soul on the first meeting, if ever.

Carson smiled and took a long pull from his paper coffee cup. "Your boss and I are pretty close and did a lot of work together once upon a time."

Sam nodded, knowing that in a public place like a coffee shop they would avoid the details.

"Then I will also tell you that I retired at age forty, at the peak of my game. Not bragging, but I was known to be pretty good at my job. All the usual skill sets at the top of my peer group. I was up for promotion to an oversight position when I found myself on a short vacation at Myrtle Beach in the Carolinas, staring at the ocean from my hotel room and wondering what in the world I was doing with my life."

He gave Sam a knowing look. "Your boss thinks you may be wondering the same sort of thing."

Sam sipped his mocha and paused before replying, meeting the man's eyes. He saw trust there and someone he might be able to relate to. When he did speak, it was with careful, low tones. "I love my work."

"No doubt," Carson replied. "I loved my work, too. What your boss and I did together made a difference. People could sleep well at night because of what we were doing and never feel the impact of what might have happened had we not been there with our special skills."

Sam nodded and sipped his mocha, then added, "That's how I see it, too."

Carson gave a slight shrug. "In my case, on that ocean beach, I found myself wondering if even that was enough for me. Was I making enough of a difference, considering the stack of wreckage I'd left behind me? Every mission I participated in was golden and justified, and I never lost any sleep over what I did for a living. But on that day at the beach, I realized that all I had with me at the end of each day were memories of what I'd done. Beyond a few close friends in the tactical squad, when the day was done, I had nothing to go home to but the man in the mirror. I started doubting my life as an operator, and we both know there is no place for that sort of self-doubt in what you do and what I did for a living."

"I don't feel like I suffer from self-doubt," Sam started.

Carson held up a hand, cutting off Sam's next words. "I'm not saying you do, but for some of us, the lives we took add up, even though what we did, we always did for the greater good. I saw operators, both men and women, crumble after ten or fifteen years as an operator with memories haunting their dreams. I did not want to become one of those people."

Carson shrugged, sipped his coffee, and continued, "It took me a few weeks to reach a final decision, but I took some time off just as you are now and headed out here for some R-and-R. I grew up a few miles up Interstate 5 from here in the town of Lakewood. I visited friends there, and while I did, I encountered two people who changed me. The first was a nice, young lady about my age who had two grown children. She is now my wife. The second was an old friend of similar persuasions as you and me who'd left the teams and moved into the world's second-oldest profession."

Sam was about to fall for Carson's joke when the pastor cut him off with a raised coffee cup. "The priesthood. He became a priest. We shared several long talks during those two weeks, and a month later, I'd submitted my retirement paperwork and enrolled in a nearby seminary. Three years later, I was called as an assistant pastor of a local community church in Lakewood. For the past nine years, I have had a church here in Olympia."

"I don't think I am cut out to be a man of the cloth," Sam said.

Carson sipped at his coffee, his thick black eyebrows knitting together in a frown as he came up dry. "Hold that thought," he said as he left the table and returned a few minutes later with a refill for each of them.

"I should buy," Sam started. "You got the last round."

"Not an issue," Carson replied, handing Sam his mocha. "You're a member of a pretty small community of current and former special operators, and I am more than happy to contribute a cup of coffee to your vacation. But as I was starting to say, I am not suggesting that you resign your commission and position with the group or enter the priesthood. Heaven knows that it is not for everyone. That said, the best warriors I have ever known have been men and women who explored faith, got in touch with their spiritual sides, and became better operators for having done so."

Sam grinned. "That includes Director Samuelson? He mentioned something about his faith just before I left his office."

Carson nodded. "Never met a more spiritual man, although most would never realize it. I consulted with him several times before enrolling in the seminary. His encouragement was what got me to hear and heed God's call to service."

"You were comfortable becoming a minister after all you had to do as an operator?" Sam asked. He let his eyes drift around the coffee shop and out to the parking lot beyond the windows. He noticed a tall, distinguished man walk across the parking lot and get into a silver Chevy Colorado pickup. He filed the image in the back of his mind. Such was the training of an operator—situational awareness never ends and is always on.

"With faith, it's not about what you've done in the past or been in the past. It's about who you become when you accept Jesus Christ." Carson shrugged. "Forgiveness from the Lord is a big step but one that is open to anyone. The famous disciple Paul was a sort of warrior before he became one of the most prolific authors in the New

Testament and a follower of Jesus Christ. Some would say he was a bad man before his conversion. I doubt that anyone would have ever called me a bad man—or you either, for that matter."

"I can only hope, but I am not looking for a way out of what I do," Sam said. "I love getting bad people off the streets so they can't harm anyone else. And I love the people I work with. They're like family."

"I get it," Carson replied. "It was, and is, the same for me. I remain in touch with my teammates to this day."

Carson paused for a moment as he considered his next words, then continued, "Your director is concerned that the loss of your sister when you were younger and the death of a young girl of similar age as your sister on a mission a while back may be a factor in how you feel today. He advised me about your team's op-tempo of late, and I know that when you don't have adequate time to breath between missions, when you're tired and worn out, that memories like that can rise and shake your soul. I saw it happen to my fellow operators too many times back in my time, although those same people came back around once they'd been given a breather and some help sorting things out."

"But I don't need any help or any time off—" Sam started, but Carson cut off his next words as he glanced at his watch, slid back his chair, and stood.

"I'm sorry, but I have to leave for a meeting. I hope you will consider what I've said. You have my number. When and if you want to talk again or even just get a coffee, I'll make myself available. You'd be surprised at how many of us are out there walking the streets like any average person and living average but fulfilling lives outside of our old community. After a period of introspection as I've described, some give up their lives as operators and discover a different path in life. Many return to their work with an even greater degree of self-confidence and commitment than before."

That conversation had happened a day ago. Sam sucked in some of the clear morning air and glanced around him at the selection of restaurants and food stands in the area surrounding the marina. His hotel sat a few blocks to the east on the edge of Washington's small but diverse capital city.

He had decided to skip breakfast and take a long jog around Capital Lake—a serene inlet from the Puget Sound that sat just below the state capitol building and not far from where he stood.

As he started a brief stretching routine in anticipation of the long, relaxing jog he was about to take, his cell phone vibrated. He lifted it out of his pocket and examined the screen: possible spam. Sam smiled and pressed the green button on the screen, answering the call. "Good morning, Director Samuelson," Sam said. He'd set the director's office to show up on his phone's contact list as "Possible Spam" as his own little joke.

"Good morning, Empty," Paul replied. "I know you are on vacation and that I promised to give you your space and time, but. . ."

Sam laughed and completed the sentence for him, "A mission just came up."

The director chuckled. "Yes, and it is in your current backyard. I could use your help."

"Of course," Sam said, happy that he could delay his forced vacation for a few more days by whatever time it took to complete the new mission.

"There's going to be a drug interdiction conference at the state capital building in Olympia tomorrow," Paul said. "Leaders from throughout the western hemisphere will be there, including delegates from the U.S., Canada, Mexico, and a host of other Central and South American countries. One of their agenda items is our agricultural conversion approach to the cartels. We have picked up chatter about potential activity in the area and have been asked by the National Security Advisor to provide overwatch for the state, local, and other federal agencies who will keep an eye on conference attendees. I will be sending Fox, Romeo, and Cap out to assist. They should be arriving at your hotel later this afternoon."

"You need me to pick them up?" Sam asked.

"No need," the director replied. "They will be landing at the Olympia Regional Airport and have a Suburban waiting for them. They will meet you at your hotel with the gear you will need this evening. Fox has the details of the assignment and can brief you once they get there."

"No problem, sir."

"Oh, and Empty . . . "

"Yes, sir?" Sam replied

"I know I forced you to take your vacation, so I appreciate you being willing to lean into this for me," Paul concluded.

Sam started to say, "No problem," but the click of the phone told him that Paul had already disconnected the call.

With a smile on his face, Sam tucked the phone into his pocket, completed his stretching routine, and headed out for his jog. He had plenty of time before his teammates arrived at the hotel, and he could not wait to see them and get back to work.

CHAPTER 8

Allen, Jess, and Leah made record time getting to the hotel, arriving around four in the afternoon. Sam met them in the lobby and helped carry four large black duffels up to the hotel's large conference room, which Samuelson had rented. The room was twenty feet by ten feet with hotel-beige walls and neutral, rough carpeting. A large rectangular conference table sat in the center of the room with six chairs surrounding it. The tang of disinfectant and carpet cleaner bit at Sam's nose as he entered.

Allen swept the room for listening devices and other electronics while Jess, Leah, and Sam unpacked the duffle bags. Allen finished his chores by setting two silent alarms and lock-pick defeaters on the doors to ensure they could leave the excess gear there when they headed out.

Minutes later, with the duffels unpacked, the conference table was covered with M4A1 carbines, pistols, ammunition, small explosives, and assorted communications devices. Jessica picked up a small communications device that resembled an old flip phone and held it up for the others to see. "Old school. Analog," she said and threw it back into the nearest duffle. "No way we're using that."

Jess hefted one of the loaded magazines, tossing it up and down in one hand. "Wait a minute. Who loaded these for us?"

Sam noticed the frown on her face. "Phil, I assume, or one of the logistics people. What's the problem?"

"The mag feels light," Jessica replied. She thumbed rounds out of the twenty-round mag onto the conference room tabletop.

"Well, well," she added as the tenth flipped out of the mag with a hollow chink, and she saw that the magazine was empty. She pointed the top of the mag at Sam and then waved it at the others. "There's supposed to be twenty rounds in here. We've been shorted."

"Whoa," Leah said and picked up two of the four mags she was about to pack into her tactical harness. She weighed one in each hand and glanced at the one on the right. "This one is much lighter than it should be. If many more are like this, we could run out of ammo before we got started."

Leah stepped over to where Jessica had extracted the bullets from the short magazine and picked up the last bullet Jess had ejected. Using a multitool from her tactical vest, she removed the bullet from its casing, finding the shell empty of gunpowder. She held it up for everyone to see. "The bullets are bad, as well."

Sam set aside his Sig Sauer 226 and picked up his cell. "I'll give Phil a call and see what's going on. Meanwhile, empty all the clips and magazines and check the bullets. If that doesn't work out, we'll need Phil to get a fresh ammo load by tomorrow morning."

Allen, Leah, and Jess got busy with the ammo check while Sam dialed Phil's number. As expected, the director's enthusiastic apprentice picked up on the first ring.

"Mike Tango. What can I do for you?"

Sam explained what they had found. "I'll dig into it right away," Phil replied. "Sounds like the logistics guys messed up."

"By a long shot," Sam replied. "I thought the director was signing off on ammo and weapon's loads personally before they went out."

"No longer," Phil replied. "I got him to delegate that to me, but I was called to the NSA and passed the job to the logistics supervisor."

"I need you to inform the director, Phil. This may have happened before. We are checking the ammo that we have and will reload our weapons and mags ourselves. In the meantime, I think it would be best if you could overnight us a new loadout of ammunition and magazines for our pistols and carbines."

"Yes, sir. I'm on it," Phil said. "I will get a fully vetted ammo load to you within the hour."

"Much appreciated," Sam replied. "We can't afford to go into harm's way with questionable gear."

Several hours later, with the ammo check and reload completed, the team secured the conference room and loaded into their Suburban to find some dinner. The plan for tomorrow called for setting up at the capitol building by five in the morning. Now, they needed a fast, out-of-the-way place to eat. The hotel concierge suggested a local pub on the far side of the city called Tugboat Annie's. In conspiratorial tones, the concierge informed him that the locals swore by its low-key atmosphere and high-quality food.

Fifteen minutes later, they found the restaurant at the end of a long, gravel road with a surprisingly full parking lot for a mid-week evening. The restaurant's white clapboard building towered above the parking lot with the restaurant located up a long wooden staircase, while the building's ground level serviced a marina that stretched out behind the building. The sound of laughter and clinking glasses drifted down from above as they exited the vehicle and headed up the stairs.

They entered through a wide, swinging door weathered by decades of service. Inside, Annie's was decorated in classic mariner style with aged, polished wood covering the walls and ceiling and mariner memorabilia hanging in every nook and cranny. To the right of the main door, a long mahogany bar ran half the length of the pub and serviced a half-dozen raised tables for two and four and several booths. A tall memorabilia shelf separated the bar area from the restaurant proper where twenty tables and booths were scattered across the large dining area and along tall windows that looked out across the crowded marina and into the southern reaches of the Puget Sound's inlet. The place smelled of fries and seafood, reminding Sam that he hadn't eaten all day.

A waitress greeted them at the door and led the way to a large booth near the bar. Leah and Jessica took seats on one side of the booth while Allen and Sam took the other. The waitress collected their drink orders and left menus that Sam had just started to examine when Allen elbowed him in the ribs. "Hey, Sam," Allen whispered. "Isn't that the Zamora woman you rescued in Mexico?"

"Right, Allen. Will you just leave that subject alone?" Sam replied, keeping his eyes on the menu.

Leah and Jessica turned in their seats, and Leah said, "Whoa, Sam. I think it is her."

"What are the odds?" Jessica whispered. She reached across the table and pushed Sam's menu down from the front of his face and onto the tabletop. "Allen's right. It is her. I'm sure of it."

Sam let out a long, exaggerated sigh and said, "Fine." He glanced to where they all looked, and there she was. Consuelo Zamora sat at a booth next to one of the tall windows, with Antonio sitting across from her. He froze as he watched her smile at something the boy said.

Sam felt an odd, unsettled feeling as he watched her. She seemed different from when he last saw her in Mexico. Her long, ebony hair was pulled back in a thick ponytail that came forward over her right shoulder. Her large, dark eyes flashed with good humor. She looked more relaxed and so beautiful.

Sam felt his face redden as that last thought arrived unbiddenly. The waitress returned with their drinks, and Sam forced himself to return to the menu.

"Look at him, Jess," Leah blurted, snorting as she laughed. "He's blushing again."

Allen lifted his drink and saluted in the direction of Consuelo's table. "You'd better hurry, buddy. I think you might have some competition for her attention."

"Let it go, will you?" Sam replied. They all knew how uncomfortable he was around women and seemed to feed on his discomfort. Despite his determination not to do so, he glanced over at Consuelo's table again and saw that a tall, well-dressed man now stood at her table. Trim, perhaps in his sixties with carefully combed, thick white hair and a thick drooping mustache, the man attempted to talk with Consuelo.

As Sam watched, Consuelo looked up to meet the man's eyes, her expression was first surprise but then shifted to hurt and anger. When the color appeared to drain from her perfect face, Sam rose from his seat. "Stand by, guys."

"Sam to the rescue, yet again," he heard Leah mutter as she and the other two team members reached to the small of their backs where their pistols rested beneath floppy t-shirts and, in Allen's case, a much-too-bright Hawaiian shirt.

Sam was still a few steps away from Consuelo's table when he heard her say to the tall man, "You are mistaken, sir. My father died several decades ago." Sam could feel the anxiety in her voice.

"I assure you, Señorita, that he did not and that I am who I say that I am."

Sam calmed his expression and stepped up to the table beside the man and said to Consuelo, "I hope I'm not intruding, but my friends and I just arrived at the restaurant and noticed you and Antonio here, Ms. Zamora. I just wanted to speak, if I might interrupt for a second."

Before Consuelo could reply, the tall man turned to face Sam, his weathered face stern and his eyes cold. "Señor, you are intruding on our conversation. Come back another time."

Sam noted the man's arms, held relaxed and loose at his side, and how his knees flexed as the older man appeared to sink slightly into the floor. Sam recognized the posture as a martial arts discipline called rooting. He was a trained fighter, regardless of his age.

For a long moment, the two men stared at each other, the tall man glaring at Sam from hazel eyes set above a blade-like Aztec nose, thin lips, and firm lean jaw. After a moment, the man took a sudden step backward, holding up one hand, palm forward in the universal sign of defense.

"My apologies for my rudeness, sir," he said. "I was just discussing a family matter with Señorita Zamora, but perhaps this is not the best time or place for me to do so. I will take my leave." He nodded to Consuelo. "Perhaps I can approach you another time under better circumstances."

The man spun on his heel, wound his way through the restaurant's tables, and exited through the restaurant's main door.

Sam watched the man leave, noting his smooth, balanced gait, and felt the hair rise on the back of his neck. A trained fighter, for sure.

"Sam? Is it you?"

Sam heard the words and turned back to see Consuelo staring up at him, her smile wide and warm.

Sam offered her his best smile, but now that the perceived threat was gone, he felt his shyness returning. On any day of the week, he'd rather face a platoon of armed bad guys than face a beautiful woman like Consuelo. He felt his throat constrict and all thoughts of conversation flee his brain.

"Yes, ma'am." He stammered the words and waved a hand in the direction of where his team sat. "My friends and I are in town and are having dinner. I noticed you and Antonio and then noticed the man and that you seemed concerned."

"Here to save me, again?" she asked, a mischievous twinkle in her eyes.

He felt like a fool, trying to talk to a woman that was so far out of his league. He gathered himself and attempted to apologize for his actions, not realizing that she was kidding, even flirting with him. "I'm sorry. I realize that someone like you needs little saving. I guess it was just an excuse to say hello."

Tiny lines crinkled at the edges of her large, deep brown eyes. "It is nice to see you, too, and I don't mind that you came to my aid. You remember Antonio?" she added, indicating the young boy sitting across from her.

Sam glanced over to see a different Americanized Antonio from the one he last saw in Mexico. Sam turned back to Consuelo and gestured to the boy. "This is the young man who saved you, as I recall."

Consuelo repeated his words to Antonio in Spanish, "Este es el hombre que te salvo."

Antonio hesitantly reached out a hand. "Gracias, señor, pero creo que nos salva alos dos."

Consuelo started to translate Antonio's words, but Sam stopped her with a smile. "I'm not fluent, but I get what he said. Gracias, jovencito," Sam replied.

They shook hands. Antonio's smile was wide. "Please to meet you, too," the boy said in surprisingly clear English for one so new to the country.

Sam smiled as he dropped Antonio's hand. "You are learning English already, and it's been just a few days since you arrived, I imagine. Very good!"

The teenager beamed. "I am trying."

They all laughed.

"Are you in town for long?" Consuelo asked.

"My friends are here for a day or so, but I'm on vacation for the next few months and thought I might spend some time here. A close friend recommended the area. Now I recall that you said you would be headed here as well."

"Perhaps we could get together once your business with your team has been completed," Consuelo offered.

Sam felt himself blush and was sure that he heard three glasses clink together across the room.

"I . . . I would like that," he replied, noticing Antonio's sheepish smile out of the corner of his eye.

"Habla mucho de usted, señor," Antonio said.

This time, it was Consuelo's turn to blush, and the color in her cheeks seemed to make her even more attractive than before.

Sam smiled, glanced at Consuelo, and then turned back to Antonio. "You say she talks about me all the time?"

Antonio nodded, needing no translation to understand the smile on Sam's face and the knowing look that Consuelo was giving him.

"I do no such thing," Consuelo started. Then she laughed and added, "Well, maybe I do a little. You did save my—*our*—lives."

"Then it's a date," Sam replied.

"You still have my number?" she asked.

Sam tapped the side of his head. "Committed to memory, Ms. Zamora."

"Please, call me Connie." She scribbled her phone number on a napkin and handed the paper to him. "Just in case."

Sam laughed and then paused, surprised at how his words now came so easily with this woman. It normally took him months to approach a woman, let alone carry on a conversation.

"Connie, it is. We should be done with our business in a day or so. Would it be okay if I call you Thursday afternoon?"

"It's a date," she replied with a warm smile that seemed to reach deep down inside him and make something there turn a little sideways. It was not an unpleasant sensation.

Sam lifted a hand and nodded to Antonio. "I'll talk to you then," he said and headed back to his teammates.

Knowing what awaited him there, Sam was not disappointed when he retook his seat next to Allen and his teammate slapped Sam on the back. "Nice going, brother. You saved her again. I did not think you had it in you."

Leah traced a small heart in the condensation on her water glass and spun it toward Sam.

Jessica tried to look serious and concerned as she said, "She is very pretty, Sam. You sure you are up to it? She may not be your kind, being a real woman and all." They all laughed.

"Fine, fine," Sam replied. "You've had your fun. Let's order some food. I'm starving, and we have a long day tomorrow."

A second later, the waitress returned, and they ordered their meals. After the laughter died down, Leah gave Sam a searching look. "You do realize that your Miss Zamora is way out of your league, don't you?" Her words were a warning and yet carried a sincere, concerned tone.

Allen nodded in agreement. "In all our time together as a team, we have seen you on a date exactly twice and, even then, not more than one time per woman. Consuelo Zamora is as famous as she is beautiful. She probably has men lined up at her door." Allen drowned his last words in the remainder of his drink and waved the waitress over for a refill.

Sam looked to Jessica, who had held her peace after her bout of laughter. She noticed his gaze and lifted her eyes to meet his. "Your choice," she said. "As far as I'm concerned, considering what we all do for a living, you need to grab all the happiness you can whenever it is offered." She lifted her water glass in his direction in a toast. "You go for it, big guy!"

Allen and Leah lifted their glasses to join hers. "Here, here," they said in chorus.

Sam nodded. "I appreciate your collective concern, all of you, and I'll be the first to admit that I am not an expert when it comes to women—" He was interrupted by the light touch of a hand on his shoulder. He looked up to see Connie there, smiling down at him with Antonio at her side.

She passed her glance across Sam's three teammates. "I remember each of you from the cantina in Aguascalientes. I presume you are not just Sam's friends but also his teammates."

When Leah was about to wave off the comment, Connie cut her off with a smile. "I have encountered people like you in my travels many times. On several occasions, I might not have survived without their help. It was a hazard of my job as a missionary. The cartels and even the government were not always pleased about outsiders like me coming into their country and helping their citizens—a sort of admission that they could not or would not help them themselves. I just wanted to thank you all again, as I did in Mexico when we met, for what you do to help people like Antonio and me."

Consuelo bent down, kissed Sam on the cheek, and then whispered in his ear. "I heard them teasing you from across the room. Let them chew on this."

She stood up and then added for all at the table to hear, "I am looking forward to our date on Thursday."

Sam started to rise, but her warm hand on his shoulder kept him in place. "I will see you then," she said, before turning and making her way across the pub and out the restaurant's door with Antonio trailing behind.

"Whoa!" Allen said after a prolonged silence, and then lifted his water glass yet again. "I take it all back. You are the master!"

They all laughed and clinked their glasses together again as the waitress returned with their meals.

As Sam and his team left Tugboat Annie's an hour later and headed for their Suburban, a tall, shadowy figure emerged from the darkness at the edge of the parking lot and intercepted them, empty hands held out to his sides to show he was unarmed and meant no harm.

Even in the dim light, Sam recognized the man as the one from the restaurant who had tried to talk to Connie. "I'll meet you at the car," he said to the rest of his team. "I believe this man wants a word with me."

"You sure?" Leah asked, her hand resting at the small of her back where she holstered her pistol. "I don't trust lurkers."

"Just stand by," Sam replied.

"If you don't mind, Señor, perhaps we can step into the light by the restaurant stairs. Perhaps your friends will be more comfortable if they can see us," the man said.

His accent carried the smooth, melodic accent of the Spanish language but with a harsher edge. Sam followed the man the few steps to the stairs, noting again how he moved with the fluid grace of an athlete.

They stopped at the base of the stairs, Sam keeping his distance.

"My name is Fernando Zamora," the man said, running a long-fingered, scarred, calloused hand through his long hair and letting it drop to his side with a sigh. "I am Consuelo's father."

"You can't be Fernando Zamora," Sam replied. "I know that story. And you can't be Consuelo's father. Both those men are dead."

The man lifted his hands from his sides and gave a slight shrug. "And yet, here I am."

Sam gritted his teeth. "You told Consuelo that in the restaurant, didn't you? That's what upset her."

Zamora shrugged, again. "You don't have to believe me, but you need to know I will be around to ensure my daughter's welfare." He gave Sam a knowing look that projected cold certainty. "I will let no harm come to her."

Sam's mind spun into gear, sizing up the situation. Either this man was crazy, or he was one of the most famous ghosts in intelligence history. He was rumored to have been the owner of one of the largest haciendas and rancheros in central Mexico and also an agent working for the Mexican government. To Sam's recollection, no one ever figured out if Zamora was an honest man, a criminal, an assassin, or worse.

Sam examined the man's face. Perhaps he was who he said he was. If that was the case, then Connie's father was indeed alive, and he'd just met one of the most wanted men in the western hemisphere.

"If you are Fernando Zamora, you're taking a big risk being here," Sam said.

Zamora pursed his lips and gave a single nod. "You are correct of course, but only you and Consuelo know I am not bones in a shallow grave somewhere, although I doubt that she yet believes me."

"She has a lot of reasons not to believe you. She thinks you died almost twenty years ago. That's a long time to leave her and her siblings fatherless."

"It was the one way I could protect them," Zamora replied. "It actually is none of your business, but Consuelo and the rest of the family never wanted for anything as they grew up. I made sure of that, and her mother and I have been in contact for all that time. If I had been with them, their lives would have been in constant danger."

Sam raised a hand to glance at his smartwatch. "I am sure there is more to this story, but my friends and I have somewhere we need to be."

Zamora reached into his front pants pocket and withdrew a small business card. He handed the card to Sam. "Everything you need is on that card. I will be close by."

Sam glanced down at the card, memorizing a phone number with a Virginia prefix. "This isn't a lot to go on . . . " he stated as he lifted his eyes, but the man who called himself Fernando Zamora was already gone.

Sam walked over to the Suburban and got into the back left seat. As Jess fired up the vehicle and pulled out of the restaurant's parking lot, he ran through his conversation with Fernando Zamora. When he finished, he held up the business card. "He said all I needed to identify him was on this business card."

Allen, sitting next to Jess in the front passenger seat, reached into a pocket and pulled out a small sandwich bag. "Did you memorize the number on the card?"

"Of course," Sam replied.

"Was the Zamora guy wearing gloves?" Allen persisted.

"I don't think so," Sam replied.

"Then he probably did give you everything you need. Put the card in the sandwich bag. We can hand it over at headquarters once we return, and Phil can run the DNA and the fingerprints. If this guy is the real Mexican Ghost, we will know for sure."

"Wow!" Leah exhaled. "The famous Ghost of Mexico, right here in the neighborhood. The man is a legend."

"Yeah," Jessica said. "And Sam chose his daughter for his latest crush. What are the odds?"

Yeah, what are the odds, Sam thought.

CHAPTER 9

Morning came early for the team. By 5:30 a.m., they were all in position in the capitol building. Sam crouched a few yards to the right of the conference room door on the second floor of the rotunda where the conference attendees would meet. He played the role of a maintenance technician repairing a chip in the building's rare and beautiful Alaskan Tokeen marble walls. His goal was to survey the attendees and provide the first line of defense for those individuals attending the conference.

The Washington State Capitol building was an impressive structure. Sam had visited many famous capitol buildings over the last ten years, but the Washington State Capitol ranked in the top three or four on his list for its simple beauty. The building's floors and walls were covered in brilliant white Alaskan Tokeen marble, streaked through with veins of dark gray and black. High-arching walls reached up from the floor of the capitol rotunda to a small central gathering on the first floor. Wide, marble stairways led up to two brass-railed balconies. Hanging from the peak of the tall rotunda was a five-ton Tiffany chandelier, the largest ever manufactured by that company.

From his position on the second floor next to the conference room entrance, Sam could see Allen on the opposite landing, polishing its burnished brass railings. On the floor above Allen, Sam got a glimpse of Jessica's head as she paced a circuit from the ground floor to the third floor and the hallways beyond. Leah worked near the peak of the tall rotunda some forty feet above, touching up artwork in the tall ceiling, her sniper rifle set to provide internal overwatch for the team.

"Home Team report," he said into his wrist mic as he pulled out a putty knife and marble patching materials and feigned work on a foot-long crack in the expensive marble wall.

"Cap, status one," Jessica replied.

"Fox, status one," Allen added.

"Ditto, Romeo," Leah said.

Sam smiled at Leah's response and glanced at his tactical watch: a few minutes after seven. Time to report in.

"Overwatch, this is Home Team. We are status one," he said into his mic.

"Roger, Mike Tango. Move to status two," Overwatch replied. Sam recognized the higher-pitched voice as Phil's. The usual intelligence analyst must have been called away.

As Phil said his last word, a tall, young state trooper in the traditional blue uniform and Smokey Bear hat of the Washington State Patrol approached and took the position of attention on the far side of the conference room door. He cast Sam a casual nod, which Sam returned. A trooper stationed at the conference room door was a pleasant surprise. The Washington State Patrol was known for its high-quality training programs and top-rate law enforcement officers.

A few minutes later, the six-feet-three bulk of a man that Sam recognized as the chief of the state patrol approached the trooper who, if it was possible, stood a bit taller as his boss approached. With skin as dark as night, the chief was a pioneer in the law enforcement world as one of the first and longest-serving African American chiefs in the business.

The chief paid Sam little notice as he shared a few whispered words with the trooper and then passed through the door and into the conference room.

"Overwatch, the guests are arriving," Sam whispered into his wrist mic. "Moving to status two and standing by. All stations report."

"Fox, two," Allen replied, signaling that his position was set and secure.

"Romeo, two," Leah responded. "And for the umpteenth time, I want a new call sign."

"Cap, two." Sam noted a chuckle in Jessica's voice as she added, "Get over it, girl."

"All stations, roger," Sam acknowledged. "Overwatch, Home Team is status two?"

"Roger, Mike Tango," came Phil's reply. "We are tapped into the capitol CCTV system and have you all on visual. You are go for the mission with full latitude."

"Home Team, we are now status three," Sam said.

CHAPTER 10

Paul Samuelson sat in a coffee shop twenty miles from his office in a tiny, one-street, northern Florida town. The air outside the shop was humid and damp despite the clear, cloudless sky. Beetles and other bugs the size of his thumb clung to the shop's dirty, fly-specked windows. An old, rusted, and dented blue and white Ford pickup passed by as he sipped a cup of passable black coffee, leaving a plume of red-brown dust in its wake.

The directions provided in the text he'd received on his secure phone that morning identified the meeting place as Who Done It Coffee.

Only the National Security Agency director, the Secretary of State, and FBI director possessed the number for the phone as far as he knew. When the text woke him from a deep, dreamless sleep, the phone displayed no name or origin for the call. The text message gave him the name of the coffee shop, the time for the meeting, a designation as potential spam, and a code that Samuelson recognized as a high-level authentication that was unknown to him but not to be ignored.

Samuelson sat in a well-lit corner of the coffee shop with a wall to his back and a large picture window on his left side. He shifted in his chair to unbind the belt holster on his right hip from the chair's armrest while still keeping it well-hidden beneath his gray, herringbone sports jacket. It felt a little odd, carrying a gun again after so many months without it.

Samuelson resisted running his hand over his close-cropped hair, a bad habit and a tell for anyone who might be watching. He had not been in the field for more years than he liked to admit and found that he was a bit nervous.

He sipped his Americano—light cream, no sugar—and set it on the small, round table before him as a delivery man in a brown uniform and baseball cap, pulled low over his eyes, entered the shop and approached him. The man lifted a clipboard, examined it, and then handed Samuelson a legal-sized, white envelope.

Samuelson accepted the envelope without a word as the man turned on his heel and departed. He ran a thumb under the envelope's flap. He should have it scanned for biological and chemical agents, but anyone who knew who he was and how to reach him at this place could have taken him out in any number of ways, so why drag the mystery out any longer?

Inside the envelope was a single sheet of paper with three lines of print in large font:

> We know who you are. We know the names and locations of your team members and their families. We know every mission that your group has scheduled. You need to put all planned missions on hold. In two weeks, you will receive further instructions. Follow those instructions or your team members will be eliminated, one each day, until all are dead. Tell anyone about this communication, and the executions will begin immediately. We are watching.

Samuelson retrieved his secure phone from the side pocket of his sports jacket, glared at it, and stuffed it back. He pulled out a second cell phone and a burner he kept for emergencies when communications might be compromised as they were today. He punched in the number for the secure line in his office.

Phil picked up on the call. "Your code, please," Phil said.

Samuelson recited an eight-digit code that changed daily but offered a safe and secure method for validating the person at the other end of the call.

"Proceed with your message, sir," Phil continued.

"Suspend all missions. Do it now. Highest priority. All teams already in the field are to relocate to secondary, safe locations. Family members are to be put under observation and protection now."

"Yes, sir. What about Home Team?" Phil asked.

Samuelson drummed his fingers on the tabletop. "Empty is already compromised, and Olympia is a low-level support function. Let them complete their mission."

"On it, sir."

Samuelson drained his coffee in a single long draw, crumpled the cardboard cup, and tossed it in a waste can as he stood and departed the coffee shop.

CHAPTER 11

At 7:15 in the morning, Jessica signaled that a small crowd had entered the rotunda from the first-floor front entrance. Once in the building, they gathered in the small ground-floor receiving area of the rotunda as a young woman in a smart business suit arrived and pointed out the many historic features of the building. One man of dark and swarthy complexion dressed in a tailored, navy pin-striped suit split off from the group and headed toward the wide marble stairs that led to the conference room.

Sam whispered into his wrist mic, "Lone man leaving the group. Eyes on him."

"Fox, three. I see him," Allen said over Sam's cochlear receiver.

"Romeo, three," Leah added from her position in the high reaches of the rotunda. She had the man covered as well.

Sam tracked the man as he mounted the final steps to the second floor and approached the conference room door. Sam ran his practiced gaze over the man as he paused to check in with the trooper at the door. The man's suit looked expensive and well-tailored. As snug as the suit fit, Sam could see no bulges or obvious indications that the man was armed.

"Tango is clear," Sam whispered into his communicator. Three clicks in his cochlear receiver told him the others got the message.

As the group's tour of the rotunda ended a few minutes later, the crowd mounted the marble stairs to the conference room door. Sam scanned the crowd as the trooper checked each person in. He recognized the director of the U.S. Drug Enforcement Agency and his aide from years of collaboration with that agency. Following behind the DEA chief were his counterparts from Canada, Mexico, Guatemala, and eight other Central American and South American countries. An officious-looking aid accompanied each dignitary. With such a large group to size up in one pass, it was impossible to tell whether they might or might not be carrying weapons under their clothes or in the briefcases. The team would have to trust the metal detectors built into the conference room's doorframe.

Sam had previewed the governor's conference room layout on his tablet computer the night before. He called up the image on a small tablet computer he carried in a box of maintenance supplies, much as any repairperson would do when finishing one job and preparing to move on to the next.

The diagram on the tablet showed a long conference table centrally located in the room. Eight high-backed, brown leather chairs lined each side of the table with another at each end. One of the end chairs was taller than the rest and embossed with the seal of the state of Washington. Smaller leather chairs flanked the walls. Thick crimson wall hangings framed the room's three windows, edged in rich, gold brocade and embroidered with the hand-stitched state seal in gold thread.

"Overwatch, this is Home Team standing by. Nothing to report," Sam whispered.

"Overwatch, roger," came the reply.

As Sam and the team settled into what looked to be a boring, eventless day of watching attendees enter and leave the drug interdiction conference, a green cargo van with the Washington State logo on both doors turned down a narrow road and driveway at the back of the capitol building. A tall, gray garage door lifted as the van approached and disappeared inside, then closed behind it.

Sam's cochlear hummed twice, indicating an emergency call. "Ears on, Home Team," he said into his wrist mic.

"This is Overwatch," Phil said over the radio. "An unscheduled van just entered the sub-basement garage at the back of the capitol building. We have a drone above that location and two CCTV cameras that show the van in place in the garage now. I repeat, this is unscheduled and should be considered a threat."

Sam felt his pulse quicken. "Overwatch, please advise Capitol Security of the situation."

"Already done, Empty. Standing by."

"Fox, Cap, abandon your positions and clear the rotunda of civilians as quietly and quickly as you can. Romeo, remain in position," Sam said.

"Cap, roger."

"Fox, roger."

"Showtime," Leah added.

Sam set down his putty knife and can of marble patch, stood and stretched like a worker too long in the same position, and wandered over to the trooper standing next to the conference room door. "You know who I am, trooper?" Sam asked.

"I was briefed," the trooper replied without taking his eyes off the rotunda he was ordered to watch.

"We have a situation," Sam whispered to the man. He saw the color drain from the trooper's face, and then the man's jaw set with renewed determination.

"We identified an unscheduled van that pulled into the subbasement garage a few minutes ago. If anything is about to go down, the bad guys will have to come up the stairs or service elevator to get to the conference attendees. Campus Security has been notified. Just wanted you to know in case things get dicey."

"The Washington State Patrol should be told," the trooper replied.

"That is being taken care of," Sam responded.

"There are two public elevators and fire escape stairs on the backside of the rotunda that they could use," the trooper said.

"Good to know," Sam replied. "If you can, please get word to your chief in the conference room to let him know our concerns."

The trooper nodded, his wide-brimmed Smokey Bear hat following in response, and then turned smartly on his heel, quietly opening the conference room door and stepping inside.

"Home Team, the conference room is as secure as we can make it," Sam announced and then relayed the elevator and emergency escape stairway information to the team.

"That's a lot of ground to cover," Fox concluded.

"Home Team, this is Overwatch. The State Patrol's Rapid Reaction Force is standing by and is five minutes out once you give the word."

Sam scanned the rotunda and saw a set of elevator doors open on the second-floor balcony behind where Fox had been stationed. Two men in green overalls, carrying what looked like older AK rifles, jogged out of the elevator and headed for the stairs leading to the ground floor.

"Two tangos confirmed on the east balcony," Sam whispered. "They are armed. Home Team going status four and tactical."

"Roger, Home Team," Oversight replied. "Alerting the State Patrol RRF and Campus Security now."

"Belay that, Overwatch. There are too many people in this space. Give us a few minutes before you bring them in. I think we can handle what shows up."

"Acknowledged. Will comply," Overwatch replied.

Leah clicked her mic twice for a priority communication. "I see three more tangos entering the ground floor reception area from the elevator on the west side of the building. I see another half-dozen emerging from a hallway from the south, headed for the ground floor reception area. All appear armed with long guns and a few submachine pistols of some kind. There might be some older M16s in the crowd."

As Leah finished, the trooper emerged from the conference room door in time to be met by two high-velocity rounds to the chest. The man staggered backward and fell through the open doorway.

Sam raced to the downed trooper's side, seeing no blood seeping from three fresh holes in the man's uniform shirt and noting the thick bulletproof vest underneath. Sam dragged the trooper into the room and then turned to the conference room attendees. "He should be okay, but the building is under attack. We need you all to stay calm and remain in the room so we can handle this."

He glanced around the room until his eyes met those of the state patrol's chief. "Go do your job, son," the chief said. "We'll hold things together in here."

Sam left the conference room in a crouch, grimacing as he turned, his tactical vest pressed against the bruise on his rips from the battle in Mexico. He pulled the door closed behind him and was pleased when he heard the inside door bolt thrown.

"Fox, Cap. Where are we on the evacuations?" he whispered into his smartwatch's mic.

"It's all clear, as much as we can determine," Jessica said. "It's early in the day. Not too many visitors, but someone mentioned a small school group in the building. I have not been able to confirm that or locate the group."

"Keep an eye out for those kids," Sam replied.

"Orders, Mike Tango?" Fox requested.

"The trooper at the door is down, but I think he's okay. Romeo, stay in position. Let's do the tag drill so that we can take them down but not give away too much. Jess, Allen, and I will find our best locations and paint the tangos as we see them, one by one. When you see the red dot on a tango's chest, Leah, you take the shot. Let's see how many we can take out before they realize how many of us are here and where we are located in the building."

"Roger that," Leah replied.

"Fox on the hunt," Allen added.

"Showtime!" Jessica said.

With Jessica's last word, the attackers opened fire in earnest. Some hunkered down next to the ground walls of the ground floor's reception area. Others stood in plain sight, making Sam wonder just who they were facing. From his position, Sam identified the attackers as a collection of tall and small males and females randomly firing on full-automatic in all directions. It appeared that their goal was to create fear and pandemonium for anyone in the building, rather than focus on any specific target.

"Tag, left side, ground floor," Sam heard Allen say.

That was followed by a soft *phutt* as Leah triggered her suppressed sniper rifle and a man on the ground floor dropped.

"My turn," Jess said. "Paint on the east side. Same floor."

Another *phutt* sounded, and another tango dropped.

The rest of the attackers noticed their compatriots dropping around them and stopped firing, milling around in place without any specific direction in mind.

"I'll take the west wall. Jess, you take the east wall. Allen, the north wall. We light up as many as we can and as rapidly as we can. Leah, you take them down in cycle: east, north, west. Keep an eye on that south wall. Keep cycling through east, north, west, and south for as long as we can keep knocking them down."

"Roger," Leah said. "Show me the color!"

Six attackers dropped in the next few minutes before the assailants figured out their strategy and took cover behind stairway corners and doorways and reopened their random, automatic fire.

"I think tag is over," Sam whispered into his wrist mic. "I think the people on the ground floor are a distraction for something else, probably directed at the conference room. If I'm right, we should see something happen soon."

Sam heard the suppressed *pop-pop-pop* of his team's M4A1s as Allen and Jessica opened fire, mixed with the softer coughs of Leah's sniper rifle as they took down attacker after attacker. Still crouching, he scooted his way to the edge of the marble stairway leading up to the conference room from the ground floor, noting its thick, cool marble surface. Leaning around the marble column at the edge of the stairs, he saw two attackers charge up the steps side-by-side.

"Two tangos headed my way, toward the conference room. Stay on your targets. I've got them," Sam said into his mic.

He counted the attacker's loud footfalls as they pounded up the wide, marble staircase. When they were a few feet from the top, he slid on his right side into the open above the top stair, swinging the butt of his M4A1 into the legs of the attacker nearest him. As that man fell, he lashed out with his left foot to catch the second attacker on the knee. The joint cracked, and the man went down next to Sam.

Sam jumped to his feet, bent forward, and launched a punch at the first attacker's temple with the middle knuckle of his fist extended. He heard the crunch of bone and felt the soft tissue of the man's head give way. The man's eyes rolled up, and his body drooped across the top step.

Sam spun and lashed out with the butt of his M4A1 again, this time straight into the second attacker's forehead as he recovered from the kick in the crotch. The man screamed as bone crunched and the man's skull fractured. Sam silenced him with a palm strike to the forehead. The man whimpered as he lost consciousness and fell atop his fellow attacker.

"Two tangos down," Sam reported.

Sam's report was followed by the grunt of hard-blown air over the comms. Another quick beat and Jessica added, "This is Cap. Two more down at my end. Some clean-up will be needed on the second floor. A lot of blood up here."

Jess had taken out two as well. How many were left?

"Overwatch, do you have a count?" he asked into his wrist mic.

"We have the drone in the high reaches of the rotunda. From what we can see, you have taken out a dozen attackers. Heat signatures identify at least eight more in the areas around you and moving."

"Roger, Overwatch. Use the drone to light them up. Get the drone's lasers on the tangos for Romeo's shot."

"Roger, Empty," Overwatch replied. "They are getting much better at staying out of sight, but we will do what we can."

"Romeo, work with Overwatch. Tag as many as you can," Sam said.

"Roger, Empty," Leah replied, followed by the cough of her M21 Special sniper rifle firing another suppressed .338 round. With its customized M14 frame, twenty-six-inch barrel, and six-inch silencer/suppressor, the rifle was durable and reliable and the perfect size for both field use and in tighter spaces like the overhead catwalk in the capitol building's high ceiling. "Tango down," she said.

Three more shots followed, along with three more reports of attackers taken down under Leah's sharp eye with the help of the drone.

Sam remained at the top of the stairs guarding the entrance to the conference room, using the stairway's thick corner post for cover, M7A1 in hand. He heard a loud yell, glanced to the second-floor stairs on the opposite side of the rotunda, and saw Allen grappling with an attacker. The two went to the ground in a flurry of fists and feet, followed by the flash of Allen's long-bladed assault knife as it rose and pounded down into his adversary once and then again.

"Tango down," came Fox's labored report.

With a scream, another attacker flew over the brass rail of the second-floor balcony. Sam glanced up in time to see Jessica's head peer over the rail. "Tango down" came her report a second later.

As the falling attacker hit the marble floor with a dull thud and clatter of weapons, Sam glanced to the floor below in time to see a thick head of ebony hair and Consuelo Zamora peering around the white marble post at the bottom of the stairwell. Four teenagers,

Antonio among them, followed her glance as the remaining attackers opened up with full-automatic fire in their direction. As the gunfire echoed across the cavernous rotunda floor, he saw Connie reach out a hand to pull the teens back behind the marble wall.

Sam vaulted over the staircase wall and flew down the remaining steps, paying no heed to the bullets flying around him or the stabbing pain in his ribs. He hit the bottom floor flat-footed, knees flexed, landing nose to nose with Consuelo. "You need to get out of here, now. This place is under attack."

"Sam?" Consuelo asked.

"We're under attack?" one of the teens asked and raised his cell phone to take a video. "This is so cool."

Sam ripped the cell phone from the kid's hand and pocketed it, turning back to Consuelo. "I need you to get these kids out of here."

Recalling the map of the building to mind, Sam raised an arm to his left. "Go down this hall and you will find an exit. Take the kids and get going. Please."

Consuelo turned to the four boys and Sam could see the steel in her eyes. "Let's go, boys. No talking. Follow me. Do it now and keep your phones in your pockets."

"Thank you," Sam whispered as she headed down the hall at a jog, the four boys falling behind.

"Found the school group," Sam whispered into his mic.

"I saw. It was Sam's girlfriend," he heard Leah say from her perch high in the rotunda. "She had a bunch of teenagers with her. That woman just can't stay out of trouble."

"Fox, here. Bad guys heading up the stairs to the conference room."

"Can you mark any of them, Romeo?" Sam asked.

"Give me a sec," she replied, followed by a soft *phutt, phutt.*

Sam edged up the stairs and glanced toward the landing at the top in time to see two armed attackers fall halfway up. Four more carrying rifles and a third attacker in a heavy overcoat ran to the conference room door beyond where the first two fell. Three more tangos swarmed up the base of the marble stairway to join their compatriots, trapping Sam between the two groups until Sam heard a loud volley of M4A1 fire and the three below him crumpled to the ground.

Sam keyed his mic. "Thanks, guys. The lead tango is wearing a thick overcoat."

"A little warm for that," Jessica replied.

"Roger that," Sam said. "There has to be a suicide vest underneath. I need a tunnel."

"Roger" came the reply, repeated three times.

"Lay down the fire on my mark and push those four tangos away from the one in the coat. I'll take that one myself, but give me a path there," Sam said. He paused a beat and then whispered, "Mark," and began his sprint up the remaining stairs leading to the second-floor landing and the conference room door.

Allen and Jessica's M4s and Leah's sniper rifle opened fire up both sides of the stairway, blazing a path for Sam as he took the stairs two at a time. One attacker dropped immediately as bullets pinged off the marble floor and walls, catching him in a ricochet. That was followed by the loud crack of a smaller caliber weapon that Sam couldn't place as a second armed attacker dropped next to the conference room door.

Head down and legs churning, Sam made the top of the stairs and slid to a stop outside the conference room door as the conference room door crashed closed. He pushed aside an AK47 and the leg of a sprawled, motionless attacker to clear space next to the door for him to stand. A glance down at the attacker revealed long, blonde hair in a thick braid hanging down from what might have been an attractive woman's face, except for the gaping hole where her right eye had once been.

"Three made it into the conference room," Sam whispered into his wrist mic

"This is Fox. I'm on my way."

"Cap, en route," Jessica added.

"No time," Sam replied. "I think that one in the long coat is wearing a suicide vest."

"Wait for us, Sam. We can go in as a team," Jessica offered.

"That bomb could go off any second. I'm going in now. Overwatch, this is Empty. Do I have a go?"

"You are status four, Empty," Phil replied over the radio. "Proceed as you see best."

"Roger," Sam replied.

Sam racked a round into the chamber of his M4A1 and then shifted his carbine to his left hand. With his right hand, he reached to a loop on his tactical vest and pulled out a steel Smith & Wesson expandable baton. He swung the baton down with a snap, expanding it to its full twenty-four-inch length, then paused for two beats and sucked in a deep breath.

The attackers surely would have the door blocked on the inside. Negotiation was never a good idea when someone wore a suicide vest, so he dropped his right shoulder and charged the door. The wood door cracked under his attack, and the already-splintered wood bent around several chairs positioned against the wall, creating an opening wide enough for Sam to follow into the room.

Sam came in low, head on a swivel and eyes scanning the room. Sam located the state patrol's chief on the far side and sent the M4A1 carbine through the air in a high arc, trusting the old chief's reflexes were good enough to catch the weapon on the fly and do what needed to be done.

In two ground-eating strides, he was at the conference table and vaulted onto its top, just missing the shoulder of an elderly woman in a brightly colored dress. She gasped and dodged out of his way, tumbling to the floor.

Pumping his legs and scattering glassware and papers in every direction, Sam sprinted down the length of the table toward the man—no, he saw now that it was a woman—at the far end, still wearing the trench coat with the bomb vest visible beneath it. As he fixed his eyes on her, she reached for what he assumed was the trigger mechanism located at her belt.

Behind him, Sam heard two three-round bursts from the carbine he'd thrown to the chief. He prayed the man's aim was still good.

Reaching the end of the table, Sam launched himself at the woman in the suicide vest. Her eyes widened as he reached her, extended his left hand, and clamped down on her right as she fumbled with the trigger mechanism.

He raised the steel baton in his right hand, pulled the attacker toward him, and crashed the rigid, steel baton down on the suicide bomber's trigger arm with all his strength. The woman screamed as the steel bit into her arm, breaking bones and tearing muscles. Her grip on the bomb's trigger mechanism went limp. Sam let the baton drop and ripped the trigger mechanism from her grasp, careful to keep his fingers well away from the central, black button.

Sam came down hard on his wounded side atop the woman, whose screaming stopped abruptly. Ignoring the stabbing pain from his bruised ribs, he lifted the trigger mechanism high in the air and away from any potential struggle that might ensure should she resume consciousness. She didn't, remaining inert below him.

Silence enveloped the room as Sam struggled to his feet. The smell of cordite from the rifle shots spoiled the air, and a gray haze lay over the stunned conference attendees, many of whom remained in their chairs, too shocked to move. That silence lasted only a beat before everyone in the room let out a collective sigh, followed by a round of applause.

Sam stood on shaky legs over the downed suicide bomber, being very careful with the bomb's trigger.

The state patrol's chief walked over to him, the M4A1's barrel still wafting its smoky exhaust from the barrel. "Nice job, son," the chief said. "That was good work."

"Thank you, sir," Sam said as he sucked in great gulps of air.

A trooper appeared at Sam's side a moment later, accompanied by a beefy German Shepherd and two additional troopers who wore the signature padded uniforms of an explosive ordinance disposal team. "I'll take that," the first trooper said, nodding to the bomb trigger.

"Of course," Sam replied.

The two troopers bent over the still motionless suicide bomber and did a cursory exam of the bomb vest as several other troopers escorted the conference attendees from the room. The bomb ordinance disposal officer raised a thumbs-up to Sam and the chief. He reached down and then snipped the wires leading from the trigger mechanism to the vest. "Simple setup on the vest, sirs. No problem. It is now inert. We'll blow it in the explosives yard once we get it out of here and have a good look at it."

"Thanks, guys," the chief said, then clasped a massive hand on Sam's shoulder. "I suspect you would like to get back to your team. I'm pretty sure the people you work for would not appreciate you being present when the press shows up, as it undoubtedly will."

"Nice toss, by the way," the chief continued. "A nice little gun, too, that M7A1. A bit small for my hands, but it did the job just fine, thanks to you."

"Good shot, taking out the two tangos and the suicide bomber," Sam said.

"I got the two attackers with the guns, but as for the suicide bomber, that wasn't me," the chief replied. "That was all you. I figure she died right after she hit the floor."

"She's dead?" Sam said, glancing over to where several troopers and EMTs loaded the vestless suicide bomber onto a metal gurney.

"What I did should not have killed her. I wanted her alive for questioning," Sam said.

"Who knows?" the chief replied. "It could have been a simple heart attack. I've seen it before. In any event, my thanks to you and your team for all you did today."

"Thank you, sir," Sam said, accepting his M4A1 from the chief. Sam wracked back the carbine's bolt back, clearing the round still lodged in the chamber, dropped the carbine's magazine, and slapped a full magazine into place. That done, he whispered into his analog wrist mic, "Home Team, exfiltrate."

"Romeo, roger," came Leah's reply.

"Cap, roger," Jessica added.

"Fox roger, but moving slow. Pulled something during that fight."

"Your ride is outside the south ground level exit door, away from the gathering crowd," Overwatch advised.

"Roger, Overwatch. Home Team clear," Sam said and headed for the door.

CHAPTER 12

The group jet sat ready, engines warmed up and whining for a quick departure as they pulled up at the small but serviceable Olympia airport thirty minutes later. Four and a half hours after that, they were wheels down at a small, abandoned Air Force field near the group's headquarters in northern Florida and ushered into the headquarters' small conference room.

"Nine p.m. eastern time," Jess grumbled. "What could be so important that we couldn't take time for a quick shower and a change of clothes?"

Director Samuelson met them in the conference room with a fresh pot of coffee, four mugs, and an assortment of doughnuts and other pastries. Tired from the mission and the rapid transit across the continent, the four operators piled their mission-duffels next to the conference room door and took seats around the green, metal conference room table. Cups of coffee and fresh-made doughnuts were passed around.

Samuelson sat at the far end of the table, a stained Styrofoam coffee cup in one hand. He picked up a remote control and punched a button. Behind him, a screen recessed in the conference room wall was filled with a familiar face. It was Sam, frozen in mid-air on CCTV in the capitol conference room as he dove for the suicide bomber.

"Welcome back, heroes," Samuelson said, cutting off anything Allen or the rest of the team might have added. His tone was dry and not at all happy. "It seems that you not only saved the day in Olympia, as you were supposed to, but you also have now made it onto national TV."

"Nice Superman dive, Sam," Leah said.

"Yeah, nice pic, buddy," Allen added, wiggling his thick eyebrows. "Superstar form!"

"Not so quick, Fox," the director said and hit a button on the screen's remote control. Sam's picture was replaced by one of Allen charging down the capitol building's hallway, M4A1 in hand and teeth bared. Samuelson hit the button several more times, catching each of the operators in turn in various dramatic poses. Even Leah was highlighted as she sat crouched high in the capitol building's dome with her eye glued to the scope of her rifle.

The director took a long pull of coffee and tossed the cup into a waste can across the room. "It seems that all of you are famous, now that our little low-risk mission has been completed."

Jessica sat forward in her chair, her expression intense and not pleased. "I scanned the area for cameras that morning, and I can tell you where each of those cameras is in that building and none of them, including the one in the conference room, could have captured those images. There is something more here."

"She's right, sir," Sam added. "We reviewed the CCTV camera locations the night before from the diagrams provided for the mission. None of these pictures could have come from those locations."

Samuelson nodded. "I figured as much, but I wanted to hear from each of you."

"What about the ammunition loads, sir?" Leah asked. "Our loadout for the op included defective rounds and light-loaded magazines and clips."

Phil entered the room with a yellow legal pad in one hand and took a seat on the director's right. "I tracked the errors in the ammunition load-out back to our own resources. Earnie, in logistics, was in charge of getting you the ammunition for the mission."

"Error, nothing," Leah replied. "Someone wanted us to run short on ammo at a bad moment."

"As I was saying," Phil continued, unperturbed as he stared at notes on a yellow legal tablet, "the last person to check the loadout was the logistics supervisor. The issue rests there, whether it was a simple mistake or sabotage."

"You're saying Earnie Ross shorted us ammo?" Sam asked. "That is hard to believe. He is so compulsive he would not let anyone else pack my chute for the HALO mission into Brazil last year."

"And thank goodness for that," Jessica added. "Those high altitude, low opening chutes need to be packed just right, or there can be a lot of problems. I'm with Sam on this one. It can't be an Earnie issue."

Phil held up the yellow tablet and tapped it with a finger. "My information suggests it could be only him."

"I still find that hard to believe—" Sam started but was cut off by Samuelson, who raised a hand for quiet.

"We will get to the bottom of your load-out issues in time. Whether it was Earnie Ross or someone else, I will follow up."

"But, sir," Phil started.

"But nothing," the director replied. "This is my group, and I am the one who delegated the loadout. Ultimately, I am responsible for everything that goes on in the group. So, until I can get to the bottom of this, I want you all to take two weeks' leave, starting now."

All four members of Home Team groaned in unison.

Samuelson stood, hands on his hips, and let his glare go from Jess, to Allen, to Leah, and finally to Sam. "Your op-tempo has been severe for the past six months, and the last two weeks of that have been a whirlwind. That's on me, and I need you fresh for some missions coming up in the next month. I need you rested. Stash your gear in your cages and get out of here. There are three open-ended tickets for anywhere in the country for Allen, Jessica, and Leah on the counter in the lobby. The three of you let Phil know where you'll be once you figure it out. And I don't want to see any of your faces until you've had two weeks off."

Jess, Allen, and Leah stood, grumbled three "yes, sirs," and filed out of the room, grabbing their duffels as they went.

"Sam, stay behind for a minute, if you will." The director turned to Phil. "Phil, I need the room with Sam. Please close the door behind you when you leave the room."

Phil started to protest the director's direction but gathered himself, stood, and exited the room.

Samuelson dropped back into his chair and gestured for Sam to do the same. "You and your team did a good job in Olympia."

"Thank you, sir," Sam replied. "But I still don't understand—"

Samuelson cut him off with a raised hand. "I know you and the team did what was needed, and as usual, you all went well above and beyond . . . "

"I hear a definite 'but' coming with that comment," Sam said.

"I have no problem with the team's performance," Samuelson continued, "but I remain concerned about your reluctance to pull the trigger during an operation. From what I saw in the mission recordings taken by the drone, you had the opportunity to shorten numerous enemy engagements had you pulled your sidearm or used your carbine. Instead, you chose direct, hand-to-hand engagement with your targets."

"There was no need for me to shoot those people," Sam replied. "Everything was up close and personal, where a weapon would have gotten in the way. If the suicide bomber hadn't had a heart attack and died, we might have captured a valuable source of intel. If I'd shot her outright, there would have been no chance for that, let alone a greater chance of her triggering that suicide vest."

Samuelson waved away the remarks. "Look, as always, your actions carried a good portion of the mission, regardless of whether you pulled a trigger or not. The chief of the Washington State Patrol testified to that point when we talked after the mission. That is why I'm not removing you from the team."

Sam stood up from his chair. "Not removing me from the team?"

"Correct. I remain worried about your actions, even as effective as they were yesterday and always have been. I need you on the team, but the bottom line is that I want you to take the time and think through things and figure out why you hesitate to pull a trigger. As of right now, you are to take those two months of paid leave that we talked about earlier. That will give you time to come to grips with anything that might stand in the way of you being a fully functional operator."

Sam could not believe the words he heard and stood from his chair. "I am a fully functional operator, sir. I've never failed on a mission, and Home Team is your best team. You've said it yourself."

"I understand how you feel, Sam. I do," the director replied, "but I need you to work this out."

Samuelson lifted a thin folder from the table in front of him. "We have a new computer program that the NSA has asked us to use to assess team resources. It factors in history, training, experience, personal history, current performance—everything. Each team member is given a score once they have been run through the program and is assessed regarding their suitability for ongoing operations. This is your assessment. It suggests you are a potential risk to your fellow team members."

"Why haven't any of us heard about this assessment program?" Sam demanded. "For that matter, why are you relying on a computer to tell you about us when you've seen our work?"

Samuelson dropped the folder onto the tabletop. "I have been directed to use the program by my boss, the Secretary of State. You were the first operator run through the program, and only Phil and I have known of its existence until now."

Sam dropped back into his chair, feeling defeated and betrayed. "This is so wrong. That program has it all wrong."

"When you return from your vacation, we'll talk about that. I do not want to lose you from the group," Samuelson said, climbing to his feet to conclude their meeting. "But I will do what I have to do to ensure the safety of our operators and the success of our mission."

Sam sucked in a deep breath and met Samuelson's gaze. "I can tell you right now that, for me, it's being on the team or nothing at all. If you have some idea of pulling me off of the teams and putting me in training or behind a desk because of all this, I'd rather leave the group and return to the Special Forces."

"I understand your feelings," the director replied, stepping around the conference room table and stopping a few feet from where Sam sat. "I would feel the same way in your shoes. Just do me a favor and take that time off. I'm sure everything will come together in time, and we will both have a better idea of what we need to do then. I cannot emphasize the importance of you not doing anything rash during that time."

Sam stood from his chair and turned toward the door, then paused as his hand reached for the knob. "I'll do that, sir, but I think you already know where my heart is."

Without another word, Sam stepped from the room and paced out of the building.

CHAPTER 13

Sam made his way across the group's small courtyard behind the headquarters to the logistics building where each operator's equipment cages were located. As he reached for the padlock on his cage, he found a yellow sticky note attached to it. "Usual place. One hour."

One hour later, he found Allen, Leah, and Jessica at McCarthy's Tavern. A classic Florida dive and a favorite meeting place for military and law enforcement officers in the area. A cold soda awaited him as he took a seat with his teammates. He downed half the glass in a single pull.

"Whoa, boy," Allen said. "That must have been some talk you had with the boss."

"Whatever," Sam mumbled and drained the rest of his soda.

Leah lifted her half-empty glass and waved it in the direction of a couple sitting at a small table near the door. "Look at those two," she said. "The man's Bermuda shorts, black socks, sandals, and lily-white legs say *civilian* all over. The woman's couch-potato smock backs it up."

"That's you in another day or so," Allen said, saluting Sam with his glass. "You're on the way out the door, buddy. I can feel it in the air."

Sam glared at his empty glass, moving it around the moisture ring formed on the tabletop. With the other hand, he reached into the peanut basket in the center of the table and popped a peanut into his mouth—shell and all.

"Ewwww," Leah protested. "How can you eat that with the shell on? It's not human."

"He just does it to bug you," Allen said, saluting Sam as he spit out two halves of the peanut shell onto the floor.

"As opposed to not pulling the trigger on my carbine right and left, peanuts are what I do," Sam replied. "Do you guys think I'm holding back when we're on assignment?"

Jessica responded first. "We have not failed a single mission. Whether you pulled a trigger or not, our success rate is off the charts compared to the other teams in the group. Team Two, as good as they are, are huge leaps behind us."

"So, then what's the problem?" Sam persisted.

"I've been snooping around the group's database," Leah said.

"You mean, you've been sucking up to Phil in the front office and prying out information," Allen said.

Leah fluffed her hair, which flowed down her shoulders in a thick cascade of red bronze. "Like any good operator in the field, I use the tools available to me."

Sam gestured for her to continue.

"What I learned from Phil is that three teams went out about the same time as we did for our last Mexico operation. One team's vehicles experienced issues, and they never got to their destination. That mission was aborted. A second team had an ammunition load issue as we did but didn't identify the problem until they were already in a firefight. They lost two operators. The third team was ambushed at a small covert airport in Brazil when they landed. Three of the four people on that mission died in place. And now there's a new software program that the group is using to assess operator competence. Only one file in that record." Leah pointed a finger in Sam's direction.

"So, I just heard," Sam said. "The program designated me a risk to the team."

"That's bogus," Allen replied.

"So wrong," Jessica added.

"Maybe the director feels that sending you on an extended vacation is a way to get the issue of that assessment off the table while he deals with the larger situation of what looks like three compromised teams," Leah said. "He's always been good to all of us. I bet he'll come around once things settle down."

Allen's chair creaked as he leaned back and ran a hand across his face. "Three teams were scrubbed before they could even start their missions, and operator lives were lost? With our screwy ammo load in Olympia, I think we all need to know what's going on."

"There has to be a leak inside the group," Jessica said, tossing her thick, black braid over one shoulder. "That would explain why we are being cleared out for two weeks, and none of us got word about any of this."

"Either way, I am out of action for at least two months. You three need to be careful once you get back from your vacations. All of our jobs just got a lot more difficult."

CHAPTER 14

Two hours later, Sam sat in the Northeast Florida Regional Airport staring at its stained pastel green walls and long rows of cracked plastic seats. The floors were dirty and scuffed and showed the abuse that so many small, regional airports experienced with too much demand and too little budget to keep them up. The place smelled of anti-bacterial disinfectant.

Tiny as it was, the NFRA's runway handled several daily flights to Denver. Sam would connect there for the final leg to the Seattle-Tacoma Airport. Before heading for the airport, Sam had made a last trip to his equipment cage, retrieving a few personal possessions and stuffing them into the ruck that was his only carry-on. As he packed his gear, it was impossible not to reflect on the last time he was forced from a place he loved.

Sam was seventeen when he had lost his little sister in a senseless playground accident. He and his brother Carter had watched helplessly as a sunny summer day turned into a nightmare. Their beautiful, five-year-old baby sister climbed to the top of a tall slide, unsupervised as both the boys and their parents were distracted, and then slipped off the top, crumpling to the ground to breathe her last breath. The trauma left both the boys and their parents grieving and withdrawn.

His parents' deaths followed closely on the heels of their sister's death, his father dying while on an army deployment and his mother following her husband a short time later. The boys were split by the courts to live with separate uncles. Each withdrew into their worlds and lost touch with each other.

Sam enlisted in the army right after high school and buried himself in his training. In a manner, he found a new family in an organization where his quick intelligence, natural athletic abilities, and guileless sincerity served him well.

Sam fast-tracked through the early days of his military career and was commissioned as an officer through the army's Green to Gold program after two years on active duty and an intense, concentrated college program. He qualified for the Army Ranger program after three more years and was recruited for Special Forces immediately after graduating from Ranger school. He distinguished himself on his first two missions as a Green Beret, and the Extreme Operations Group identified him as a candidate for their operator training program. Throughout that fast-paced time, Sam gained a reputation as someone to be relied upon no matter the cost, no matter the strain.

But Sam knew Director Samuelson was right. Something was missing. He loved his work and knew he made a difference in the world, but he needed something else. He knew Leah, Allen, and Jessica had active social lives, and he lived vicariously through the stories they shared about their experiences outside of work. Each time he heard those stories, they wondered why he had so little to share.

The announcement for his flight blared through the waiting area, interrupting his thoughts. As he swung his ruck over his shoulder and headed for the gate, he promised himself he would use the time to discover how he might fill that void in his life. How hard could it be?

The plane left on time, and the connection in Denver was nearly perfect, with just enough time for a quick meal before boarding for the final leg to Seattle. As he took his seat near the back of the crowded Boeing 737 stretch aircraft, he glanced at his cell phone and noticed a new text from Jim Carson, Director Samuelson's friend in Olympia.

He opened the text. "Heard you are headed back this way. Also heard about your adventures in Olympia from our mutual friend. Talked to another friend with a waterfront cottage for rent north of downtown. Small but a nice view. He's holding it in case you might be interested. No pressure. Just one old warrior lending a hand to another."

Waterfront? Sam imagined sitting on a deck looking over the water and relaxing. It sounded pretty amazing, so he texted back immediately. "Thanks. Please tell your friend that I'll take the place. I trust your judgment. Two-month lease is all I can handle right now."

He sent the text, and the response from Carson was swift. "Will lock down the rental. If it's okay, will meet you at the airport and give you a lift to the place once you've landed. I have your travel flight info from our mutual friend. Blue Prius."

"Sounds perfect. Thanks." Sam sent the response and shut down the phone. He'd made his own flight reservations, but the director was the director—an old spy who seemed to have his finger on everything going on around him, including Sam's flight reservations.

The flight to the Seattle-Tacoma Airport went as scheduled and Sam managed a long-overdue catnap. Three-and-a-half hours after leaving Denver, he stepped onto the arrivals curb and flagged down Pastor Carson. Late afternoon had settled by the time he dumped his rucksack in the back of Carson's Prius and climbed in. Carson had the car moving before Sam clicked his seatbelt into place.

"Thanks for picking me up," Sam offered, bracing himself as Pastor Carson dodged and weaved up International Boulevard, which fronted the airport and was congested continuously. Sam noticed the pastor's white-knuckled grip on the wheel as he dodged back and forth between lanes, barely missing one of the many aggressive drivers using the four-lane road as their own Grand Prix racecourse.

"Not a problem," Carson replied after several blocks. "I had a meeting up this way, so it all worked out. Your flight? Was it okay?"

"People still wearing face masks from the pandemic, which seems odd a year after the Covid vaccinations have been out. I had to locate one in the airport in Florida just to fit in but otherwise, pretty uneventful."

"The aftereffects of the pandemic will remain with us for decades to come, I am sure," Carson replied.

They held their silence as the pastor turned onto the main thoroughfare that took them from International Boulevard to Interstate 5 and then navigated the two-lane on-ramp onto the freeway. The pastor blew out a long breath as he settled the Prius into the second of the four southbound lanes of the interstate. "Thank goodness that's over," Carson said in a low whisper.

"Amen to that," Sam said.

"About that," Carson replied. "Maybe we could talk as we drive to Olympia. It's about an hour."

"Not sure what you mean, but I'm game," Sam replied, drawing out the last syllable.

"What are your plans while you're here? Your boss said he sent you this way for some rest but that he interrupted that with the

Olympia assignment, which," Carson added, "went well from what I've heard."

"It *ended* well, anyway," Sam replied. "A little iffy for a few moments, but the team pulled it off. You've run the gauntlet a few times yourself, so you know what I mean."

"You know my background?" Pastor Carson asked.

"The director filled me in some but not the full story. Much of your history with the agency is classified."

"And so, it should remain," Carson added. "But yes, I did run the gauntlet more than once, as you say. More to the point, how do you plan to address the situation the director sent you out here to consider?"

"You mean, my supposed reservations about doing my job the way he wants me to do my job?" Sam felt anger and resentment toward the director building as he said the words. "I don't think there's any way to address that situation positively. I do my job."

"You could always become a training officer. Training new operators and refreshing those already in the field is an important task. You could make a real contribution."

"Hardly," Sam said, glancing at Carson as the man drove, then redirecting his eyes toward the passing brightly lit billboards, evergreens, and offramps lining the interstate. "I'm thirty-one. I'm at the peak of my game, and my team . . . "

"Your team is like family," Carson finished the sentence for Sam. "I know. I felt the same way about mine when I left. Still do."

"Yep. Then you know I did not grow up with much of a family life. I think the army filled some of that need. Felt like I'd found a home. When I moved from the Rangers to Special Forces and then started working for the director, I *knew* I'd found my place. Now, to lose all that."

"But he's not pushing you out. He just wants you to consider where you're at right now and how that might affect things," Carson said, his eyes remaining front and center on the interstate as he spoke.

"Because he thinks I'm afraid to pull a trigger," Sam said. "He'd take it all away because of that misguided perception on his part."

"Are you?" Carson asked.

"Am I what?"

"Afraid to pull the trigger?" Carson asked. "A pistol or rifle is just another tool for an operator in the field. If operators reject any of their tools, the rest of the team could pay the price in critical moments."

Sam blew out a long breath as they passed a large boat dealership to the right of the highway. "I just haven't needed to use a gun on the last couple of missions."

"You didn't answer the question," Carson prodded.

"You're right," Sam replied. "But it's the truth. I haven't needed to use a gun in the past year or so. I saw other ways to get the job done." Sam found his attitude shifting as they talked, from hesitant to introspective. There was something about Carson's tone, the way he talked, that settled and focused his thoughts. Was he unwilling to pull the trigger? Could he have put his teammates into jeopardy? He ran through the last bunch of missions in his mind as they continued south on I-5.

How many times had he come close to pulling his Sig and using it or the carbine and decided to go a different route? He'd pulled the Sig during the last mission in Mexico, but had he been willing to use it? No. That incident had been an idle threat to illustrate a point with the old cartel boss. Was the director right, then? Had he lost his edge since that little girl died during that one mission? Did that take him back to his own sister's death?

"I don't know," Sam said.

Pastor Carson snapped his fingers. "That's a good first step," he said.

"What do you mean?" Sam asked.

"You've heard the old saying that a journey begins with the first step."

Sam nodded.

"Recognizing you might have a conflict that could disrupt what you do is important. That's exactly what happened to me and probably why Director Samuelson asked me to talk to you while you're here. When I retired, it was because I felt empty with a sense that life had to be more than the next mission, the next trigger pull. I never doubted the importance of what we did, but even with the support of my teammates, I felt kind of hollow between missions—during the times when it was just me and the four walls of my apartment."

"But what we do—what you did—is important," Sam protested.

"You bet, and I was good at it." Pastor Carson's passionate tone surprised Sam. "A lot of people slept more soundly because of what my team and I did—what you and your team do. And most never knew about it."

Sam turned in his seat to face Carson. "I don't follow. If you knew your work was so important, why did you leave?"

"Oh, my work was fulfilling, but I didn't feel fulfilled. There's a difference between the two. When I wasn't with my team, I felt alone. Who, besides us, can relate to what we do—or what I *did*—for a living? My team was my life during our times in the field, but between missions, I realized I had little else in my life. I never intended to leave the agency or my team. I found I needed something more in my life than what I did as a professional. That led me to where I am."

"I get what you're saying when you put it like that. There is no work I'd rather do than stop bad guys and help other people, and there's no one I'd rather work with than the people on my team. The work is fulfilling, as you say, but I do feel as if something's missing."

Carson paused for a moment, as though gathering his thoughts, then said, "For me, it was more a collection of things that led me to retire. I think it was the combination of the enemies killed, the friends left behind, and no one else to turn to when I was away from my team."

"Are you referring to the 'Thou shalt not kill' thing that comes with religion? Is that what caused you to retire?" Sam asked.

"Not at all. The literal Hebrew translation is 'Thou shall not commit murder.' It's a big difference. I have no murder in my past. I had a job to do, and any lives taken were in self-defense or the defense of others."

Sam gazed at the landscape streaking by as they passed Tacoma and then the gates to the Joint Base Lewis-McCord where the combined forces of the army and air force lived, worked, and trained.

"I feel the same about what I've had to do in the past," Sam said, finally.

"That's good news," Carson replied. "You're not the first person to face what you are facing—being a skilled soldier and looking for something more in your life."

"Thanks," Sam replied. "But I do not see myself becoming a minister like you did."

Carson laughed. "Fair enough, although that's what I said when I retired. Now look at me, an old Tier One operator serving as pastor of my small flock of Christians. The bottom line is that I'd never felt so alone during those times of deep introspection when I pondered why I was feeling the way I was. Then I found Jesus. Now, I know I'll never feel alone like that again."

They pulled off I-5 at the Olympia/State Capitol exit, turned north on Plum, the major arterial leading to the city, and followed the road through the east edge of Olympia. They continued when that road narrowed and became a residential street, making its way along a silvery-gray inlet with sparkling waters. They pulled in at a small, gray cottage perched on a sizable lot overlooking the inlet. Carson fished his hand through his car's glove compartment and produced a key and small file folder and handed both to Sam.

"The key will get you into the place. The paperwork is for you to sign and return to the rental agency tomorrow. The address is on the paperwork. I stocked some things in the kitchen, so you won't go hungry in the meantime. Also in the file is the name of a friend of mine who rents cars at a price that won't break you. Give him a call in the morning, and he'll set you up with a vehicle."

Sam took the key and papers. "Thanks for doing so much."

"It's not much between brothers," Carson replied. "And we are brothers. No one other than operators can understand the unique bond you build in the field."

Sam reached across the car, and they shook hands. "Brothers for sure," he said.

Sam unlocked the door to the cottage, waved as Carson pulled away, and then stepped inside. He dropped his ruck and flipped the light switch next to the door.

The kitchen area to the right of the door was small, compact, and homey. It contained a small gas stove and range, a full-sized refrigerator, a dishwasher, and a small stack of cupboards surrounding a large, white farm-style sink. The counter space was limited but adorned with a white granite surface next to the sink. A small peninsula separated the little kitchen from a living area that held a leather couch, recliner, and wing-back chair that faced wall-to-wall and floor-to-ceiling windows looking west across the still silver waters of the inlet. The view was breathtaking.

Picking up his ruck, Sam turned left down a short hallway to find a small but functional bathroom with a sink, toilette, and large, glassed-in shower. The large bedroom across the hall from the bathroom held a king-size bed and chest of drawers and, like the living area, had wide floor-to-ceiling windows that revealed yet another spectacular view of the water. A small closet with sliding doors flanked the south side of the room.

Sam dropped his ruck in the closet and glanced at his watch. Almost midnight, not counting the three-hour time difference from where he'd started his journey in Florida, which made it three in the morning his time. He splashed his face with warm water in the bathroom, moved back into the living room, and dropped into the thick, leather cushions of the recliner. Sleep overtook him seconds later as the long days and intensity of the past few weeks caught up with him.

CHAPTER 15

Back in Florida, Director Samuelson turned over in his bed, careful not to disturb his wife of forty-five years. He glanced at the clock on the nightstand: three in the morning. He growled under his breath. He'd had too many sleepless nights lately. He swung his legs over the edge of the bed, just as his cell phone lit up and vibrated on the nightstand. He slid his feet into a pair of well-worn moccasin slippers, wrapped himself in a thick terrycloth robe, and picked up the phone and glanced at the screen. It was his assistant, Phil. What would cause him to call this early in the morning?

"This had better be good," he whispered into the phone as he stepped out of the bedroom and closed the door behind him.

"It's not good, sir," came Phil's reply. "Team Two was just ambushed in Argentina on the emergency rescue mission that went out this morning. Three dead at the landing strip. Their plane was destroyed by a rocket as it prepared to lift off. It's a miracle the other two survived. They exfiltrated over land and managed a flight to El Paso. They are on their way home now. Alpha Dog, the Team Two leader, is pretty beaten up. The extra team member came out without a scratch."

"What extra team member?" Samuelson asked, the already uneasy feeling in the pit of his stomach growing worse.

"I don't have any record of a fifth person being deployed, so I thought you arranged it," Phil replied.

"Never mind that for now. Did they recover the bodies of the other three operators from the wreckage?" Samuelson asked.

"Negative, sir. All were incinerated in the explosion. There were no remains to recover."

"Shoot," Samuelson replied. "I knew it was a risk sending them out while the other teams were on lockdown. Have them in my office as soon as they land in Florida. Better yet, route them from El Paso to Tampa. I'll meet them there. Get us a TSA conference room at the Tampa airport for debriefing. Take a team there to provide additional security and make sure the space is clean and secure. Something's going on here, and I don't want to take any chances."

"TSA can provide security, sir," Phil offered.

"I understand that, but at this point, I wouldn't trust my mother," the director replied. "Get the group jet fired up. I'll be at the airport in . . . " He did some quick mental calculations and then discarded the jet as an option. "Better yet, get someone from the standby team to fire up my Suburban and pick me up at my house. I'll go to Tampa directly from home. I need to do some work on the way, so make sure the secure comms in that vehicle are functional and that the Suburban has been sanitized for listening devices. I will meet the team there after they arrive. You say you have no idea who the guest operator was on that mission?"

"I don't, sir. Whoever it was, they were reportedly under orders directly from the Secretary's office. And I just got an update. The fifth person is already headed to home station using a separate flight out of El Paso. They will not be available to you in Tampa," Phil said. "You will find only Dog there when you arrive."

"Shoot," Samuelson said. "More secrets."

No sooner had Samuelson disconnected the call than the lights came on in the kitchen. His wife stepped into the room with his "go-bag" hanging from one hand. "You go shower. I'll make the coffee," she said.

CHAPTER 16

The next morning, Sam spent a quiet hour sitting on the living room couch, staring at the water. What was it about water that seemed to settle the soul?

As he watched, a tugboat, several sailboats, and one large yacht made their way in and out of the marina. The tugboat looked more like a pleasure boat conversion than a working vessel as Sam watched it chug into the marina and tie up at the public pier to the south of the cottage.

He checked the date and time on his watch. Thursday. The day triggered something at the edge of his memory. As he was about to shove the thought aside, his cell phone chimed with a calendar reminder: "Call Consuelo Zamora."

It was already mid-morning. He punched in her number, and she picked up on the first ring. "Hello, Sam."

"Good morning," he replied. "I'm back in Olympia, and as promised, I am calling."

"That's fantastic!" She sounded both excited and a little tentative. "Would you like to get together for lunch?"

What was it about this woman that made him instantly feel comfortable? The memory of her at Tugboat Annie's and then at the state capitol building flashed through his mind. She was an amazing woman but was, perhaps, way out of his league.

Consuelo sensed his hesitation and added, "If you have changed your mind about getting together, I will understand."

"No, no, not at all," he stammered, gathering himself and determining to not let his normal tentativeness around women get in the way this time. "I am still a bit jet-lagged, but it would be great to meet for lunch."

"Do you have a car?" Consuelo asked.

"Not yet," he replied. "That is on my to-do list for today."

"Then I'll pick you up." The tentative tone in her voice was replaced by the confident tone he remembered with just a hint of a musical Spanish accent. "I know several great places. When we're done, I can take you wherever you need to go to arrange for a car."

"That would be amazing, but only if you let me buy lunch," he said, smiling as he gave her his address and ended the call.

He had no sooner showered and dressed than he heard her car's tires crunch on the gravel drive behind the cottage. He stepped out to greet her, feeling awkward and uncertain in his usual faded jeans and polo shirt. Normally, he wouldn't give it a second thought, but for right now, he cared about how he looked when she saw him.

"Nice car," he said as he climbed into the passenger seat of what appeared to be a new Subaru SUV. "Even has that new car smell," he added.

Consuelo flashed him a bright smile. "I treated myself," she said as she backed out of the drive. "I left my job with the foundation the day before I saw you at the capitol. I needed a new start, and a new car seemed like a good first step."

"You left the NGO?" Sam asked. "I got the impression you were pretty committed to that organization."

"You thought right," she replied, turning down the narrow road leading into downtown Olympia. "After I found Antonio in Mexico and you pulled us out of that situation, something clicked. I wanted something more than traipsing across the backcountry of Mexico at this point in my life. I thought I'd try something different and landed here in Olympia."

"The foundation was faith-based, right?" Sam asked.

"It was Christian and rewarding to work with, but I can practice my faith in a lot of different ways. When I met you, it wasn't the first time I'd been kidnapped. That last time, I think God was sending me a message that it was time to make a change."

She paused, and Sam let the silence linger for a few beats, then said, "I read your State Department file. You made a big difference providing medical care in small, often-forgotten communities."

"My team and I did make a difference, but my days in Mexico already seem like a long time ago," she replied. "I saw the news reports about what happened at the capitol. It's been a busy week for you and your friends."

"It was at that," Sam replied as they continued the drive along the inlet and watched the expensive waterfront homes lining the street. "I'm not sure how it sounds to you, but I could use a big old burger and fries. I've been on the road so much lately to so many locations where they don't have burger joints."

"Me, too," Consuelo replied. She cast him a sideways glance and a smile. "I know just the place."

They wound their way back onto Interstate 5 and followed the three-lane interstate north several miles before getting off on the Hawk's Prairie exit. A moment later, she pulled into a broad parking lot.

"The Ram Restaurant," she announced as she set the parking brake and turned off the car's ignition. "Best burgers anywhere."

"Now that sounds perfect," Sam said as he climbed out of the SUV and followed her into the warm, wood-toned interior of the restaurant. The richly-appointed restaurant was littered with flickering flat-screen televisions, broad tinted windows, and several dozen tables and booths. The place was almost full of the local lunch crowd.

As they entered, Sam saw the entrance to a bar area on the left with subtle lighting, high tables and stools, more large-screen televisions, and less of a crowd. The air was filled with the cheerful chatter of the patrons and the clinking of glasses, ceramic plates, and silverware. Consuelo found them a table for two in a secluded corner near the entrance.

"Great place," Sam said as they slid onto their tall stools at a small, round table. In another few minutes, they each had a drink in their hands and were clinking their glasses. "To strange reunions," Consuelo said.

"I guess we've had a few," Sam replied.

"Twice, you were my rescuer. It's enough to make a damsel swoon." She gave him a mischievous smile across the top of her glass.

"Just doing my job, ma'am," he replied with a horrible imitation of a Texas drawl.

Consuelo laughed at his weak attempt at a joke, and Sam decided he liked the sound.

"It still surprises me a little that you quit your job with the NGO," he replied. "Paloma Blanca."

"White dove," she said. "The dove of peace and hope that the Lord provides. I will always cherish those memories."

The waitress arrived with their orders, a petite woman who reminded Sam a bit of Leah with her all-business approach to her work. She set the plates before them. She flashed them both a broad smile and disappeared back into the mass of people.

Sam sampled a fry and held one up as though examining a priceless treasure. "Spicy, tangy. Now that's great cuisine."

Consuelo laughed. "Told you you'd like the place."

"So, what do you plan to do with your time here in Olympia?" Sam asked before taking a huge bite of his burger.

"Just after I saw you in Aguascalientes, I learned about a nursing position at the community center here. There's a growing retired population in the area with a lot of over-fifty-five apartment buildings going up. They needed a wellness nurse. I gave them a call, went through a brief telephonic interview, and got the job. I start next week."

"How's Antonio handling all this?" Sam asked, pausing between bites of his burger. "I admire you bringing him to the States and giving him a home. There's no telling where he would have ended up back with the cartels."

"He's a good boy, and it's not his fault he was put into that position," she replied, her eyes flashing in the dim light of the restaurant.

Sam leaned back in his chair. "I am sorry, Consuelo. I didn't mean anything negative by that remark, and you are giving him a chance that he might not have had otherwise."

Her expression softened, shifting back to the relaxed beauty that routinely seemed to take Sam's breath away.

"No, I should apologize, and please call me Connie. It's just that there is a mountain of paperwork and a maze of bureaucracy to wade through if I hope to adopt him. I've already met resistance with the local school district, given Antonio's need to learn English at his age. I guess I'm a little on edge about it all. He idolizes you, by the way."

"I'm the last guy anyone should idolize," Sam replied.

"He's fourteen, and you came through that window in Mexico like some sort of ninja. What boy his age wouldn't idolize someone like that? You're Rambo in the flesh."

"That's a stretch . . . " Sam started, but paused as a man strode up to their table. Medium height and build and dressed in a well-tailored business suit, the man set off a dozen alarms in Sam's mind. Maybe it was his pallid complexion, thin face, or slicked-back, mouse-colored hair, but Sam didn't like him at first sight.

The man pushed his way up to their table and laid a business card in front of Connie. "I hope this is not an imposition, but I need a moment of your time."

Sam saw Connie's complexion darken and her eyes narrow to slits. "Actually, it is an imposition. My friend and I are having lunch."

The man waved away her words, obviously disliking her response. *Another strike against him,* Sam thought as he shifted to the side on his barstool, both feet on the ground beside the table.

"My name is Wayne Parsons. I own several condominiums and two apartment complexes near the community center where I understand you will soon work."

"Mr. Parsons, I—" Connie started, but Parsons interrupted before she could go further.

"I have researched your background, Ms. Zamora. I know you are an experienced nurse practitioner with a good sense of the world and will hold an important position in the community center when you start work. I represent a group that is submitting a proposal to the Olympia city council to rezone the property where the community center sits. Our goal is to tear down the building to provide more housing for our city's growing retired community. The manager of the community center has shown some reluctance to cooperate. I'd hoped to gain your support for the proposal and encourage you to talk with the center's manager. Your support for our efforts would mean a lot to me and my investors."

Connie slid her plate of burger and fries to the side of the table, folded her hands before her, and glared at Parsons. She slid his business card back toward him. "I do not know you, and I certainly have no interest in any sort of business proposal you might be considering. I was hired by the community center to provide healthcare services for seniors and others, not to become involved in a real estate deal. During my job interview, I was briefed on the center's plans for expanding its support to the city's older population and the homeless, not reducing those services."

"If I could pull up a chair and explain . . . " Parsons persisted.

"You may not," she countered. "I would like you to leave, now."

Parsons grabbed the back of a stool near their table. As he did, Sam left his stool, stepped around the table, and imposed himself between Parsons and their table. "I believe Ms. Zamora said now is not a good time." Sam's voice came out as a soft, low growl.

Two men Sam had not noticed before emerged and positioned themselves behind Parsons. Both sported closely cropped blond hair and suits that matched their boss' attire. Their suit jackets strained against broad shoulder muscles, and the butts of pistols peeked out from their shoulder holsters.

Sam ignored the men and covered the hand Parsons used to move the barstool with his own, tightening his grip on the man's fingers. When Parsons attempted to pull his hand away, Sam held his grip fast and moved his face to within a few inches of Parson's face. "I think we would all like to avoid a scene right now. How about if you call off those trained dogs behind you and leave before this goes any further?"

Sam removed his hand, and Parsons jerked it back, cradling it and rubbing it with his other hand.

"Of course," Parsons sputtered, meeting Sam's glare with barely contained fury. "Perhaps another time." Parsons nodded curtly to Connie and stepped quickly away, his two men following closely behind.

Sam slid back onto his stool, picked up his glass, and took a sip. His hands shook slightly from the adrenaline still coursing through his veins. After a few calming breaths, he set the glass down and turned his eyes to Connie. She met his gaze with a mixture of emotions he found hard to interpret. She waved over their waitress. "I think we'll have refills," she started to say, but the waitress was already carrying a tray with them. She placed them on the table. "These are on the house," the waitress said.

Sam lifted his glass in the direction of a tall, Hispanic waiter who gave him a one-handed salute in return. Sam noticed an unmistakable tattoo of a Navy Seal on the man's arm and nodded.

"Well, I'm glad that's over," Connie said as the waitress departed.

"Me, too," Sam replied. "I'm supposed to be on vacation."

"How long are you here for?" Connie asked.

"Two months," he replied. "It came up suddenly, so I don't have any specific plans. I heard about the area when I was here for training. My boss suggested the place and that I connect with a friend of his who lives here." Sam paused, and then said, "And then I saw you again, and that was a real bonus."

Connie smiled and reached a hand across the table to cover his. "I am glad you are here, too. And not just to defend my honor, although that seems to be a trend with you."

Sam turned his hand over and, in a gesture that surprised even him, laced his fingers through hers. She didn't pull away, and when he met her eyes, she was blushing slightly.

"Not forward at all. I'm glad, too," he replied.

The rest of their lunch went without interruption. Sam found that talking came easy with Consuelo. When they finished their meal an hour later, and since neither of them had any plans for the day, Connie gave him a short driving tour of Olympia. As they wound their way through the city, Sam commented several times about the city's old-town charm with its small shops and restaurants lining the streets and architecture that dated back to the 1940s. The sidewalks were amazingly clean. Little evidence existed of the homeless hangouts, panhandlers, and drug victims normally found in large cities.

"That's one of Olympia's big accomplishments, and they did not get the city in this condition at the expense of the homeless and the disenfranchised," she explained. "Olympia received a series of grants and creative funding initiatives that allowed them to invest in both their underserved populations. They used the money to study and mitigate the downtown homeless issue, which was bad a few years ago. From what I read, they had an explosion of crime and riots in the area, so businesses left in droves. The homeless occupied the city to fill the void and effectively took over the city."

She drove east along Fourth Avenue, the city's major east-west arterial, and they passed a half dozen multi-story apartment buildings. "These apartments house a large percentage of what used to be Olympia's homeless population. They were moved here a year ago by an innovative city ordinance specifying that homeless individuals and families were no longer allowed to sleep on Olympia's streets. If someone is found on the streets, they are taken into custody by the police and moved to a closely guarded, secure shelter. Within twenty-four hours of their arrest, a caseworker sees them. The caseworkers assess the individual's needs and direct them either to the courts to resolve open warrants, to mental health resources if that's what's needed, or to one of these units. In the latter case, they are given food and shelter and assigned to city work units cleaning the streets, parks, and so on. It's called the Olympia Work/Life Program, and people accepted into the program are provided with work and a chance at a new life. If they have children, their children are placed in state-funded schools or daycare. Workers are paid minimum wage for their efforts and required to attend job training and life-building classes. Once they are working, they pay a small amount for their lodging and meals to ensure that they recognize that the program is not a free ride."

"Sounds a bit like involuntary servitude," Sam said, although he admired the cleanliness of the area and the large number of people who entered and left the buildings, nicely clothed and apparently at ease.

"It's not that at all. People in the program can leave whenever they want, but if they are picked up off the streets again, they face stiff charges. It seems to make a difference. The downtown area has bounced back, and the homeless population in Olympia is a small fraction of what it was two years ago. Of course, it's a new program, so the jury is still out on it. It could be that a lot of those impacted by the program simply moved on to other towns."

"Even so, that's pretty incredible," Sam replied, flashing back to his times as a youth and the homeless kids he'd known back then, many who had entered the military to escape their situation. "You seem to know a lot about the program."

She nodded. "I'd considered trying for a position in the program, but it has no religious affiliations and has no plans to put medical staff on the site." She glanced at her watch. "I need to pick up Antonio in an hour. How about if you call about your rental car, and I drop you off there?"

"That would be great, but I do have one additional request," Sam replied.

She shot him a glance, her dark eyes meeting his for only a moment before returning to the road. "And that would be?"

"I'd like to see you again."

She stopped for a red light and cocked her head in his direction. Her smile was warm as she lifted a hand to pull aside stray strands of ebony hair that had drifted across her eyes. "I'd like that," she said. "I'd like that a lot."

CHAPTER 17

Wayne Parsons stalked out of the restaurant after finishing what he considered a lackluster meal compared to the crow the Zamora woman and her friend had just fed him. He held his cell phone to his ear as his stretch Hummer pulled up to the door, and he climbed in.

"I want that woman fired," he demanded of the person who answered his call. "I know you have a person working in the community center, so use your leverage and get her fired!"

The voice at the other end was female, low, husky, and unrattled. "What woman?"

"The Zamora woman. The new nurse who is going to work there," he growled.

"I am not going to do that, Wayne. She's a legend in Mexico and within the NGO community. She is well-known and cherished by many of our business associates. We cannot be associated with any harm that might come to her."

Parsons ran a finger around the tight shirt collar at his neck and tugged the knot of his blood-red tie loose. "You said she would be a good person to have on our side. I introduced myself when I saw her at the Ram a few minutes ago. It did not go well."

"As usual, Wayne, you jumped the gun. You need to be patient. I have some interesting information regarding her past employer's funding and cooperation with some, shall we say, undesirable people back in Mexico. When the time is right, I will leverage what I know, and she will come around to see our perspective."

Parsons slammed a fist on the car door's armrest. "We don't have a lot of time," he growled again. "Things are going to hit a head soon if we want to get the land purchased and the permits in place. We have only two weeks, or the funding window will close with our investors."

"You exaggerate. I don't think a week or two will matter either way with our investors. There are bigger moves in play right now than the building project and more involved in this than you know."

"Our investors? You mean *my* investors," Parsons returned. "I brought those people to the table for . . . "

"Oh, my dear Wayne." Her tone took on a flat, boring quality. "You cannot think that I would leave managing relations with the investors up to you, do you? You could not manage a lemonade stand on your own, let alone as big a venture like the one currently going down with our people. I have our investors' assurance that we have the time we need to acquire the community center property without raising undue concern with the city council. And we need that extra time, anyway, so I can move some additional pieces on the chessboard and secure a handsome profit for each of us."

"You made a new agreement with them? You went around me?" Parsons' tone grew loud as he felt the project slipping out of his control. "I thought we were partners."

"We are partners, my dear, as long as you continue to demonstrate your value to me and our investors. In the meantime, leave Ms. Paloma Blanca to me."

CHAPTER 18

Connie's schedule with Anthony's adoption paperwork and settling into her new home delayed Sam from meeting her again for several days. He filled the time jogging, working out on the cottage's deck, and exploring the city with its extensive farmer's market, shops, and restaurants. Climbing into his rental SUV with plans for a day trip to the Pacific coast, Sam plugged his cell phone charger into the car's 12-volt outlet just as his cell phone rang. He glanced at the number and, not recognizing it, declined the call. As he started the vehicle, the phone rang again. This time his curiosity got the best of him, and he accepted the call.

"Sam, it's Connie. I'm calling you on another person's phone. I wonder if you might have a free moment."

He glanced at his watch. It was only ten-thirty in the morning. "Of course," he replied. "Where should I meet you."

"I'm at the community center. I stopped by this morning to get my bearings before starting work on Monday, and that man from the restaurant was here with five other men. He's giving the woman in charge of the center a bad time and making threats. She's in tears and . . . "

"Give me the address." He jotted it down as she read it to him, and then he keyed it into his phone's map application.

Ten minutes later, Sam walked into the center through the wide glass double doors to find Wayne Parsons and five large, tough-looking men in the reception area. Parsons was yelling at a kindly woman who looked to be in her late sixties. Sam took her to be the community center director. Her face was pale as Parsons ranted, standing only a few feet away from her. Connie stood next to the center's director with their arms linked in mutual support. The two women eased back a step as Sam closed in on the group and placed himself between them and Parsons.

Parsons sneered. "Ah, the hero from the restaurant. My issue is with Mrs. Carsworth, not you." He reached for Sam as if to push him to the side. "Now, get out of my way!"

Sam grabbed Parsons' arm with one hand, pinching the forearm muscle tightly and turning Parsons' arm over and down, leveraging the man's weight against his elbow and shoulder joints. Sam's voice was level and calm as he said, "This has gone far enough, Parsons."

Parsons attempted to wrest his arm away, but Sam's grip was too strong. In a smooth move that no one besides Sam and Parsons could have noticed, Sam slid his hand down to Parsons' wrist, placed his thumb on the back of Parsons' hand, and wrapped his four fingers around the palm in a full lock. Sam pinched down hard on both sides of the man's hand, then twisted it ninety degrees to the outside. Sam used his leverage on Parsons' wrist and shoulder to turn the man fully around so that he faced his five men and then said in a calm, soft voice, "I suggest that you and your friends leave. When I release you, I will give you to the count of four before I call 911. Nod if you understand."

For emphasis, Sam twisted Parsons' contorted wrist ever so slightly. Parsons winced against the pain and nodded. "We'll leave," he said.

Sam gave Parsons a little shove and released the man's wrist, stepping back as the man stumbled, gathered his feet beneath him, and spun to face Sam. "This is not over."

Sam pulled his cell phone from his pocket and pointed a finger at the number display. "One, two, three. . ."

Parsons spun on his heel, pushed his way between two of his thugs, and headed out the front door. Four of the five men followed him immediately, but one with a severely broken nose and a week's worth of beard paused before following his boss out. He gave Sam a wicked smile. "I know you, even if you don't remember me, and I already owe you from before. We'll settle this between us another time."

Sam felt a twinge of recognition but shrugged it off as he turned back to Connie and the director. "I don't suppose you'd have any CCTV coverage of what just happened."

Mrs. Carsworth nodded and smiled. "Thanks for your help, young man, and yes, we do have cameras in this area. I will send a copy of the tapes to the Olympia P.D. right away, along with a complaint against that man. It won't be the first, so I'm not sure what good it will do. Mr. Parsons is closely connected with the city council."

Sam returned her smile. "It would help if you could also get a copy to the chief of the Washington State Patrol. Tell him it would be a favor for the man with the M4. He'll know what you mean. If there has ever been anyone likely to lend a hand with something like this, he would be the one."

Mrs. Carsworth nodded. "I will see to it, personally," she said, turning to head for her office.

Sam stopped her with a gentle touch on her arm. "Connie and I have encountered Parsons before. What exactly is the issue with him?"

Mrs. Carsworth sighed, her shoulders drooping and the fatigue showing in her eyes. "About the time we hired Consuelo, Parsons and some other people involved in local government approached me about shutting the community center down so they could build retirement condos in its place. I explained to them that we are funded by a five-year federal grant that has four more years on it, and even if I did support such a thing, going along with their plans would waste all that funding. For the last week, I have been getting constant calls and visits and threats from Parsons and his people. I am committed to this community center, but I don't know how much more I can take."

Mrs. Carsworth turned and headed down a long hall extending off the reception area. Connie laid a hand on Sam's arm, and he glanced over to see her smiling at him. "I'm so sorry, Sam. It seems as if you are always pulling me out of some tough spot, but I didn't know who else to call. That man was antagonizing Mrs. Carsworth. She has great hopes for building a wellness clinic here with me running it and expanding that to provide services to the city's homeless program."

Sam covered her hand with his hand. "I'm not sure what I can do to help beyond what I just did, but I'm glad to do whatever I can. Don't ever worry about calling me when you need me. If nothing else, it's a good excuse to see you. Then again, I saw how you stood beside Mrs. Carsworth. I'm not sure you needed my help at all."

"You're being kind," she replied. "But seriously, thank you." She went up on her toes and gave him a soft kiss on the cheek.

Sam flushed and recognized this as a good time to leave. "Can I see you Saturday?"

"You bet," she replied. "How about coming over to my place for dinner with me and Antonio?"

Sam's eyebrows shot up. "I'd love that. Can I bring something?"

"Some dessert maybe," she replied. "Otherwise, just bring yourself."

"Thanks," he said. "I haven't had home cooking in a long time."

CHAPTER 19

Director Samuelson's long day at the group headquarters got even longer as his secure cell phone rang. He glanced at the number on the screen, which displayed as "unknown" again. Before he accepted the call, he shouted for Phil to start a trace.

"On it, sir," came Phil's business-like reply.

"Director Samuelson," a scratchy, hardly discernible voice said as he placed the phone to his ear.

"I'm here," Samuelson replied.

"You have no doubt noticed the difficulties your teams have experienced of late."

"Go on," Samuelson said.

"That is only a sampling of what will happen if you do not hold off on any remaining missions scheduled for Mexico and Central America."

Samuelson let his silence speak for itself.

"Very well," the voice said. "Stay out of Central and South America for the next thirty days. After that, you can resume business as usual as you wish."

"And if I don't stand down?" Samuelson asked.

"Then additional deaths will be on your conscience, Mr. Samuelson. You will not be able to do anything to protect your teams if you force our hand. We know who your teams are, where they are headed, and what they are doing at all times. We can get to them whenever we wish. Go look out the front door of your office."

The location of the group's headquarters compound was a closely guarded secret, except to a few people highly placed in the government. He walked to the building's front door window and waved for Phil to join him.

A late-model pickup was parked across the road in front of the headquarters' entrance. As they both watched, the truck exploded in a ball of flames that sent metal, tires, and glass twenty feet into the air. A truck fender landed only a few feet from the door where they stood.

Samuelson placed the cell phone to his ear and said, "You have my attention."

"Very good. Do as we say for the next thirty days, and all this will pass."

"But . . . " Samuelson started, but the line went dead.

Phil returned to his desk as the call disconnected and called out, "We've got something on the trace of that call, sir."

Samuelson leaned over the reception counter to examine Phil's computer screen. The young operator pointed to a series of numbers listed there. "It was a voice-over-internet call. I have an IP address for its origin. No, wait." Phil punched in a long string of computer commands, then paused and glanced up at the director. "The call was bounced around the country a half dozen times. It's a pretty sophisticated setup; but give me a little time, and I'll identify the point of origin."

"Good. Keep at it," Samuelson said. "Call in Jessica Falcone from Home Team to lend a hand. The woman's a whiz at this sort of thing.

Between you and her, you'll stand a better chance of figuring out where the call came from."

"Of course, sir," Phil replied. "Jessica is on two weeks' leave, but I'll dial her in right away."

"And put a stop on any outgoing teams, effective immediately. If they're in the air, call them back. If they are on the ground, call them off their targets. I need everyone on lockdown, and I need that to happen now. And give me a detailed list of where all the team members are, team-by-team, member-by-member."

"On it, sir," Phil replied, again.

He would lock down his teams, all right, but not for the reasons the person on the call said. No one outside the group could have that much information about his teams' missions. It had to be someone on the inside, and he intended to find out who.

CHAPTER 20

Saturday morning broke sunny and warm, with the waters of the inlet beyond the cottage's back deck as smooth as glass and the chill air tasting clean and fresh. Remembering the kayak stand next to Tugboat Annie's restaurant, Sam decided to head for the water before his date with Connie later that day. The kayak rental shack opened just as Sam arrived. Twenty minutes later, he was on the water, gliding across its glass-like surface. With smooth, even strokes that beat a soft dip and swish rhythm, he pushed his bright yellow fiberglass kayak along the inlet's shoreline east across the inlet and toward the towering loading cranes of the bustling Port of Olympia.

Half an hour later, with the water clear and free of craft, Sam found himself considering whether he could make it to his cottage's beach and back before his two-hour rental was up. Deciding to go for it, he headed out into the wide heart of the inlet, several miles across. Halfway there, he caught the flash of glistening black and white slicing through the water just below his kayak. At first, he thought the morning sun was playing games on the gently rippling waters. Then it happened again a few yards to his right and then twice more to his left. The last flash of color was accompanied by a long, black dorsal fin slicing through the water alarmingly close to where he sat on the water in his kayak.

Sam slipped his paddle across his lap and let the tiny craft drift, cutting a slow smooth path across the water. His patience was rewarded when, some fifty yards distant, a large orca rose out of the water, shot straight into the air, arched to one side, and crashed back down into the water. The impact sent a wave that set his kayak rocking.

"Amazing," he whispered, bracing himself to stay upright. Like so many people, he had seen killer whales on television but never expected to see one so close. The sleek lines of the orca arcing out of the water with its distinctive black and white markings, and its sheer size left him silent and thoughtful. The orca was the supreme hunter of the ocean, and he knew that a resident pod frequented the Puget Sound and the Olympia area from time to time.

It occurred to him that perhaps the orca and he were not so different. Orcas were the ocean's great hunters. For both the orca and him, the hunt was their purpose in life. The orcas hunted to feed and, in the process, culled the weak from the ocean's depths. For his part, he and his teammates hunted evil and removed it from the world so that others could live and thrive.

Sam's kayak rocked ever so slightly, breaking him from his thoughts. He glanced down to his left and saw an enormous orca head gently nudging his kayak with its huge, bulbous nose. The orca nudged his kayak again, and Sam suddenly recalled stories he'd read about sharks attacking kayaks. Sharks responded to sudden movement and thrashing, so perhaps orcas did the same. If he could stay very still. He forced his breathing to a slow, calm cadence and his muscles to a point of total relaxation as he did so often during his martial arts training.

He was repaid for his efforts as the orca adjusted position and moved alongside the kayak, rolling onto one side so that a single, large, dark eye looked up at him. Sam reached a hand down to touch the smooth, slick skin. The killer whale did not flinch at the touch but simply sank away from his hand. Sam relaxed, then froze again as the orca rose again on the opposite side of the kayak, this time nudging a tiny version of itself to the surface next to Sam's kayak. A baby orca. A calf a fraction of the size of its parent, but otherwise, a perfect match in shape and coloration.

The orca calf duplicated its mother's earlier position, rolling on its side so that a single eye glanced up at Sam from not more than six feet away. Sam wondered just how many people got to see an orca and its offspring up close like this. He knew it was a memory he would keep for the rest of his life.

Deep in the moment and becoming more thoughtful by the second, Sam watched the baby orca roll over so that its air hole breached the surface. It blew a long snort of water with a sound like an air compressor letting off excess pressure, soaking Sam from head to waist.

Sam laughed as the baby orca suddenly turned head-down, flipped its tiny tail fluke into the air, and slid into the depths. The mother orca lingered just a moment longer before she tipped her nose up into the air above the water and then slid down, tail-first, and disappeared into the waters after her calf.

Sam sat there for a long moment, letting his breath return to normal and considering just how special the morning had turned out. Deciding he would be hard-pressed to top the experience no matter how far he paddled, he headed back to the dock.

Thirty minutes of steady paddling later, Sam crawled out of the water and onto the marina dock. He was met by the kayak rental shack's owner, who gave him a nod. "Watched your little adventure unfold out there with the orcas," the man said. Tall and slender with weathered skin and long, windblown hair, his voice sounded like gravel tossed in the bottom of a rusty metal bucket. "Watched through my binocs." He gestured to an expensive set of binoculars, resting on a life vest box standing near a kayak rack with a dozen brightly colored one- and two-person kayaks.

"It was something special," Sam replied.

"Yep. Doesn't happen much around here. The orcas visit occasionally, but I never heard of a local orca visiting with a kayaker as that one did with you. Something special, for certain. Some people feel that when an orca approaches you up close, they are there to tell you something." The man paused and then added with a chuckle, "Then again, maybe it was just hunting up something tasty for lunch, and you were on the menu."

The man nodded and handed Sam a towel. "Thought you might need that after the young one hosed you down as it did. Got to say that I laughed hard at that one."

Sam grinned, wiped his hair and face, and handed the towel back.

"Friend of mine retired from the army back in 2000," the man continued. "He was an operating room nurse in the Army Medical Department to the north of here. Bought himself a place on the water over in Gig Harbor. On the first day of retirement at his new house, he put a lawn chair on the dock behind his place and took to sitting, trying to free his mind of all those memories of war, death, and operating room issues.

"He told me later that while he was sitting there in that chair, an orca pulled right up alongside his dock, rolled over on its side, and gave him the eye, just as that mama and baby orca did to you. He said he just talked to that orca as if they were old friends, and that orca lay there in the water all the while, rolling over now and then to blow a little air and then returning to where it could keep an eye on him.

"Before long, he'd talked out all his issues with that killer whale just lying there in the water listening. The upshot of it was that when he'd finished talking, that orca just slid into the water and eased itself away from his dock. He decided his time as an operating room nurse wasn't done yet. He had some tough memories, for sure, but at only forty-five, the work that created those memories was too important to leave behind at such a young age. He called up the same medical center he'd retired from and got himself a part-time job working in the operating room there."

"That's quite a story," Sam replied.

"No more special than what you just experienced," the man replied.

"You think those orcas were trying to tell me something? I don't think. . ." Sam started, ready to end the conversation and head back to his car, but he paused as the man continued.

"The Native Americans around here have stories about orcas communicating with humans, even saving them. Maybe those orcas were trying to tell you something. You got some big thing on your mind?"

Sam didn't respond.

The man nodded and tossed the wet towel into a basket. "Not my business, but God is everywhere, and I figure those orcas are as likely to act as His angels as much as anyone else. I'm a God-fearing man, and I believe everything happens for a reason. As I said, not my business, but that was something special today, what you saw."

"Thanks," Sam replied, turning away and heading for his car. "It was."

CHAPTER 21

An hour later, Sam's cell phone rang as he unlocked the door to the cottage. Juggling two bags of groceries from a stop at the local Safeway, he kicked the door closed behind him, dumped one bag on the small kitchen counter, and fumbled the other onto the floor. He pulled out his cell phone and answered the call on the fifth ring as he bent to retrieve apples, oranges, and a six-pack of diet soda from where they'd spilled out of the bag.

"Hello, Sam."

He recognized the voice at once. "Good morning, Pastor Carson," Sam replied, cocking a hip against the counter and crunching into a crisp, red apple.

"Sounds like I've interrupted your lunch."

"It's been a busy morning," Sam said.

"I'd love to hear about it. That's why I called. Thought we might get together later today."

Sam glanced at his watch as another call came through on his phone. He glanced at the caller ID. It was Connie. "Can I put you on hold just a moment, Jim?"

"Not a problem."

Sam switched to the incoming call from Connie. "Good morning."

"Good morning, sir," she replied.

"So formal," Sam replied. "I'm on another call, but I'm glad you called. Some things happened this morning that I'd like to tell you about."

"That's why I called," Connie replied. "I wondered if you might be able to come over a little early. I know I invited you over for dinner, but Antonio would love to see you, and he's told some of his new friends about you. You're quite the hero to him—and to me. If it's not too much of an imposition, I had hoped you might talk to the boys about the military and other things teenage boys like to hear about."

Sam laughed. "I'm not sure I have much to offer, but I'd be happy to spend some time with the boys." He glanced at his watch. It was one already. "How about two p.m.?"

"That would be great. We can plan on dinner for between four or five," she replied and provided him with her address.

Sam ended the call with Connie and reconnected with Pastor Carson. "Sorry about that, Jim. That was a friend of mine."

"A female friend?" The pastor's tone was light and teasing.

Sam laughed. "Guilty. It's a long story, but it looks like we're going to spend the afternoon together with her son and his friends."

"My, oh, my. Only a few days there, and you've already been invited to dinner."

"As I said, it's a long story," Sam replied.

"Obviously, our get-together is not going to happen today. How about tomorrow? I get done at the church around three. Maybe we could meet after that."

"That sounds great. Why don't you come over to the cottage, which, by the way, I am thoroughly enjoying. I can barbecue some burgers on the deck."

"It's a date," Carson replied. "Or should I save that term for your events of later today?"

"Very funny," Sam said as he ended the call.

Sam put the groceries away and moved to the deck, lowering himself into one of the patio chairs. His thoughts turned back to the kayak rental owner's words about those experiences with orcas having special meaning. Was it just a coincidence that he was dealing with questions about a job that he loved and what he now recognized as a hole in his life? Or his reluctance to pull the trigger in a firefight? Was that even an issue? His work filled his life with travel and adventure, and guns were just the tools of his trade. He was grateful for his friends on the team, and hadn't he pulled his pistol many times in the past?

His cell phone rang again. "Busy phone," he muttered, picking it up. The screen read, "Secure ID."

He pushed the green button to accept the call, knowing it would likely be the director. Sam surprised himself with the bluntness of his words as he said, "I wasn't sure I'd hear from you again after our last talk."

"Totally understood, Sam, given the situation," the director replied. "But I sent you away for several reasons. Any concerns I might have about your performance as an operator were the least of those. I need the people around you to feel you were cut off from the group so I could call on you to help with a situation that requires special handling."

A light went on in Sam's mind. "You wanted it to appear that I was away for disciplinary reasons."

"Exactly," Samuelson replied. "I am going to text you a secure file. You will need to download it to the secure memory card in your phone and then upload it to the partitioned area of your laptop. We've had a breach of security, and I need your help to nail it down. I want people to think that you're off the net with me and the group, that you're no longer a part of your team. That may enable you to dig into the situation and get information from others that you might not otherwise be able to secure."

"A disgruntled employee?" Sam questioned.

"Exactly," Director Samuelson replied. "It would be a big favor to me if you would take this on."

"What's the timeline?"

"I don't have one. I want you to take at least one more week of your vacation to keep up appearances and then attack the situation in whatever manner you deem appropriate. I am going to give you a blank check for this one. You may be able to do a lot over the phone or email, or you may need to come here or somewhere else to do what needs to be done. You will report only to me and no one else."

Sam didn't hesitate with his response. "I'm in, of course, sir."

Sam remembered the business card handed to him by the man claiming to be Connie's father. Before the director could terminate the call, he said, "If you have a moment, I could use a favor."

"Name it," the director replied.

"That business card I gave you during the Olympia out brief?"

Sam heard papers being shuffled in the background. "Right," Samuelson said. "I got the results of the fingerprint and DNA analysis this morning. That business card you gave me came back positive for Fernando Zamora, a Mexican spy and fugitive long believed to be dead. Both the DNA and the fingerprints on the card were an exact match to what's on file. Where, exactly, did you get that card?"

"From the man himself," Sam replied.

"Now, that is interesting," Samuelson replied. "He and I have a long history. When you have more information, I'd like to hear about it."

Samuelson ended the call before Sam could say more. A moment later, Sam's phone chirped as the encrypted file arrived via secure text. Sam checked his watch. If he was going to pick up a dessert before heading for Connie's house, he'd have to get going. The file would be safe enough for now.

CHAPTER 22

"Antonio, I need you to get ready," Connie called from the kitchen. "Sam will be here in a little bit. Why don't you take the lemonade and cookies to the porch for you and your friends?"

Connie glanced at her watch, tossed a thick, ebony braid over her shoulder, and made the final preparations of a large platter of beef enchiladas. "I hope he likes Mexican food," she muttered.

"The way he looked at you, I think he would like anything you made," Antonio said with a giggle. She pitched a leftover piece of jalapeño at him.

"Chico gracioso!" she replied.

"Speak English, Mother. English. I am trying to learn the language," Antonio replied as he retrieved the snacks and lemonade and carried them outside.

"Funny boy!" she repeated in English. *Did he just call me mother?* She thought her heart might burst at the thought.

She dropped her spatula and grabbed Antonio into a big hug. "Mom," he protested and wriggled in her embrace.

"Now, go join your friends outside," she said, releasing him.

She followed him out the wide sliding doors to the pergola-covered patio, making sure he didn't spill the lemonade and snacks. His friends chatted quietly on a bench near the back of the garage that bounded the patio and the small patch of grass and colorful gardens beyond.

The doorbell rang, and she called to Antonio as she stepped back into the kitchen, "It's probably Sam. Can you please let him in!"

"Is that Tony's ninja?" called the tall, fair-complexioned, blond boy with shaggy hair. The other boy, a second-generation Korean pre-teen with a thick mop of black hair sticking out in all directions, elbowed his friend in the ribs. "Of course, he's not a ninja. They come out only at night."

Both boys laughed as Antonio headed for the front door.

"He's not a ninja," Antonio mumbled as he reached for the door, "but he is pretty cool."

CHAPTER 23

As Sam pulled the Subaru up to the curb in front of the address Connie had given him, he glanced at his rearview and side mirrors before shutting down the car's engine. Nothing in sight, except for the usual smattering of vehicles seen in any neighborhood, parked in driveways and on curbs in front of houses that looked strikingly like one another.

He punched the doorbell, and the front door opened before the bell had a chance to chime. "Welcome, sir," Antonio said with a broad smile and dramatic bow.

"Thank you, and please call me Sam."

"Entiendo. Gracias," Antonio said, with a slightly formal air. "Please call me Tony."

Sam was about to reply when Connie called out. "Sam, welcome!" Wiping her hands on a pretty apron, she hurried around a large kitchen island to the front door and drew him into a brief, warm embrace.

Sam's smile was involuntary as she released him, stepped back, and let their eyes meet. She looked radiant in her tomato-smudged, yellow apron, faded jeans, and brightly flowered sleeveless blouse. Her hair had come loose as she came to greet him and flowed across her shoulders in a thick cascade of ebony. He felt his face grow warm and then heard two teenage boys standing in the kitchen let out a long, "Oooohhh."

Tony went over to meet them and elbowed the blond-headed boy hard in the ribs. "Knock it off, you two." The other two boys quieted immediately, although the blond one elbowed Antonio right back.

"Come in. Come in," Connie said, taking him by the arm and leading him to the broad, white, quartz-topped island that separated the kitchen from the rest of the wide, high-ceilinged great room that contained a heavy, wooden dining room table and chairs and a large sectional couch facing a big-screen television.

"Can I get you something to drink?" Connie asked as she pointed him to one of four tall stools pulled up to the kitchen island.

"A bottle of water would be great," Sam replied.

She stepped over to a stainless-steel fridge, pulled out a bottle, and handed it to him.

"I'm in the final stages of preparing dinner. I hope you like enchiladas and fried rice with vegetables and cilantro."

"Sounds amazing," he replied as he slid onto the barstool.

She paused and gave him a pleading look. "Do you think you might join the boys on the patio? They seem excited to meet you after all Antonio has told them about you. I'll give you all a yell when I'm done putting the dinner together."

"Glad to," Sam replied as he stepped through the sliding glass patio doors and into the yard. A tall, oak pergola transitioned from the patio doors into the yard. The brightly colored flowers of the yard's scattered gardens and the sunny feel of things fit Connie to a tee. *Beautiful,* he thought again. The yard contained just a touch of the exotic in Connie's diverse selection of flowers with just the right touch of simple yet elegant homeliness in how the gardens surrounded a small, circular, green yard.

Sam found a low chaise lounge and lowered himself into it. "I know, Tony, but I do not know either of you," he said, nodding his head in the direction of the other two boys.

Tony pointed at the tall, skinny, blond kid with the fair complexion. "That's Randy. The other one is Phillip. His parents are from Korea. We play soccer together."

"You play on your school team?" Sam asked. He'd developed a taste for the sport while traveling throughout Central and South America.

"We do," Tony replied, swelling his chest a little. "Ninth-grade team. We are all on the first string, but Phillip is the real star."

"Hey," the blond Randy replied. "I got a goal last week."

"You're a defender," Phillip replied. "You wouldn't have been anywhere near the goal if the coach hadn't decided to press the other team."

"Lucky shot, too," Tony added.

"I hit that shot from ten yards out. It was sweet!" Randy said, fixing his arms across his chest and frowning.

Sam held up his hands. "Whoa, guys. Every member of the team counts. No position on any team is more important than any other. It's what you do together that matters. If a defender didn't do his job, how would that work out for the team? If the attackers weren't fast on their feet with the defenders to back them up, how would that work out?"

"I guess so," Phillip muttered reluctantly. "Sorry, Randy-man."

"No sweat," Randy replied and then grinned. "I can still kick your tail on the pitch."

"I still think it was a lucky shot," Tony added.

Randy lunged from his seat and landed on Tony. In seconds, the two were tangled, wrestling on the grass beside the concrete patio and laughing hysterically. Another beat, and Phillip jumped in and joined the free-for-all.

Sam smiled as he watched the boys. It reminded him of long-ago times with him and his brother, Carter.

"Are you on a team?" Randy asked, his face turned serious as the boys climbed to their feet and resumed their seats.

"I am," Sam replied. "And we are all close, just like you three."

"You're in the military, right? Tony said you were in the military," Phillip said, his breath still coming in great gasps. "My dad just retired from the military."

"Please thank him for his service for me," Sam replied.

Phillip nodded. "I will. "

"Yes, I am in the military," Sam continued. "I am part of what they call a Special Operations Group."

"Like the Green Berets!" Tony cheered. "Like Chuck Norris!"

"I do have a green beret," Sam replied, "but I am not much like Chuck Norris."

"My dad was an Army Ranger," Phillip added.

"Then we might know each other," Sam said. "I was a Ranger before I became a Green Beret and before I joined my current team."

"Tony says that you are a ninja," Phillip continued.

"I never said he was a ninja," Tony protested.

"Some people do practice a form of martial arts called Ninjitsu," Sam replied, "but I am not a ninja. I am trained in what we call 'empty hand' martial arts, which is sort of like what ninjas do."

"Empty hand?" Phillip asked.

"It's where you learn to fight without weapons—just your hands, your feet, and your mind. We all know how to use a lot of weapons, but my specialty is unarmed self-defense. The other members of my team specialize in weapons, explosives, computers," Sam replied. "I'm the team's empty hand specialist."

"Can you show us?" Tony asked. From the eager look in his eyes, Sam could tell he was anxious to prove to his friends that Sam was someone special.

"It's not the sort of thing I can stand here and do for you. When I practice, I spar with other skilled partners and do things called poomse and kata, which are forms of shadowboxing. It can be pretty boring to watch."

Sam paused and then remembered how watching martial artists break boards and bricks had excited him when he was young. "There is one thing I could do. Do you have any spare wooden boards around here, Tony?" Sam asked.

"Sure do," Tony said and climbed to his feet.

"How about a couple of cinder blocks?" Sam added.

"We have those, too, from when Mom worked on her gardens," Tony said. He tugged Randy up from his seat, and the two boys disappeared around the edge of the garage. A moment later, they reemerged with two cinder blocks and two three-foot lengths of two-by-six pine board.

Sam set the two cinder blocks on end about two feet apart and laid the two boards across the top. Sam shoved the short sleeves of his polo shirt up a little higher and faced the boys who had formed a half-circle around him and the boards.

"Breaking boards is one of the skills you learn in most types of martial arts. It's an important skill because it requires a lot of concentration." Sam tapped the side of his head with one forefinger. "People think it's about strength, but it's more about the mind."

"Like Chi flow?" Randy asked. "I learned about it in Tai Chi class. My dad makes me take it."

"Exactly," Sam said. "Now, which one of you would like to break these two boards for me?"

"No way," Phillip said. "I'm not breaking my hand."

"Me either," Randy added. "I've seen people get hurt trying to break boards like that."

"I'll try," Tony said.

"Okay," Sam replied. "You come over here and give it your best shot. I suggest you try to break it with the heel of your hand." He raised his hand and tapped the thick part at the bottom of his open palm.

Sam demonstrated by slowly raising his hand up and down toward the center of the boards, coming down each time with the heel of his palm and then stepping back.

Tony stepped up to the boards, imitating Sam's movements. He raised and lowered his hand twice, and on the third try came down hard on the center of the top board. His hand bounced off the board with a soft thud. Tony stepped back and gripped his sore hand. "Me lastimé!"

Connie stuck her head out the patio door. "In English, Antonio," she called, smiling widely.

"I hurt myself," Tony said, still holding his hand. "No way anyone can break those boards!"

Sam gently nudged Tony aside and stepped up to the boards. He crouched slightly and placed the heel of his right hand on the center of the top board. Inhaling deeply, he raised his right hand a foot above the boards, then exhaled loudly as he shot his right hand down. With a loud crack, the two boards broke cleanly in two.

Sam inhaled deeply, then turned and faced the boys. "And that's how you do it."

"Can you teach us?" Randy asked. Tony and Phillip nodded eager agreement.

Sam remembered having that same eager expression on his face more than twenty years ago when he first encountered martial arts, but any response he might have made was cut off by Connie's next call. "Dinner's on, boys!"

All thoughts of breaking boards with Sam disappeared as the three gangly teenagers sprinted into the house. Sam picked up the broken boards and cinder blocks and set them at the edge of the patio.

As he finished, Connie stuck her head through the open patio door. "You coming, Sam?"

"On my way," Sam started to reply and then noticed the strained expression around her eyes, where a happy sparkle had been only a few minutes before.

Sam stepped over and took her hand in his. "What's wrong?"

"I got a short call a moment ago while you were with the boys. A woman called and said she has information that could ruin my career. She said she'd release that information if I don't support Parsons' efforts to close down the community center."

Sam took both her hands in his. "They are just trying to bully you. The director of the community center won't play ball, so they're trying to get to her through you. They're grasping at straws."

Connie raised her eyes to meet his, her expression hurt and sad. "There are some secrets in my past that could ruin things for me if they get out. It could mean the end for me adopting Antonio, for my work, and maybe even for me starting a new life here."

CHAPTER 24

After dinner, the boys settled into the upstairs game room while Connie and Sam enjoyed cups of coffee as they perched side-by-side at the kitchen island. The soft glow of bronze pendant lights suspended over the island created a warm, intimate setting. The aroma of jalapeño, rice, and warm tortillas hung in the air.

Sam glanced up from his coffee to meet Connie's eyes and set his cup aside. She seemed close to tears. "It may not be any of my business, but what was the woman referring to when she said she could ruin your career and your chance to adopt Tony? You don't have to tell me, but maybe I can help."

Eyes downcast, Connie touched the edges of a delicate cup, hand-painted with pictures of hummingbirds in flight. "A year ago, my team and I spent some months providing medical care to the indigenous people living in the forests of Chihuahua, Mexico. The people are poor, and when we arrived, we found a virus had decimated the village. Although the virus is considered common here in the States—and there is a vaccine—those people had no such access to the vaccine.

The trip into that village required a full day of riding over rough roads in a truck and then another day on foot with us packing in everything we needed. By the time we arrived, a lot of people had already died, and many of the remaining elderly and young dangled at the edge of death."

"My team's been in that area many times. A lot of cartel traffic originates in that state."

Connie nodded, her dark hair waving across her face and catching on eyelashes dampened by tears. "If it hadn't been for our calling, my team never would have gone in there. But our work was so important for those people."

"The medical help you brought. . ." Sam began, but a gentle hand on his arm stopped him.

"But there's more to it than that. We provided medicine, yes; but more than that, we brought them hope. This hope drove us to take such a difficult trip, and the same hope drives me today, even though I am no longer with the NGO."

"But how could helping that village ruin your career?"

"When we found all those people infected by the virus, I didn't know what to do. If we would have hiked out and driven to the nearest source for the vaccine and returned, many more people would have died. If we didn't try, the village would sustain even greater losses. It was a lose-lose situation. While we prayed and wrestled with what to do, one of the people we hired to carry our equipment and supplies snuck off and met with her brother, who worked for one of the cartels in the area. The next thing I knew, a helicopter landed at the edge of the village. A man and three bodyguards emerged with two boxes of the vaccine we needed. I realized the vaccine probably was stolen from a humanitarian shipment hijacked a few weeks before, but what could we do? As the mission leader, it was my decision to make, and without that vaccine, the people would have died."

"You accepted the vaccine? A gift from the cartel?" Sam asked, knowing what her answer would be.

"I did." Her eyes finally rose from her cup to meet his gaze. "We saved lives with that vaccine!"

Sam gently laid his hand over the one she used to cradle her cup. "You saved lives. It's what both of our careers are about. Then again, the cartels don't offer anything without strings attached."

Connie nodded. "This was no exception. In exchange for us accepting the vaccine for the villagers, I agreed to vaccinate the men in the cartel's compound, which was located nearby. Aiding a cartel is against the law in Mexico and against the charter that our NGO had on file with the U.S. State Department. If anyone finds out, I could be extradited and convicted of aiding and abetting in Mexico. I would lose my nursing license."

"You think the person who called has that information?"

Connie continued to meet his eyes, although the look in her eyes took on a sadder appearance. "It's the only thing that makes sense. I can't act against the community center, and I won't cooperate with Parsons. I'll have to resign, and I may have to relocate to start again."

Sam watched a tear slide down her cheek. "I don't think you should give up so quickly. I'll bet that whoever you talked to came by their information through criminal channels, maybe even a direct link with that cartel. The last thing they would want is to have that link exposed to the public."

"But I did do those things."

Sam squeezed her hand. "They must have a lot resting on getting the community center's property. Approaching you, threatening you as they did. . . Maybe we can work the situation from another angle—turn the deck around on them."

Hope returned to Connie's eyes. "You have an idea?"

"I might," Sam replied. "The cartels and their leaders are complicated. I once saved a cartel boss' son when we took down a grow operation. The boy was caught in a crossfire between my team and the cartel's security force. I recognized the kid from a picture I had seen of the cartel boss and his family. I could have shot the kid when he charged our position, but instead, I knocked him out and cuffed him. Once the fight was over, we captured the cartel boss and torched his grow fields. Once that was over, I handed him his son with only a bruised jaw instead of as a corpse. The cartel boss thought he'd lost his only son in that fight and broke into tears. He promised whatever I wanted in exchange for his boy's life. When everything was over, he flew my team back to our demark point in two of his choppers. On one hand, we were his enemy and destroyed much of his livelihood. On the other, we spared his son and gained his loyalty, of sorts."

Wiping her eyes, Connie laughed softly. "I heard that story. That was your team?"

Sam nodded. "I bet the border patrol and DEA folks are still talking about that one."

The conversation lapsed for a second as Connie's thoughts drifted. When she spoke again, the uncertainty had returned to her voice. "I don't know . . . You're on vacation, and you've already done so much."

Sam's gentle smile cut her off. "You helped that cartel boss and his people, as well as those villagers. I suspect he had more than one family member in the crowd you vaccinated, and he became fast friends with the villagers after he helped you save them. I'll bet if he ever heard that someone here was using that information to threaten you, Paloma

Blanca, that he might not take it well. On the other hand, he might not care at all."

"So, what do I do? I feel stuck between a problem and a disaster."

"Give me a week. If that woman or Parsons calls again, put them off as long as you can to give me a little time."

"I don't want anyone hurt over this."

"That would not be part of the plan," Sam said as he drained the last dregs of his coffee.

Sam glanced at his watch. It was almost six, and he had calls to make to people in Florida. He stood from his stool. "It has been amazing spending time with you and the boys. I hate to do it, but I have to get going."

Connie took him in her arms. "I'm sorry if I said too much tonight. I don't mean to bring my troubles to your door."

Taking her hands in his, Sam said, "It's not about that. I will help if I can because of how I feel about you and Tony."

Hand in hand, they walked to the front door. "I may be out of the area for a few days, but I'd like to see you before I go."

"How about joining us for church tomorrow? It's a ten o'clock service, so you won't have to get up early. And we could grab some lunch afterward."

Sam reflected on Pastor Carson's words and Connie's earlier words about her faith driving her work. "Why not?" he replied. "I've got a friend who keeps suggesting there might be more to life than what I do for a living. Several of my closest friends suggested I might benefit from church. If Tony won't mind me tagging along, I think I would enjoy it."

"I've been going to our church for only a short time, but the pastor is great," Connie said. "He seems a bit like you in some ways, so you might like him. And it's an informal, come-as-you-are service. You don't need to dress up."

"That's a good thing since all I brought on this vacation were jeans and polo shirts. Your pastor's name wouldn't be Jim Carson, would it?"

Connie smiled. "That is the one. He's a tall man. African American. Great sense of humor and a big, broad smile. How'd you know?"

"Just a guess, but I think there might be a conspiracy between God and my friends to get me to church."

Connie laughed, and Sam enjoyed the musical quality of the sound. "It might be, at that. He does work in mysterious ways, you know. Besides, worse things could happen. In my most difficult times, God got me through. Maybe you'll find something there for you, too."

"Already have," he replied, hoping the smile in his eyes clearly expressed his feelings.

Connie tiptoed and placed a soft kiss on his cheek. "Maybe we both have."

As the front door closed behind him, Sam heard a car door open not far down the street. He saw the tall, gray-haired man from Tugboat Annie's standing next to a gray sedan. Sam covered the short distance to where Fernando Zamora stood and extended a hand. "You seem to be everywhere, Señor Zamora," Sam said as they shook.

"Then you have confirmed my identity?"

"We have. An old friend asked me to say hello."

Zamora's eyebrows raised slightly.

"My boss," Sam said. "Seems you worked together on a case back in the day."

"Ah," Zamora replied. "I am so old and there have been so many. However, please pass on my regards to Director Samuelson when you next talk to him."

Sam's eyebrows shot up at the mention of his boss' name.

"It is a big world but a small community in which we work and live," Zamora said. "I plan to be anywhere my daughter is, especially right now."

"Fair enough." Sam nodded in the direction of Connie's house. "I'm joining her and Tony for church tomorrow if that's of interest."

Zamora tried but failed to suppress a brief smile that curved the corners of his thin lips and lightened his expression. "Anthony. The boy she rescued from the cartel in Mexico. I am glad he is with her. Consuelo was always one who cherished family, and now she is making one of her own. It is a good thing. And as for you, know that Consuelo's mother did not invite me to join her at Mass until we had known each other for two years. You are moving fast, my young friend. Move carefully."

Sam held up a hand in self-defense. "We've known each other only a few weeks. But don't worry. I will behave myself."

"That is a good thing, Mike Tango," Zamora replied. "Remember, this old spy will be nearby."

"Understood," Sam said. "All jokes aside, are you aware that your daughter has been threatened by people in the local government who want her to cooperate in some sort of land scheme? They come off as pretty rough people and are attempting to blackmail her."

"I was not aware of this," Zamora replied. "I assume you plan to help her?"

"Of course," Sam replied. "I will keep you in the loop as I get more information, but I can tell you it may involve one of the cartel bosses we have both fought."

"I am aware of the man in Mexico whom she aided," Zamora replied. "I also know he would not do anything to jeopardize my daughter's welfare."

Zamora stuck out his hand again. They squeezed hands briefly. "I am grateful for the information and for anything you can do to help my daughter, señor. I am aware of your skills and have observed your good judgment from afar, so I will trust your efforts now. In the meantime, I will be nearby."

"Guarding her against guys like me?" Sam chuckled.

"From men just like you, yes, and others."

CHAPTER 25

Sam glanced at his watch as he arrived at the cottage and stepped through the back door. Locking the door behind him, he headed for the couch facing the gray waters of Puget Sound, anxious to make several important calls before the evening progressed further. Six-thirty in the evening here meant nine-thirty in Florida and a good chance Jessica would still be available. He pulled out his cell phone and punched in the code to encrypt the call and route it over the group's secure satellite frequency. She answered on the first ring.

"Hello, stranger." Jessica's clipped tone told him she was deep into something.

The word "stranger" told him someone was nearby who could overhear her words. The sound of fans in the background suggested she was in the tech room at group headquarters.

"Working late?" he asked.

She laughed. "Nothing I'd rather do on a balmy Saturday night."

"I need help with a couple of things."

"Name it, big boy, and it's yours," she replied.

Sam laughed. Jessica could lighten any mood, no matter how dark the situation. "Two things. I'm still curious about that defective ammunition load we received for the Olympia mission. It had to be extreme neglect by the logistics team or something more sinister, considering the same thing occurred for another team."

"Read your mind on that one," she replied. "Hang on while I change locations."

Sam heard quick footsteps and a door closing before she continued. "I can confirm that Earnie in logistics had no part in it. He was at his son's grade school concert in another city at the time our load was checked and dispatched. So someone else prepped that ammo load."

"It sounds like the boss had you working that angle already," Sam said.

"Affirmative," Jessica said. "Are we working the same thread?"

"I think I can confirm that," he replied.

"Understood." Jessica snorted. "I figured there was no way the boss was going to toss you off the team like that. He had to have you working something special with all of us thinking you were off the grid. What else do you need?"

"I wonder if there are any data points to connect the cartel-work we've been doing with the failed missions. Maybe you could construct a timeline that links the types, timing, and destinations of the missions. Then, you could track back to who knew about those missions, received briefings, booked the flights, prepped the ammo loads, chose the teams, and coordinated the other logistics. I'd suggest throwing a wide net, including partner agencies. It's just an idea."

"You know how to sweet-talk a geek girl like me. I know exactly how I'll approach it. When do you need the information?"

"It's pretty important," Sam replied.

"I'm on it. I've already been digging inside the group. I'll only need to rotate my view of the data and identify correlations from a slightly different angle. It shouldn't take that long. When are you coming home?" Jessica asked. "The rest of the family misses you."

Sam chuckled. "I miss you all, too."

Sam ended the call and immediately punched in the speed dial for Allen's encrypted number. The phone rang a dozen times with no answer before Sam gave up. It was unusual, although not totally unheard of for an operator not to pick up a call. Protocol demanded that any call on the group's encrypted line be answered, regardless of the circumstance. Of course, he might have been in the bathroom. If that was the case, Allen would return the call as soon as he was available.

Sam's final call was to Leah. She picked up on the first ring.

"Well, well, well," Leah said in her best mocking tone. "The hero finally decides to reach out to his lowly little sister in arms. Will wonders never cease?"

Sam laughed. "I love you, too."

"You see that Zamora chick recently?"

Sam paused before replying, and Leah picked up on it. "You hesitated. That means you have been seeing her. You are a fast-mover."

"I may have seen her a few times," Sam admitted.

"That is serious." Leah's voice became soft and less mocking. "I'm glad. It's about time you found something or someone outside kicking down doors to fill your time."

"You should talk," Sam replied.

"Can't argue that. Won't argue that. You are interrupting my private Brazilian Ju-Jitsu lesson right now. You know that I always meet the guys at the gym on Saturday evenings. It's a high point of my week, kicking large male butts across the mats."

"Only you, little tiger," he replied. So long ago, her small size had sucked him in the first time they'd spared. Her attack-attack-attack approach and uncommon physical strength reminded him of a tigress he'd once seen on a mission during his Ranger days.

"I could use some help," he said.

"Name it, brother," she replied.

"You know the guys in the other teams pretty well. I wonder if you can see what the rumor mill is saying about the missions that have gone sideways recently."

Her tone shifted to a near-whisper. "What are you digging for?"

"I'm curious if anyone has picked up on any common elements in those missions."

"My, my, you are suspicious," she replied.

"You know me: the consummate worrywart."

Leah called out, "Time to wrap it up, boys. I've punished you enough for one night."

He heard muffled complaints in the background, then slamming doors as her training partners departed. "I've already been talking around, digging on my own. It's bothered me, too."

"That's my nosey teammate," he said.

"Funny, but here's the scoop. Team Two and its leader, Alpha Dog, have been in the same area a half dozen times in the past year. On that last mission, where Dog and one other person were the only survivors, they were reportedly attacked by well-trained, well-armed cartel muscle. Dog reported opposition who worked well above standard for cartel goons—professionals with high order fire and maneuver skills. More like Rangers or SF than cartel."

"Not good news," Sam said.

"But there's more," Leah added. "Several of the teams were taken out using shoulder-mounted rockets."

"We've seen Light Anti-Tank Weapons, LAWs, and other portable rockets in cartel hands in the past," Sam said.

"Not like what was used on Team Two," Leah replied. "The director sent a drone over the site where they were taken out. At one of the sites, they found a discarded case for a US-made, start-of-the-art shoulder-mounted ground-to-air missile that has not been released for general use by our forces."

"Experimental?" Sam felt a shudder form in the pit of his stomach.

"Strictly R & D," Leah replied. "Experimental. Prototype only. A highly effective, low altitude, self-directed, shoulder-mounted munition known as a smart rocket. Strictly fire and forget."

"If they have access to that sort of weapon . . . " Sam replied.

"It's a problem," Leah finished his statement. "The best I can find out is that no one is even aware the things exist outside of the National Security Agency, and they're not talking."

"Have you passed this info on to Jessica?" Sam asked. "The director has her working on something related to this."

"Not yet but I will."

"When you do, be sure to use the encrypted line," Sam said. "I'm not sure who we can trust at this point. Have you heard from Allen? I tried him earlier but couldn't raise him?"

"No one knows where he is," Leah replied.

"That is worrisome," Sam said. "He's not one to break protocol and go dark like that."

"True," Leah replied. "If I find out anything more about Allen or the missions, I'll let you know."

"Right on," Sam replied. "Later, little sister."

As Sam set his phone aside, it rang again. He glanced at the caller ID: Jim Carson.

"Good evening, Pastor," Sam said.

"So formal," Carson said. "I said you can call me Jim."

"The friend of mine invited me to attend church with her tomorrow," Sam replied. "To one apparently pastored by one James Carson, recently defected from the special operations community to serve as an agent of God."

"What a nice coincidence," Carson replied. "That wouldn't be Consuelo Zamora who invited you, would it?"

"One and the same," Sam replied. "Such a coincidence."

Sam heard Carson's sigh. "It could be your director let me know she was headed in this direction and asked for help ensuring her continued welfare."

"Once an operator, always an operator," Sam replied.

"Perhaps," Carson continued. "It seems Ms. Zamora has a loose connection with a cartel boss in Mexico, so my oldest friend and your immediate supervisor asked me to keep an eye on her. He provided me with her travel information, which I leveraged to ensure she was properly welcomed to the area. I dug into her background as a Christian missionary. I figured the easiest way to keep an eye on her might be to invite her to visit my church. Strategically placed flyers at her hotel room door and in its lobby did the job. She bit, and now I get a bonus by having you both at the service tomorrow. God does seem to work—"

"In mysterious ways," Sam said. "I've heard that a couple of times now."

"I am only His instrument," Carson said, using his best sermon voice. "You still up for that get-together tonight?"

Sam considered the events of the day and meeting Connie in the morning. It had been a busy day, and he wanted nothing more than to take a long run and get some much-needed rest. He said as much.

"Totally understood," Carson replied. "I'll see you at church tomorrow. Maybe we can connect in the afternoon, once I wrap up my day."

"It's a date," Sam replied.

Carson laughed. "Save the dates for Ms. Zamora, Romeo. You and I will just grab a coffee."

"Funny," Sam replied. "The pastor has a sense of humor."

"Always," Carson added. "That's how we operators survive when things get serious."

"True," Sam replied, ending the call.

Sam dropped into the thick cushions of the wingback chair facing the windows and felt the tiredness of the past week wash over him. Beyond the windows, the evening had set, and the water gave a shimmering silver blanket across the inlet. Lights from residences and businesses dotted the hills beyond the water. To the north, the bright lights at Tugboat Annie's danced across the rippling waves. Above, the sky rapidly darkened as he watched, with lighter gray patches of high clouds driving in from the west.

So many things on his mind these days. He knew the director was right about the little girl's death not being his fault during that mission, but it came so close to how he and Carter had witnessed their sister's death. Then there was everyone's concern about his hesitance to pull a trigger, and how that might affect his teammates' safety. And what was all that about him not having a full life? As the questions filtered through his mind, he knew in his heart that there was substance to those concerns. Who was he, anyway, beyond a door-kicking soldier?

His thoughts slowing and his eyes growing heavy, he'd just drifted off when the cottage's doorbell rang, jerking him awake. He went to the door, rubbing the sleep from his eyes. As he unlocked the back door and swung it open, two men burst in, the force of their entry shoving him back against the kitchen sink. They both wore the standard kit of Extreme Operations Group operators: dirty-green tactical overalls; superlight body armor on chest, shoulders, and back; a utility belt; and an equipment harness over that. Both men carried a sidearm in thigh holsters and A4s across their chests. They were covered in dirt and grime and heavy with sweat. One supported the other, who clutched at his face.

"We need help," the operator supporting the wounded man said as they made their way to the couch. "We were told you are one of us."

"Of course," Sam replied. He gathered himself and helped carry the wounded man the final few steps to the couch and then lowered him onto its cushions.

Sam shoved the wounded man's partner back and did a quick A-B-C check: airway, breathing, and circulation. He found nothing and saw no blood. "What's wrong with him?"

"His call sign is Sierra Papa. We call him Paul," the unwounded operator said. "I'm Alpha Juliet. You can call me Alpha. We were working the area on special assignment, hunting down some problem folks . . . you know the kind we go after . . . mostly drugs and criminal organizations. We were on a stakeout not far from here when Paul, who some say is a bit overly enthusiastic about his work at times, dropped to his knees, grabbed at his eyes, and said he'd gone blind."

Sam glanced down at Paul who still clutched at his eyes with both hands. He moaned and rocked from side to side where he lay across the couch's cushions.

"Was he tagged by some sort of narcotic or chemical?" Sam asked, kneeling beside the wounded man. He saw no burn marks or punctures on the man's neck, face, or hands. His uniform, though dirty and worn, appeared untorn.

"Maybe he got hit by some a neuro-paralyzer dart?" Sam asked.

Alpha kneeled next to Sam as they both examined Paul and rested his hand on the chest plate of his partner's body armor. "Not that I'm aware of. We never got close to our target. Have you got a damp cloth? Maybe we can wash his eyes and clear his vision. Maybe some cool water on his eyes will calm him down. Can you give Phil a call and set up an extraction for us? We need to get him some medical care."

Sam got a cloth from a drawer in the kitchen, dampened it, and returned to Alpha who laid it across Paul's eyes. It seemed to work, and Paul quieted his moaning.

"Am I going to be blind forever?" Paul moaned.

Alpha patted the side of his partner's face with a dirty, black-gloved hand. "I'm sure the boss will fix you up, buddy. Empty is getting HQ on the phone now."

Sam located his cell phone, selected encrypted mode, and entered the number for overwatch at group headquarters. Phil answered on the first ring. "What's the situation?"

"It's Empty. I have Alpha Juliet and Sierra Papa at my place in Olympia."

"Aren't you supposed to be on vacation?" Phil replied.

"Yes, but that's not the issue. They showed up looking for help. Sierra Papa's been blinded. They need medevac."

Sam heard Phil suck in a long breath. "The director told Paul he was going to get into trouble someday if he kept going at things so hard. He's always too rough and out of control during missions—too zealous and a crusader. The group shrink suggested Paul might experience some sort of hysterical disorder like blindness if he didn't get his emotions under control."

"I don't need or want to know all that, Phil. Are you going to arrange extraction?"

Phil hesitated before replying. "We have a Suburban a half-mile away. It should arrive in a few."

"You're doing ops in my area? Why didn't I know?"

"You're supposed to be on vacation," Phil replied.

Sam turned as Paul groaned, sat up, and blinked his eyes. "My sight is coming back!"

"Hang in there, big guy," Alpha said as Sam looked on, still holding his phone. "Empty is getting us a ride out of here."

"Your exfil will be here in less than five . . . " Sam started to say, then felt the cell phone vibrate in his hand. He snapped his eyes open and jerked back against the back of the wingback chair, making it rock. His eyes felt fuzzy, and his mind muddled. Rising on shaky legs, he glanced around the cottage's living room, looking for any sign of Alpha and Paul. The place was empty, except for himself.

"Empty? Empty, are you there?" The voice from the cell phone in his hand broke through the fog in his mind. He examined the caller ID. It was Phil's secure number.

Sam raised the phone to his ear. "You okay, Empty?" Phil asked.

Sam blinked hard to clear his mind. He must have been dreaming, but it had felt so real, and he'd actually dialed Phil's number. *Need to pull myself together,* he thought. *No one wants an operator who dials his phone in his sleep.*

"Sorry, Phil," Sam managed to say. "I guess I butt-dialed you when I fell asleep on the couch. Apologies." He glanced at his watch. It was 2 a.m. He let out a big yawn.

"No problem," Phil replied. "I'm just glad everything is all right out there, and I can get back to sleep," Phil said.

"Some dream!" Sam mumbled. He powered down the phone and headed for the bedroom. He needed to be up in another four hours to meet Connie and Tony for church.

CHAPTER 26

Sleep did not come easily after the dream, so Sam was up with the sun. By the time he heard the soft honk at the cottage's back door, he'd put in yet another three-mile jog—enough calisthenics to break a good sweat—showered, and eaten.

As he locked the cottage door behind him, Connie stepped from her car, gave him a warm hug, stepped back, and tossed him the keys. "I thought it might be nice to drive to church together, and if you're available after church, we could stop at I-Hop for breakfast. I have a growing teenager on my hands who will probably starve to death by the time church is out."

"I'm with Tony on that one," Sam replied with a wide grin. He followed her to the car's passenger door and opened it for her.

"Such a gentleman," Connie said, as she settled into the passenger seat. "A rare quality nowadays."

"Not sure where I get it from, but you're welcome," Sam replied. "Lo, Antonio." Sam tossed the greeting over his shoulder after he'd taken the driver's seat and started up the SUV.

"You are supposed to call me Tony," the boy said from the back seat. "Mom refuses, but it's the least you can do between us guys."

Sam caught Connie's sidelong glance and wide smile as he backed out of the cottage's gravel drive and onto the main road. "I stand corrected," he said. "From now on it's Tony, unless you screw up, and I have to give you a stern reprimand."

"Oh, save me," Tony replied and pushed himself back into the rear seat's cushions. "I am surrounded by adults."

They covered the short distance to the church in less than twenty minutes. It was a modest building, resembling the white clapboard churches of the old west. From outside, Sam could see two large stained-glass windows flanking a wide double front door. A modest bell tower loomed above the open front doors. In front of the building lay a small lawn and a sign announcing service times and the church's name: Christ's Truth Community Church.

Sam pulled into the church's half-filled gravel parking lot and parked. Pastor Carson stood out front, greeting each person with a broad smile and a handshake or hug as they approached. Sam noted how Pastor Carson's massive frame seemed softened by his long black robes. It was quite a transition to take in, from legendary CIA operator into a man of God—but it suited him.

Carson smiled broadly as he saw them approaching. He greeted Connie with a warm hug and punched Tony softly in the shoulder before turning to Sam. "And just where did you find this stray cat, Ms. Zamora?"

"Funny," Sam replied, as Pastor Carson stuck out a huge paw that engulfed Sam's hand.

"You are most welcome," Pastor Carson replied.

"Sam says you know each other," Connie said.

"We do through a mutual friend," Carson replied. "But enough of that for now. I had plans to meet Sam this afternoon after the service. Maybe you and Tony would like to tag along."

Tony started to reply, but Connie held up a hand to cut him off. "We would love to, except we're heading to I-Hop. Then, Antonio has homework. Tomorrow is a school day."

"Ah, mom," Tony moaned.

Pastor Carson clapped a strong hand on Tony's shoulder. "You listen to your mama, son. School first, right after faith and family. You keep those priorities in place, and you will do well in life."

"Okay," Tony moaned.

They sat on the left side of the church on a long wooden pew. Although the outside of the building reflected simple elegance, the inside was a marvel of craftsmanship. The walls boasted a sparkling natural wood finish with darker heavy beams crossing the high ceiling. At the front, a short pulpit stood to the left of an open area with a choir pit, a piano, and a band seating to the right. On the front wall, and well over eight feet tall, hung a beautiful oak cross draped with a simple crimson sash.

"It was built in 1936," Connie said, noting Sam's interest as he cast his gaze around the church's interior. "I was told that Pastor Carson and a crew of volunteers stripped the insides and restored the building before some well-intentioned parishioners could tear it down and replace it with a more modern structure. I'm glad he won the day and revitalized the place. I think it's beautiful."

"I agree," Sam said. He turned his gaze to meet hers but was distracted by movement at the back of the church. Three men entered as Pastor Carson started up the central walkway between the pews toward the pulpit. Sam recognized two of the men from the encounter at the community center.

Connie took his hand and squeezed it. "Is something wrong?"

"I'm sure it's nothing," he said. He suddenly felt naked, having left his pistol locked in the cottage.

Tony elbowed Sam and shot his gaze to where Sam and Connie's hands were joined. He gave Sam an exaggerated eyebrow wiggle, and Sam elbowed him back. They both laughed, but quieted when Connie gave them a stern look and pointed to the front of the church.

The church's small choir, backed by a rock band with a surprisingly good sound, ran through a series of Christian rock songs, and Sam found himself enjoying it. He'd never listened to Christian rock until then. There was a strong contemporary beat and on top of that, a solid, faith-based message that seemed to speak to him. Once the band finished, Pastor Carson stepped to the pulpit.

"Good morning, all!" he bellowed, his arms wide and a broad smile lighting up his face.

"Good morning!" the congregation replied in unison and with so much enthusiasm Sam felt his face break into a wide grin. He glanced over at Connie and found the same sort of smile reflected in her eyes.

"Today, we're going to talk about Saul and Paul, two very different sides of the same coin," Pastor Carson started. "If you'd like to follow along, you can open your Bible to Acts chapter nine."

Carson paused, and Sam heard a rustle of people opening books and flipping pages. More than a few fished out their smartphones or tablets to look up the reference.

"As many of you recall, Saul was a Pharisee, a man deeply committed to his faith. His mission was to put down what his seniors in the Jewish church felt was a cult that threatened their position in the world. Saul had letters from the high priest to the synagogues in Damascus so that he could track down, persecute, imprison, and even kill the followers of Jesus Christ. He was on his way to Damascus when a bright light from Heaven flashed around him and knocked him to the ground. A voice called out to him and said, 'Saul, Saul, why do you persecute Me?'"

A muttering and a few amens reverberated throughout the congregation.

"Saul, prostrate on the ground, replied to that voice, saying, 'Who are you, Lord?' and the voice replied, 'I am Jesus, whom you are persecuting. Now, get up and go into the city and you will be told what you must do.'"

Pastor Carson glanced down at his notes, and when he looked up again, Sam felt he was looking right at him. "When Saul stood up, he was speechless. He opened his eyes but could see nothing. His men led him into the city where Saul remained blind for three days. But Jesus had a plan for Saul. He reached out to a believer named Ananias and directed him to go to the house of Judas on Straight Street and ask for Saul, who would be there praying."

Sam felt a chill run through his body, the hairs on his arms prickling as he remembered the dream of the night before.

Connie cast him a sideways glance with an unspoken question. "Later." He mouthed the word silently in response.

"Ananias did as he was directed, even though he was apprehensive. He knew of Saul and the harm he had done to the holy people in Jerusalem. He also knew Saul was acting with the support of the chief priests. But the Lord said to Ananias, 'Go! This man is my chosen instrument to proclaim my name to the Gentiles and their kings and the people of Israel. I will show him how much he must suffer for my name.' When Saul met Ananias and Ananias explained Jesus' mission for Saul, Saul's eyesight cleared, and he could see again. The story goes on, but as most of you know, Saul became Paul, one of the great disciples of our Lord, Jesus Christ. His writings fill much of the New Testament. The lessons he brings to us in Philippians, Romans, and other chapters of the New Testament are words we look to for guidance in our lives today, almost two thousand years later."

Pastor Carson continued his sermon for another twenty-five minutes, elaborating on the impact of Saul-turned-Paul on the Christian faith, how he started as a force against Jesus Christ and His followers, and how he was converted into a warrior of a different kind for the love of God and Jesus.

Again, Sam felt a warmth flush through his body and his limbs.

As Pastor Carson closed his sermon, he announced the service's final prayer. "Jesus, we give thanks to You for the message of Saul's conversion and how the Holy Spirit entered him and guided him through a life of peril. As Your disciple, he was stoned, almost drowned, and persecuted by the people he served through his faith. We give thanks for his efforts, for his faith, and for his work to bring the truth to us all. We know when we come to You and meet You as we are, You will shape us into warriors for the cross through our worship and love for You and God the Father. We ask that You guide us as we leave this holy place today and return to our families and our lives. We ask that You guide each of us with our unique gifts and talents so that we can serve You in the manner that best pleases You. Amen."

A chorus of amens echoed throughout the congregation. It was not hard to see the parallels between his own life and Saul's life before he met Jesus, as well as what he experienced in the dream about Paul and Alpha. He wondered if Pastor Carson, once an operator and a warrior like him, hadn't shaped the message just for him that morning, even though he could not know about the dream.

As if reading his mind, Connie whispered. "The story of Paul always affects me like that, too. Paul's story reminds me that even at our worst, when we might feel the least worthy of God's love, Jesus will be with us and call us to His service."

Pastor Carson greeted them at the door. "Did you like the sermon?"

"I think the whole thing is a conspiracy to get me to church," Sam said, smiling.

Carson chuckled. "The only conspiracy here is the one involving God's love for you and Jesus' call to service that reaches each of us in different ways." He placed a pointed forefinger on Sam's chest. "That includes you, too, brother."

Carson turned away and clapped a strong hand on Tony's shoulder. "Maybe you'd like to meet some of our other teens at the church now that you've been here a couple of times. There's a teen group meeting here this evening at five."

Tony beamed under the pastor's gaze and turned to Connie. "Can I?"

Connie sighed and gave Pastor Carson a "you are no help" look, then reached out and ruffled Tony's hair. "If you get your homework done."

Sam noticed the pastor cast a concerned glance toward the church's parking lot. "Let me walk you all to your car. Sam and I are scheduled for a get-together this evening, and we've got some logistics to discuss."

Sam followed Carson's gaze and noticed the three men from the back of the church standing behind Connie's SUV.

"Are they friends of yours?" Pastor Carson whispered.

"We've met, but it was far from friendly," Sam replied.

"Not again!?" Connie exclaimed, catching sight of the men. Before either Sam or Pastor Carson could act, she took several long steps ahead of the group and squared off with the three men standing behind her car.

Pastor Carson stuck out a hand and stopped Tony in his tracks. "Wait here, Antonio," he said.

The young man started to protest, but a stern look from Sam cut him off. "I'm not guaranteeing anything if they try to hurt my mom," Tony grumbled.

Sam and Pastor Carson took their places on either side of Connie as she confronted the three men. "I have had enough of Wayne Parsons and you men," she said. She didn't raise her voice, but instead kept her voice low and steady. Sam recalled a non-com in the army who'd talked like that and how it scared him like no other person he'd met before or since.

She took another step closer to the men, arranged in a semicircle around the back of her SUV. She stopped an arm's length from the middle man, who Sam estimated at six foot two and well over two hundred pounds of muscle. He felt his muscles relax and the events around him slow down as they always did in times like these.

"I don't know who you think you are," Connie demanded, "following us to a house of God to intimidate us. I have never seen anything more cowardly. Didn't you have a mother who raised you to respect places of worship?"

She directed her gaze to the thugs on either side of the central man, both roughly matching the size and physique of the middle thug. "And you two. What about you? Does it take three of you to stalk a single woman and her son, or are you just not man enough to stop, reconsider, and do the right thing."

All three men's eyes went wide with her last words, and they nervously slid glances back and forth at each other.

"And another thing . . . " Connie started, but the middle thug cut her off.

"We are sorry, ma'am," he said, the expression on his face growing more nervous by the second. "We seem to have made a mistake. Our apologies."

The centerman and the thug on the right turned suddenly and headed around the SUV and out of the parking lot at a quick jog. The thug on the left, with Connie standing between him and his friends, lifted both hands in an "I didn't mean any harm" gesture, side-stepped between Connie and the back of her SUV, and sprinted after his friends.

"Well, I'll be," Pastor Carson replied.

Connie turned toward Carson and Sam, and a bright smile blossomed on her face. "Take a look behind you," she said.

Pastor Carson and Sam turned to find ten men and as many women from the church gathered a few yards behind them, standing quietly but backing them up.

Connie lifted her hands in the air, palms open in a gesture intended to include them all. "Bless you all and thank you from the bottom of my heart."

Pastor Carson placed a hand on Sam's shoulder. "Now that's what I call a congregation."

"Amen to that," Sam replied.

CHAPTER 27

After breakfast and the short ride to Sam's cottage, Sam invited Connie and Tony in for a visit. Tony headed for the rocky beachline as Sam and Connie settled in next to each other on the couch facing the windows. It felt warm, nice, and natural as she leaned her head on his shoulder.

"It feels like so long since we met in Mexico," Connie said.

"A lot has happened since then," Sam said. "And it's been a busy time for both of us. On the other hand, I don't think I have ever felt as relaxed as I do now. I have you to thank for a lot of that."

Connie snuggled her head a little deeper onto his shoulder. "I'm glad your boss gave you a break from work. I like you, Sam."

Sam felt a sudden constriction in his guts. No woman had ever said anything like that to him. He'd had women he didn't know flirt with him in bars when he was with the team, but never anything like this.

"I like you too. A lot." He felt awkward saying the words but never more certain about anything.

They drifted into a comfortable silence as they watched Tony skip rocks at the shoreline.

CHAPTER 28

Connie stayed for another hour, both she and Sam enjoying the silence and the warmth of their time together. It wasn't until Tony burst through the patio doors, bellowing "I'm hungry" that the spell was broken.

"I'd better get him home before he dies of hunger," Connie said, glancing at her watch. "The teen group meets at the church at five, and it's already three-thirty."

Sam accompanied them to the car. As she stepped around him to get into the SUV, Connie gave him a lingering kiss that sent a warm flush throughout his body. He reached down to pull her closer, but she put a hand on his chest and eased him back. She stepped into the driver's seat, closed the car door, and rolled down the window. "See you soon?"

"You can count on it," Sam replied. "And you behave for your mom, Tony."

Tony flashed a thumbs-up as they pulled onto the street and sped off.

As Sam closed the cottage door behind him, his cell phone rang. It was Pastor Carson.

"Is this a good time?" Carson asked. "I'm done at the church and could use a break."

"I'm looking forward to it," Sam said. "Come when you can."

Sam reflected on the vivid dream he'd had the night before and its parallels with the pastor's sermon about Saul who became Paul the apostle. With all the talk about faith and church lately, he wondered if he was overthinking things and if it was just a dream or if it might be something more. Carson, with a past like Sam's and as a pastor, might well be the person to discuss it with.

Less than thirty minutes later, Sam heard a soft knock at the cottage's back door. He waved the pastor in, took two cans of diet soda from the fridge, and popped the tops.

"Diet soda?" Sam asked, examining the label on the bottle. "You trying to tell me something?"

Carson laughed as he accepted one of the bottles. "I doubt you have an ounce of fat on you. Me, on the other hand . . . ." He made a show of patting the small belly that was just starting to hang over his belt. "It's been twelve years since I left the game, and it's starting to show."

The thought made Sam smile. He'd known more than one man like Jim Carson, and while the pastor may have put on a few pounds, Sam would bet he could still handle himself better than many men half his age. He said as much, and Carson laughed.

"I'm afraid my prime time is behind me. A pastor's life involves a lot of sitting at a desk and sitting in a car. It's a busy life and a good one, but not all that physical. I did find a local Brazilian Ju-Jitsu club in the city, and I go there occasionally to keep my hand in it. I admit that it is fun being the old guy there, as well as a man of the cloth. No one takes me seriously, and I get a lot of takedowns from unsuspecting youngsters."

Carson had made his way to the picture window overlooking the inlet. "I bet you still have some tricks up your sleeve," Sam said. "What's that old saying? 'You can take the spy out of the game, but not the game out of the spy?'"

They clinked bottles, and Carson replied with another of his wide smiles. "Each time I make one of them submit, I figure they learn something, so if I take a little advantage here and there, so much the better for them."

Sam pulled open the sliding glass door leading to the deck. The evening was warm and the combined smell of flowers blooming in the gardens next door and the saltwater created an inviting setting. The deck stood five feet above beach level with wide steps, and a yard beyond that sloped down to the rocky beach. He waved Carson to one of the patio chairs facing the water and took the other for himself.

"I could get used to this view," Carson said.

"I am getting used to it," Sam replied. "I called the landlord last Friday and asked if they were interested in selling. They agreed to sell it to me. It was way overpriced, but we negotiated a good price. It seems there is not that much demand for one-bedroom cottages, even with the view, and they sounded anxious to sell."

"Here's to that," Carson said, raising his can to meet Sam's. "Maybe I'll be seeing you at the church again in the future."

Sam nodded. "I suspect so, whenever I'm in town. I enjoyed your sermon, by the way. Hearing it was a first for me. Your words had a decided impact on me."

"Now *that's* what any preacher likes to hear," Carson said. "Although I would have bet it was the beautiful Ms. Zamora who had your attention."

"I won't deny it," Sam replied. "I've never met anyone like her. Church was her idea, but there's more."

"This must be the part that you wanted to talk to me about."

"You'd be right, and I'd like to talk to Jim Carson the pastor, now, rather than Jim Carson the operator. Can we do that?"

Carson raised the back of his lounge chair and half-turned to face Sam. "Of course."

Sam kept his eyes on the gray-silver water beyond the beach as he spoke. "I'm no religious zealot or anything, but last night I fell asleep on the couch, and I had a strange dream. It had been a long day . . . actually a long couple of years."

"From what Director Samuelson told me, your op-tempo has been through the roof," Carson said.

"True enough, and I do think our work has made a difference," Sam replied. "But back to that dream. When it happened, I thought it was real. It was vivid. It felt as if I'd just sat down on the couch when someone pounded on the back door."

Sam walked through the dream of the two operators who showed up at his door, including the one who'd gone blind for no apparent reason. "The team call sign for the one who went blind was Paul, like the man in your sermon. Paul's partner, call sign of Alpha, described the blinded operator as over-zealous, calloused, insensitive—also much like Saul in your story. Once I got them settled down and placed some cool water on Paul's eyes, he got his vision back."

Sam closed the story with how he'd called the group headquarters for an exfil for the two operators, only to find that he'd dialed the number and had someone on the line.

Carson finished his soda and handed Sam his can. "That's quite a story."

Sam took the empty and headed for the fridge, returning with a fresh one for each of them. Carson took a sip and considered Sam's story for a few long minutes before finally responding. "Your dream could be a simple combination of your stress and feelings about your work, along with some long-lost recollection of Paul's story that you might have heard in your youth. It's common enough for distant memories to surface during stressful times."

"I admit my stress level has been a bit high of late, but not so much more than I've handled in the past. My folks and the uncle who raised me were not religious. I seriously doubt I was exposed to biblical stories of any kind during my childhood—and certainly not since I've been on my own."

"The other possibility, then, is that God has sent you a message," Carson replied. When Sam started to protest, Carson cut him off with a raised hand. "I see the parallels between your dream and the sermon, for sure, so hear me out. This is what I do for a living."

Sam nodded for Carson to continue, keeping his eyes glued to the beach below them.

"One of the consistent points of history shared by most of the world's religions is the concept of visions. The Bible records many visions and dreams. Some faiths consider dreams to be a portal to the supernatural."

Sam shot Carson a sarcastic grin. "Now you are getting into the real hoo-doo stuff."

"I'm only saying that many consider dreams to be more than the random wanderings of the mind during sleep. From the perspective of a believer, I think your dream was a special gift from God Who was reaching out to you."

"And exactly what was He saying?" Sam asked.

"That may take some more digging on your part, but I can speculate." Carson paused to gather his thoughts. "The call sign for the operator named Paul was Sierra Papa. Your dream may well be a message about your opening your eyes to faith, about clearly seeing your path forward with Jesus as your guide. Then again, it could be a warning about someone close to you who has lost their way and become blind to the truth. It seems to me a significant message was imbedded in your dream, and that it was Jesus reaching out to help you fill a need in your life."

"Director Samuelson told me his faith is what has gotten him through his toughest days, and most of my team members go to church regularly."

"Your director is a wise man, and it doesn't surprise me a bit about the rest of your team. Some of the most fearless warriors I've met and worked with have been people of faith. Your boss has saved my bacon more times than I can count, so that says a lot."

"Sounds like you two shared quite a history."

"No more so than you and your team members, I'm sure," Carson replied.

"I get that. My teammates have backed me up more times than I can remember, and I've done the same for them. It's what we do." Sam paused as he reflected on Allen, Leah, and Jessica and the times they'd spent on missions and in their off-hours. "It is strange that Jess and Leah have never talked about their faith. I always thought we were pretty close."

"Faith is a personal thing," Carson replied. "I'll bet if you asked them, they'd be happy to talk to you about it. People relay their faith in different ways. Some are more open than others. I suggest you pray about this and see where God leads you."

"I've never prayed before," Sam replied.

"When you're ready, all you need to do is just talk to God."

Carson's words dug deep into Sam's mind, and he felt a tingling sensation spreading throughout his body. It felt good . . . important.

"But what about those Ten Commandments I always hear about? 'Thou shalt not kill' is a tough one in our line of work. I've killed on missions. Does that make me a bad person, someone who can't be a Christian like you and Connie?"

"Director Samuelson warned me this topic might come up. He expressed his concern about a young girl dying on one of your missions and your apparent hesitation to pull a trigger since then."

"I've tried to deny it, but there may be some truth in that," Sam replied. "I seem inclined to take a different road on missions, one that doesn't involve taking a life. That said, I'm good with a gun and consider it a major tool in my toolbox—not something evil or to avoid."

"Understood, but let's get back to your question about the 'thou shalts' and 'thou shalt-nots' of God's laws. Do you feel that you've ever taken a life in anger?"

"Not at all," Sam replied. "When I've had to put someone down, it was always in my defense or the defense of others. I've made my share of sniper shots, but every long-range shot with a sniper rifle I made was to take out someone who was a threat to someone. I've never thought of that as committing murder."

"Twelve years ago, I came to the same question. Could I become a pastor, even enroll in the seminary, with all that I'd done as an operator? I asked someone the same question, just as you're asking me now. Here's the good news. The literal translation is 'You shall not murder.' Jesus says murder means more than killing a person. It means having an angry and unforgiving attitude. Sometimes we refer to that as revenge killing. You ever done that?"

"No. Never." Sam was adamant about his response. "I could never stomach that sort of thing. I've known those who did revenge kills. They were angry people, and not just on the job. They seldom made great operators and frequently washed out or worse."

"Trust me. Those people exist in every facet of life, not just in our profession. Or should I say, my ex-profession?"

That got a soft laugh from Sam. "You're an angel now, I suppose."

"I am definitely a work in progress," Carson replied with a grin.

As they had talked, the sun descended behind the tree-covered hills across the water. The light from the houses on the opposite side of the inlet winked as the sky streaked with crimson, orange, and gray.

"Beautiful," Sam said.

"God's an amazing artist," Carson agreed.

"So, how does this all work?" Sam asked. "This God and Jesus thing? It seems like someone is trying to tell me something. When I think about the dream, about your sermon, about God and Jesus, I get physical and mental sensations that are difficult to describe."

"You're asking what your next steps should be." Carson tossed down the last of his soda and set the can aside. "I think that should be our next conversation, after you've prayed. Besides, it's time for me to head home. I can't tell you what God has in store for you. You'll have to figure that out during your conversation with Him. But He will give you the answers."

Sam joined Carson as they walked through the house and set their empties on the kitchen counter. "What about my job? I'm an operator, a soldier. Can I be that and a Christian?"

"Of course, you can. Jesus needs people who can endure hardship as soldiers do. But enough Bible lessons for one night. I've got a busy day tomorrow, and it's getting late. Give me a call when you're ready to talk more."

They gripped hands and Carson slapped a huge paw on Sam's shoulder that staggered him, making them both laugh.

"Thanks, Pastor Carson."

"I think we're on a first-name basis by now. Call me Jim."

Sam glanced up and down the street beyond the cottage's driveway as Carson pulled away. The usual on-street parkers were in place, except for a dull gray sedan parked across the street. With the late hour, seeing whether the car was occupied was impossible, but it appeared almost too non-descript for a waterfront neighborhood normally populated by Beamers and baby Porsches. Sam made a mental note of the gray car and locked the door behind him.

CHAPTER 29

In her room at the Fort Greeley, Alaska, bachelor officer's quarters, Leah had just packed for the return trip to Florida and decided to check her laptop. She signed into the group's secure mission website and ran a quick search, her eyes going wide when the results came up. There was the record of Team Two being sent on a mission to inspect a cartel stronghold. The mission turned out to be a bust with the stronghold found abandoned. The team was ambushed as they mounted their chopper for the ride home. Team leader Alpha Dog and another person not normally assigned to his team were the only survivors.

Very bad, she thought. She'd enjoyed working with those operators during the Mexico mission. They were competent, humorous, and fearless.

The note about the fifth person assigned to the team raised her eyebrows. Taking a fifth person on any team's mission wasn't normal and implied unusual circumstances. She called up the medical report of Dog's injuries and, as she suspected, access to the file was denied. She grinned as the big red X showed over her access request. She'd dated Phil only once, but he'd been an easy mark ever since, giving her pretty much anything she wanted with the hope he'd get a second date. At the time, she had needed to access her restricted medical file.

He'd been more than happy to type in the password at his desk with her looking over his shoulder. She'd memorized it easily.

Leah tried Phil's password on Dog's medical file and smiled as it popped open. She scanned it, keying in on his latest list of injuries: a broken leg, four cracked ribs, and a mild concussion. She signed out of the website, shut her laptop down, and stowed it in her duffle. If someone like Dog set up their team members for an ambush—and Dog appealed to her as someone cocky enough to do just about anything—he would not want to take a beating like that. She struck Dog, Team Two's leader, off the list of potential traitors for her report to Sam.

CHAPTER 30

Connie's schedule with the lawyers handling Tony's adoption ruled out another date on the following Monday or Tuesday. Sam knew how much it meant for Connie to finalize the adoption, but even so, Sam found himself missing her. Her smile, strength, and kind nature felt like a balm to the concerns warring inside him.

As much as Connie filled some of the space inside him, Sam knew he needed something more in his life. When he'd been at church, some of that space felt filled by the words he'd heard and the feelings that washed over him. Jim's sermon hit a cord that sounded clear and deep inside him. But like his feelings for Connie, that feeling was new and unknown. He needed to understand it more before he could accept something so different . . . so supernatural.

During those two days, he did his usual routine of running and exercises in the mornings. In the afternoons, he ran through a seemingly endless number of mission briefs and personnel profiles stored on the secure group website. As Sam closed out Tuesday afternoon's file review, he glanced at the four remaining personnel files: Jessica, Allen, Leah, and Phil. A part of him felt disloyal even considering his friends as potential traitors. Then again, operators had died on the failed missions, and he'd known more than one of them. It had to be done.

Sam opened Jessica's personnel file first and a banner popped open at the top of the screen: "Call me."

Sam punched in Jessica's secure number. She answered on the first ring.

"That didn't take long," she said in a musical voice that held just a hint of her mother's native Spanish accent.

"The pop-up banner was a nice touch," Sam said.

"I figured we'd both be looking in the same places, so I left the note when I wrapped up my search," she replied.

"Find anything you can share?" Sam asked.

"I did. I took your suggestion and started at the far end of things where the missions took place. I also looked at the people associated with the missions over the past two years. I worked my way backward through time to when each mission was originally briefed and approved by the brass."

"Were you able to dig up anything we can work with?"

The light-hearted smugness left her voice as she replied "I did. And it's not good news. It seems that Allen may be our prime suspect."

Sam felt his stomach sink. He and Allen entered the teams through the same training program, partnered up through the tough parts, and shared too many harrowing moments for Sam to think of him as a traitor.

"Allen made a shot in Mexico that saved my life," Sam replied. "It can't be him."

"I get it," Jessica said, "but how much water can that argument hold? Backing each other up is what we do. It's not heroics; it's part of our training."

"Still," Sam replied. "It's hard to imagine Allen going traitor."

"The data revealed several issues that we have to consider. He was the mysterious fifth operator when Team Two got taken out on its last mission. He and Alpha Dog were the two who made it out."

"That is new news," Sam said.

"He's also trained in Mexico and Central America on his own time and his dime without group cover," Jessica added. "And worst of all, he's disappeared. No one knows where he is."

"He's missing?" That was not like Allen or any other member of his team.

"Unfortunately, it's all true," Jessica said. "Allen easily could have made his connections with the cartels when he was down there on his own, and he had access to important, classified mission assignment information as we all do. For all we know, he may be in hiding right now, thinking we are onto him."

It took Sam a second to process this new information. "I don't like it, but we have to take the potential seriously. I'll have to do some more digging before I'm willing to call one of our teammates a traitor. Since we're under a general stand-down, I suggest we take some more time to check this out before we call Allen out. Along those lines, could you do one more thing for me?"

"Name it."

Sam paused, considering how to best frame his request. As he stared out the patio window, a bald eagle cruised low above the still waters of the inlet, dropped close to the water, and rose with a small fish in its talons.

"Sam . . . You were saying?" Jessica said, bringing him back to the moment.

"Sorry," he said. "I wonder if you could double-check your data with any other federal and state agencies who might have been associated with any of those missions, beyond the group and the ones you've already checked? Extreme Operations is not the only group working in Mexico."

"I should have thought of that," Jessica said. "There's the Drug Enforcement Agency; Alcohol, Tobacco and Firearms; and even the Secretary of State's headquarters' office system I can dig into. I can have that data for you tomorrow. I'll send you what I've got so far so you can review it."

"I'll watch for it," Sam said.

Sam's last call of the day was to the group director's assistant. When the call went through to Phil's desk, Sam gave him Parsons' name, a physical description of the man, and outlined what was going on.

"I'll run a full background on Parsons," Phil said. "I'll get on it as soon as I can."

"Is there some sort of problem with running that check for me?" Sam asked.

Phil hesitated, covering the speaker on his cell phone as he talked with someone in the background, then came back to the call a second later. "No problem. There's just a lot going on right now. The director is taking heat for suspending operations south of the border, and we have a lot of information requests from on high that have us jumping. I'll get your answers for you as quick as I can, but it may take a little while."

Phil's response concerned Sam. If the director was taking so much heat, why hadn't he let Sam know? Jessica didn't mention it either, and she was at the headquarters. He checked his watch. It was just after four in the afternoon. That meant it was seven back in Florida. He made a mental note to call the director in the morning and returned to his review of the final three personnel files.

CHAPTER 31

Wednesday morning greeted Sam with overhead clouds and a moist nip in the air. After his morning run, he called Connie, and they agreed to meet at a coffee shop she'd found in the suburbs of Lacey near a local college. When he arrived at their meeting place, he found her standing just inside the coffee shop's side door, wearing blue jeans and a loose, embroidered blouse in aqua blue that highlighted her natural tan and ebony hair. Her wide smile and sparkling, dark eyes brought a silent sigh from deep inside him as she greeted him, and they entered the shop.

The coffee shop occupied a sizable space on a highly trafficked corner at the edge of a large, open-air shopping area. The shop's décor presented a warm, relaxed setting with two walls paneled with rough, dark wood and a dozen matching tables of various sizes scattered around a broad, open area. The remaining walls held floor-to-ceiling windows that admitted streaks of late morning sunlight across the dark, wooden tables and sand-colored tile floor. A long combination pastry counter, barista station, and cash register stood against the far wall, where two young women greeted patrons and dispensed coffee and pastries. The pungent aroma of fresh coffee set Sam's mouth to watering.

The shop's owner—a tall, athletic-looking man with a buzz cut, a day's growth of beard, and a pleasant smile—greeted them at the counter. "Welcome! What can I get you two?"

Sam started to order his usual black coffee, but, smiling, Connie cut him off. "Let me, okay?"

Sam returned her smile. "Do I have a choice?"

The man behind the counter gave Sam a crooked smile. "I seriously doubt it."

Connie ordered hot peppermint mochas and chocolate chip scones for both of them, promising he would be addicted to both once he tasted them. Sam watched as Connie paid the bill. "My treat," she said.

They made their way to a small table next to the tall windows that overlooked the parking lot. "I'm so glad you called," Connie said after he slid onto the chair opposite her. "I've put off starting my new job for another week until things settle down at the community center. I've got time on my hands, so this is a real treat for me."

"I needed the break myself," Sam replied. "I've been doing a lot of computer work the past two days, and I think my eyes were crossing."

Their server showed up and delivered a large peppermint mocha and scone. Sam paused to take a bite of the scone. "You weren't kidding. That is amazing." Sam followed that with a sip of the warm peppermint mocha. "I don't generally order fancy coffees like mochas, but now, I think I'm hooked."

"Told you!" Connie cocked her head slightly to one side, her glance questioning. "You said you're doing research? I thought you were supposed to be on vacation?"

"I was on vacation when things went down at the capitol building, but that happens," Sam replied. "In my line of business, it's hard to leave the job behind you." He drained his mocha and held up his empty cup. "I'm going to need another one of these."

Connie waved at the man behind the counter, pointed to Sam's cup, and raised two fingers. The man nodded and sent the order to the barista.

"How long have you been doing what you do?" Connie asked. "If that's an okay question to ask."

"No, that's fine," Sam replied. "I've been with my current team for four years, but I've been in the military for almost thirteen years."

"That's a long time to be in one job," Connie said.

"I have had a lot of jobs in the military. It's the best place for someone like me, who can't keep a job."

Connie's laugh held a light, soft tone that Sam decided he liked hearing. "I doubt that's true."

"I'm serious. Since I've been in the military, I haven't stayed in any one place for long at all. I enlisted right out of high school, but made it only a year before I was accepted for the Reserve Officer Training Program and spent three years at Washington State University."

"You graduated in three years?"

"I did. I studied psychology and agriculture. Kind of an odd combination, I'll admit, but I liked it. I'm also a bit of a workaholic when it comes to school and things that interest me. I also spent three years competing for the university's Taekwondo club."

"That's a lot to do in three years," Connie replied, taking a sip of her coffee and nibbling at her scone.

"It helped that I've never been a social type. Studying and working out filled the time, and the competition kept me energized. When I graduated, I was commissioned as a lieutenant in the Army Medical Services Corps, but that lasted only a year before I applied for and was accepted to the Army Ranger School. The Ranger school and test was tough but also one of the greatest experiences of my life. It showed me I could do many things I'd never considered before my time there. I served as an Army Ranger for one year before I was recruited for Army Special Forces."

Connie laughed, again. "You seriously can't keep a job, can you?"

"Seems like."

"What then?" she prodded.

"The Green Beret training, test, and a follow-on assignment lasted just over two years. That was when I first felt as if I'd found a home in the military. The people in Special Forces are the smartest, most well-grounded people I have ever known. I got to see a lot of the world in my short time with them that I might never have seen if I had gone a different direction."

"I gather you don't work with them now?" Connie asked.

"The short answer is no, but I can't say much more without breaking security."

"If you tell me, you'll have to kill me?" Connie asked, a smile tugging at the corners of her mouth.

Sam glanced up from his scone in surprise but adjusted as he noted the playful look in her eyes. He reached a free hand across the table to take hers. "Never that. But before I went to work with my current team, I was accepted for a master's program at Baylor University in Texas, funded by the army. I did my graduate work in organizational psychology. My graduate thesis addressed foreign government reactions to U.S. covert operations over the last fifty years."

Connie's eyebrows shot up. "A master's degree at Baylor? That's an amazing Christian school. I graduated from there, too."

"Small world!" Sam replied. "It was a great school. They had a great football team, and the men's and women's basketball teams are top rate."

"I got my registered nurse degree there, as well as a master's degree in nursing," Connie said. "I went there right out of high school. Did you start with your team after you graduated from Baylor?"

"I did," Sam replied. "I was picked up out of the Baylor master's program by the people I work for now. My thesis seemed to have caught their eye. I've been with them for a few years now."

"I know you can't say any more about who you work with, but are you still in the military?"

Sam nodded as the server delivered their second round of mochas. "I am a major. I have worked in coordination with the Army Medical Department on a couple of assignments in the past but have little connection with them currently. Pay and promotions are pretty automatic, and I haven't worn a uniform in a long time."

"I am having coffee with an official military officer. This is a new one for me," Connie said.

Sam wasn't sure if she was teasing or not and was about to ask when Connie's next words cut him off. "Seriously, you've done a lot with your life. You've accomplished so much, and you've made your life count for something."

"Look, who's talking," he replied. "You're Paloma Blanca, a virtual legend. I read your file. You've worked in some of the harshest, most dangerous areas in the Western Hemisphere and helped a lot of people who might have not survived without you."

"I suppose we've both done our share, and I do appreciate your sharing your story with me. It gives me an idea of the kind of man you are." She reached over and squeezed his hand. "I like what I've learned about you."

"Ditto," Sam replied. "The funny thing is that I've never laid all that out for anyone before, not even my teammates."

A comfortable silence lingered for several seconds before Connie finally said, "You told me about your background, so I suppose I should share a little more about mine. It's not as exciting as yours. I come from a large family in Mexico. I was number ten of twelve kids."

"That's a lot of kids," Sam replied, not letting on that he'd thoroughly vetted her background as a part of the group policy addressing operators who got involved with someone outside the organization.

"It was a lot of kids, but it was nice, too," she replied. "My oldest brother and sister were out of the house and on their own before I was born. Every day was a family day for us with a lot of people, noise, and fun. My mother is an amazingly strong person, and my father was a great man before he passed."

"I lost my father and my mother when I was in high school," Sam said, not yet feeling ready to drop the news about her father still being alive. "I used to daydream about being a part of a big family like yours."

"I'm so sorry," Connie replied.

Sam shook his head and sipped at this mocha. "It's all right. That was a long time ago."

She squeezed his hand again. "Do you have any brothers or sisters?"

Sam glanced out the window to the parking lot and the gray sky beyond. It was just starting to drizzle, and the water slowly dripped against the glass.

"I had a brother and a sister," he said. "My sister died when she was six in a playground accident, a year before my parents both died. My brother and I were separated after that and sent to live with different uncles. We both took it pretty hard. We haven't had any contact since then."

"I am so sorry," Connie said.

"As I said, it was a long time ago. I was only seventeen, and Carter was twelve. I haven't seen my brother since the day they sent us off to live with our uncles. I have no idea where he is or what he's doing. Have you and your family remained close over the years?"

"Some of us have. My mother lives near San Diego. She immigrated there after Papa's death. After college, I went to work for the foundation I was with when we met and have seen little of my family since then. We talk on the phone now and then. We've tried to get the family together a couple of times for a reunion but haven't been able to pull it off." Connie paused and then added, "I hope you and Carter get together someday. Family's important."

The comment took Sam by surprise. He hadn't considered that possibility for some time. He simply hadn't had the time to give it any thought. "I guess I hope we do, too."

Changing directions, Connie asked, "In the capitol building last week, I thought I heard someone call you 'Empty.' Pastor Jim, when I talked to him on the phone after church, also referred to you by that name. Is that some sort of nickname?"

Sam felt his face flush, recalling how his cover seemed to break down by the day. Careful with his words, he explained. "Each member of our team has a nickname like that. My official call sign, as you already know from our time in Mexico, is Mike Tango. When you use the first letters of each word, it comes out as M-T. Say that real fast and it sounds like the word 'empty'."

Connie nodded. "Ah, I see."

"Exactly," Sam replied. "But there is a little more to it than that. Each member of our team brings a special set of skills to the team. For me, it's what they call empty-hand martial arts. That means I'm trained to fight and defend others and myself with . . . " He paused and held up his hands. "With my empty hands."

"Ah," she replied again. "My father trained us to defend ourselves at a young age. He always said the world could be a dangerous place and that we needed to be able to defend ourselves with whatever was at hand, even if it was just our hands."

An image of her father's face in the weak light of the restaurant stairs at Tugboat Annie's and then later in front of her house flashed across his mind. *Such a man would train his kids like that,* he thought.

"Your father was a smart man. People in my job need to be able to use any tool at their disposal, and sometimes, all you have is your hands. I'm proficient with most of the tools of my trade, but I often do my job without them."

Connie lowered her voice to a whisper and leaned forward in her chair. "I've seen you in action. You are fearless, but you are also humane. You could have easily killed the boys who held me hostage in Mexico, but you didn't. I have to think that you are the best kind of soldier."

Sam dropped his eyes to the tabletop. "I appreciate that."

Connie reached over and cupped his chin in her hand, raising his eyes to meet hers. "For that matter, the term 'empty hands' has a lot of other potential meanings for someone like me, doing what I do.

When you reach out an empty hand to a stranger and they take it, it's a greeting or an offer of help. When you reach out your empty hand to me and I fill it with mine, it means affection, even love."

Sam felt his face flush again, which drew an immediate smile from Connie as she continued. "Hold up your empty hands when you face someone, and you tell them you come in peace. When we lift our empty hands to God, He fills them with the living water that quenches our thirst and feeds our hungry souls."

Sam felt the passion in her voice as she spoke, along with that now-familiar, warm sensation gently easing its way through him.

"You believe that about God filling you up like that?" he asked as she settled back in her chair.

"With every fiber of my being," Connie replied with a look in her dark eyes that was more sincere and loving than any he'd seen before. She leaned forward again, reached across the table, and placed the palm of her hand on Sam's heart. "And I think you feel it, too."

Was that what he needed to do? Lift his empty hands to God and let Him fill his needs? Connie believed that. Both Pastor Jim and Director Samuelson were men cut from the same cloth as he was, and that's where they turned.

As Sam sorted through his thoughts, he glanced out the window again and noticed a nondescript, gray sedan ease down the street next to the coffee shop. It looked like the same car he'd seen parked near the cottage a few nights ago.

Connie caught his look. "Is something wrong?"

He nodded toward the car, which pulled into the coffee shop's parking lot and parked a half-dozen spaces from the door. The driver made no effort to leave the car to enter the coffee shop. "That car's been parked near my cottage several times this week."

"Maybe it's just a coincidence," Connie said. "This place is popular."

Sam drank the last of his mocha and set the cup aside. "I'm not a big fan of coincidence for several reasons. The first is the folks who have been giving you a bad time for the past week."

"Maybe I should give up on the position at the community center and be done with all this. It seems like wherever I go around here, trouble follows," she said, her voice hardly a whisper.

"I don't think you should do that at all," Sam replied. "There's something bad going down, beyond you taking the job at the center. The people I work for don't generally get involved with local issues, but my director thinks highly of you because of your work in Central America and Mexico. I know he'll be willing to help out with your situation once I have enough information to act on."

"That's very kind," Connie replied. "If you think it will help, I suppose I can hold out for a while longer before I make any decisions."

Connie's look changed, and the tone of her voice pleaded when she spoke again. "You know that I've met people like you before—people in your line of business."

Sam nodded. "You mentioned that down in Mexico."

"I know how committed you all become to a cause and how much you're willing to put on the line. I don't want you to get into any trouble or get hurt on my account. If anything happened to you. . ."

Sam put on what he hoped was his most confident, winning smile. "Thanks, but you don't need to worry about that. I am a careful man."

Sam looked again at the gray car in the parking lot. Then, remembering he might need to leave the area for a time on his current mission for the director, said, "Given all that's happened, I'd like to give you the number of some friends of mine. I may be leaving for a few days, and I would feel better if you had someone you can call if Parsons shows up again."

"I'm sure I won't need—" Connie began.

"Please humor me. If nothing else, it'll make me feel better. The numbers I'll give you are for the members of my team you met in Mexico at the cantina. They are aware of your current situation, although not the story you related to me about the cartel boss you helped."

Connie handed him her cell phone, and he entered Jessica and Leah's numbers. Sam slipped Connie's cell phone into his back pocket. "I'm going to step outside for a minute." He gestured toward the gray car. "I do not like being followed, and I think the driver of that car has been doing just that. I'm going to have a word with him. Maybe you could get us both another mocha for the road while I do that?"

"Please be careful," Connie replied.

"Always am," Sam replied.

Sam jogged the distance from the coffee shop door to the rear of the gray car, arriving just as the man inside started the engine. Sam thumped a fist hard on the car's trunk several times before the driver shut down the engine. A man in his late sixties stepped out. He looked like a classic set of eyes for hire: thin and wizened, nose rosy and pocked by too much alcohol and cigarettes, clothes wrinkled and askew from too much time cramped in the driver's seat of the small sedan.

"You don't need to dent the car. It's not paid for," the man complained as he closed the car door behind him and moved to within a few steps of Sam. The man held his open hands at shoulder height, palms toward Sam. The man's easy confidence demonstrated that he was a pro, accustomed to approaching sensitive targets to show them that he carried no weapons and intended no harm.

"Retired cop?" Sam asked.

The man slowly lowered his hands and gave Sam a crooked smile. "Thirty years. Retired a few years back. Got bored and started up again as a P.I. to pass the time and earn some extra cash. Guess I have a lot to learn about the private investigator business. When did you get on to me?"

Sam leaned a hip against the man's car. "I saw your car near my house a few times," Sam replied.

"Who are you?" the man asked. "I tried to run your background, but it's like you don't exist. I found your military record, but that was sketchy at best, and you caught onto my surveillance like you were born to it. You a spook or something like that?"

Sam smiled but let his silence answer the question.

"How about if you tell me who hired you?" Sam replied.

The elderly private investigator shrugged. "You probably know what my response will be to that question."

Sam gave a slight shrug and pulled a thin credential case from his pocket. He tossed it to the man. "Take a look."

The man caught it with one hand and flipped it open. The card and badge inside identified Sam as an agent of the U.S. Secret Service. Seldom required where Sam went, the cover story was well established within the Secret Service and often curtailed a lot of avoidable questions in situations like this.

The man examined the badge and card, then folded the case and tossed it back to Sam. "If I don't tell you who my client is, I suppose you can make things pretty rough for me."

Sam only kept the thin smile on his face and remained silent as before.

The P.I. sighed and nodded. "Fine. I'll terminate the contract with my client once I leave here. I won't jeopardize my career and my pension with the Olympia P.D. for anyone, not when it runs up against the U.S. government. The name I was given was Fernando Ramirez, out of Mexico. He mentioned business interests in Olympia and that you might be a threat to those interests. He asked me to watch you and send him any information I might uncover about who you are and why you're in the area. He contracted my services over the phone and deposited a substantial retainer directly into my bank account."

"I know the name," Sam replied. "But it's not the sort of person I'd identify as having local interests in this area. Florida or the Gulf states, maybe, but not here in the Northwest."

The P.I. shrugged. "That's all the information I've got. I've provided him with two reports indicating who you've met with, where you've gone, and what you've been doing. He asked for additional information about Ms. Zamora, but I have not given him any of that and, as of now, will not do so. He did seem interested in her."

Sam thought about that. Connie had a lot of connections in Mexico, and Ramirez was well known in the drug trade there. He wondered if there might be a connection between her activities on behalf of the NGO she worked for and the drug dealer. Maybe he was the one she helped with the vaccinations.

Sam stepped away from the car. "Can I assume that you and I will not be meeting again soon?"

The P.I. surprised him by stepping forward and holding out a business card. "Guaranteed, unless you need some help with anything legitimate. The name's Dale Prospect. It was never my plan to work for anyone of questionable character."

Sam stuffed the card in the pocket of his jeans. "I'll keep it in mind," he said and headed back to the coffee shop. By the time he sat at their table, Connie had received their third round of mochas. She handed him the one without the whipped cream. "This is two more cups than I usually have," she said. "I'm going to have the caffeine jitters all day. How about a walk? It's damp out, but at least it's not raining."

They walked half a long city block in comfortable silence before Sam asked, "Did you know Manuel Cruz during your time in Mexico?"

Connie dropped her eyes to the sidewalk as they made their way around a corner and toward a local shopping area. "He's the cartel boss I helped in exchange for the vaccine for that village."

Sam repeated what the private investigator told him about Fernando Ramirez hiring him to follow them and report on their actions and having business interests in the Olympia area.

"That certainly gives me a creepy feeling, but I'm not familiar with Ramirez," she replied.

"I'll do some digging into Fernando Ramirez," Sam said. He reached out with his free arm and encircled her waist, drawing her close as they walked. "Your familiarity with Cruz might work in your favor if Ramirez is involved in things up here. If he's Cruz's competitor, and if Cruz still holds you in high regard, we may be able to leverage that to get them working at odds. Then again, cartel leaders can be pretty notional. You never know which way they'll go until they finally take action, and you have to be ready for anything."

She slipped her arm around him as they walked. "It would be a relief to put this all behind me."

They filled the rest of the morning with window shopping, strolling through a large outdoor shopping area, but not spending much more than their time. They paused for lunch at a taco truck parked near the largest of the area's stores and, after a brief lunch, continued their wanderings. They walked slowly, enjoying the sunshine and each other's company in a way new to Sam but growing on him rapidly.

Neither brought up the troubles at the community center or their past adventures for the rest of their time together. It was approaching four in the afternoon before they found their way back to where they'd left their vehicles in the coffee shop's parking lot. By then, Sam felt as if he'd finally had some of the vacation time his boss had recommended.

They stopped at the back of Connie's SUV. "Thanks for the nice day, Sam," Connie said, leaning a hip against the side of her SUV as she spoke and holding his hand in hers.

"I'm the one who should be thanking you," Sam replied. "I can't remember the last time I felt 'off duty' like this."

Connie's smile was soft and wide. "You should do it more often. Relaxed looks good on you."

Sam stepped forward and drew her into a long, lingering kiss. They clung to each other well after the kiss was done, holding each other closely.

It was Connie who finally pushed away and looked up to meet his eyes. "I need to get home. Antonio will be home from soccer practice soon."

She gave him a light kiss and slid into the car. "See you later?" she asked as she closed the car door.

Sam felt an easy smile cross his face. "Count on it."

She gave him a shy wave and closed the car door. Sam stepped aside as she started the engine, backed out of the parking spot, and pulled away.

His guard down for the moment, Sam didn't notice the dark blue Ford F150 that had trailed them from a distance for the last ten minutes of their walk. As he got into his rental vehicle, the truck stopped at the intersection adjacent to the coffee shop, then sped off in the opposite direction as the traffic light turned green.

CHAPTER 32

Sam enjoyed a leisurely drive home and thirty minutes later pulled into the cottage's gravel drive. As he shifted the car into park, his senses went on full alert.

Rolling in from across the inlet, the sun faded behind a low bank of clouds. Not yet sure what had alerted him, he retrieved a small flashlight from his SUV's glove compartment. He eased his way around the right side of the cottage, using the flashlight to highlight the ground at his feet, looking for footprints or a scrap of paper. Anything that might help him understand the situation. Coming around the water side of the cottage, he shot the flashlight's beam beneath the deck, his gun's barrel paralleling the path of the flashlight's beam. Nothing.

He switched off the flashlight and looked down the slope of the cottage's backyard to the water, which rippled in the evening breeze, a fractured, silver mirror in the fading afternoon sun. Seeing nothing, he moved to the other side of the cottage, inspecting the trees at the property line and shining his flashlight under the deck once more. He began to think he'd let his instincts get rusty during his time off.

Maybe his uneasiness came from the past few weeks, along with letting his guard down with Connie. He'd enjoyed his time with her. She had gotten his mind off his work for the first time in too many years.

He holstered his pistol and made his way back to the street side of the cottage. Inserting his key into the door's bolt lock, he stopped suddenly when the key encountered a slight resistance. He carefully turned the key back to the locked position and eased the key out. The lock had always opened smoothly. It might be nothing, but he was taking no chances.

He stepped off the small porch and made his way to the back deck and the sliding glass doors. He examined the frame of the sliding glass doors with his flashlight, looking for wires, putty, or anything unusual. Finding nothing, he unlocked the door. It opened smoothly.

He froze at the threshold and looked around the cabin's small living area and then back to the kitchen. Nothing appeared amiss. He eased his way deeper into the cottage. He inspected the bedroom and the small bathroom but found nothing suspicious. Back in the kitchen, he had almost concluded that the whole thing was a figment of his over-active imagination when he noticed the bottom drawer of the kitchen cabinet beside the refrigerator. He had never opened that drawer.

He walked over and shone his flashlight inside. He could make out the edge of a small box with two wires leading to the drawer's metal handle. He smiled. Those wires and that metal drawer handle would make a makeshift radio antenna.

He stepped to the cottage's back door, examined the deadbolt, and ran his fingers along the door's frame. He found a tiny lump of putty, carefully shaped and colored to blend with the doorframe and the wall. With a fingertip, he found a microscopically thin wire that led from the lump of putty across the door's frame and into the gap between the doorframe and the deadbolt where the two made contact.

The design was easy enough to understand. If he'd turned the key further when unlocking the bolt, a signal would have transferred from a micro-transmitter buried in the putty to the jerry-rigged drawer handle antenna, setting off the bomb in the kitchen drawer.

Sam stepped back to the kitchen drawer and inspected the slides on the outside of the drawer. He found no additional wires as a booby trap for anyone attempting to defuse the bomb, although there could always be others he couldn't see.

Whoever designed the bomb had done a quick job, wanting to be in and out quickly. If that were true, disarming the bomb should be a breeze. But if his assumptions were wrong . . .

With no one to call and unwilling to alert the locals and draw more attention to himself, he decided to take a chance. Besides, who could he call? Allen, the team's explosives expert, was in the wind and unreachable.

Sam eased out the drawer, relieved that he heard no clicks or snaps indicating he'd tripped a booby trap. When the drawer was completely open, he saw a four-by-four-inch cardboard box. Inside were two one-inch-wide by three-inch-long sticks made of plastique explosive and set against the box's opposite sides. Between the bricks of explosives was a single AAA battery, wired to what looked like a tiny radio receiver. Two wires led from the receiver to two fuses stuck into the blocks of explosive. The final wire, which Sam noticed earlier, led from the radio receiver to the drawer's handle, using the metal of the handle to expand the antenna's effective range.

Sam recognized the design of the bomb as a standard group configuration, taught in the basic explosives course that all operators attended. This one, however, looked rougher and messier than what

Sam saw in the classes. The blocks of plastique had jagged edges with splinters of explosive hanging off each end. Excess wire stuck out beyond the connections, as though the bomb's creator was in too much of a hurry to trim them and clean up the mess.

Following the two wires from the radio receiver to the explosives, he found the ignitors positioned at the ends of the two sticks of explosives. The radio signal receiver had been stuffed into the box at an odd angle, as though jammed haphazardly. The wire leading to the drawer continued off the handle, piled at the bottom of the metal drawer.

Sloppy, yes, but that would not have impacted the device's killing potential. If he'd turned the key in the lock any further, he would be dead now.

Sam eased the igniters from the plastique, rendering the device harmless. He pulled out his cell phone, took several pictures of the bomb, and sent copies in a group text to Jessica, Leah, and Allen along with a simple note: "Found this when I got home. Thoughts?"

The first response from Leah was instantaneous. "Whoa! On my way, if you need me. I can ETA late tomorrow."

Jessica replied a second later. "That's interesting. Important info at my end. I'm there if and when you need me."

Allen responded with a simple, "When and where?"

When Sam saw Allen's response, he breathed a sigh of relief. So, Allen was not off the grid.

Sam placed the bomb on the kitchen counter and tapped a response to the group. "Okay, now. Stand by. Will call."

Sam sent another set of photos to the director's phone along with a text. "Things have gotten much hotter at this end. Your issue may have reached my locale, or it may be related to local doings equally concerning. Please advise regarding disposal of my surprise package."

Director Samuelson's response was as prompt as the team's. "A trusted resource will drop by later this evening to dispose of it. Things are developing at this end. Keep me apprised of your progress and needs related to any local issues."

Sam shut down his phone. "Some vacation," he mumbled as he made his way to the fridge to rustle up some dinner.

CHAPTER 33

The group's jet was warmed up and waiting when Paul Samuelson arrived. In a short time, he landed in Baltimore. The Secretary of State's executive assistant had called him, requesting the meeting. In all the time he'd worked for the Secretary of State, he'd received only a dozen such calls. She had also served as a member of a CIA tactical assault team before turning in her tactical gear for a more political career path, and her experience had served her well. He trusted the Secretary of State implicitly, and she had hand-picked him to lead the Extreme Operations Group. He reported to her and her alone, and when she called, he responded. It was as simple as that.

As Paul pushed open the heavy oak doors, he was surprised to find the Deputy Secretary of State sitting at the Secretary of State's antique desk. The man leaned back in the Secretary's chair with an air of nonchalance that triggered warning bells in Samuelson's mind. Deputy Secretary Carl Emmerson removed his feet from the desk and stood as Paul approached. With no other greeting, Emmerson gestured to two leather couches that faced each other on the right side of the expansive office.

As he lowered himself onto the thick cushions, Paul wondered how someone so void of physical appearance and personality could make it so high in the executive ranks of government. The Deputy Secretary stood two inches below Paul's five-ten and held an excessive amount of bureaucrat padding around his waist. Thin, wispy gray hair floated across a blotchy, bald head atop a round face with a pasty, colorless expression. Squinty eyes of pale blue looked out over multiple layers of fat that hung beneath the man's chin and swung back and forth as the man moved. He smelled of cheap strong aftershave.

Deputy Secretary Emmerson leaned forward in his seat across from Paul. "Welcome, Paul. Thank you for coming. Would you like a drink? Perhaps some coffee?"

"No, sir. Thank you. But I am a little confused," Paul started.

Emmerson waved off Paul's next words with a raised hand. "You thought you were summoned to speak with the Secretary," Emmerson said. "I can understand your confusion. The Secretary is leaving for a tour of eastern European countries in the morning and is not available. You can assume that I speak for her when it comes to this evening's discussions."

He then paused, pulled a cell phone from a pants pocket, and keyed in a number. Samuelson heard the call go through. When the person picked up at the other end, Emmerson said, "Please come and join us."

A minute later, Pamela Thorensen, the Deputy Director for Central American Affairs for the National Security Agency, entered. She was a slender, tall woman and wore a shapeless, gray pants suit. She also wore a pinched expression. Her dishwater-blonde hair was pulled into a tight bun. As much as her presentation did little to impress from a physical sense, Paul knew Thorensen possessed one of the sharpest minds in the intelligence field.

Paul stood as she approached, noting that Emmerson remained seated, his expression disinterested.

"Director Samuelson. I am pleased to see you," Deputy Director Thorensen said, nodding as they briefly shook hands. She took a seat on the couch next to Emmerson, sitting primly at the edge of the cushion, her posture painfully erect.

Paul nodded and shifted his gaze from her to Emmerson. "This is a surprise," he said. "As you suggested, when I was summoned at this late hour from my office in Florida by the Secretary, I assumed I would meet with her. Instead, I meet with both of you."

Neither of the two who faced Paul was friends of the EOG. They had openly expressed that the group would be better united with Army Military Intelligence, Special Operations, or even the CIA. The saving grace of their tenuous relationship with Paul was the Secretary of State's own strong feelings about the effectiveness of the EOG and the level of trust she had in Paul. Paul glanced at his wristwatch, bringing a frown from both Emmerson and Thorensen.

Emmerson crossed his short, stubby legs. "I can understand your confusion and your curiosity, so let me get to the point. Pam and I are aware of the failed missions your group has experienced of late and the warnings you have received from anonymous parties to suspend operations in Mexico and Central America. We are also aware that one of your team members recently located an explosive device in his quarters in Olympia, Washington, which was, thankfully, disarmed before it could do any harm."

Paul wondered how he knew about the bomb in Sam's cottage. To his knowledge, only Sam and he were aware of that—except for Phil, of course. Paul made a mental note to have the group headquarters swept and their communications systems checked thoroughly before the end of the day. It would not be the first time one government agency had bugged another.

Thorensen picked up the conversation after tugging a mousy, gray strand of hair into place behind one ear. "The NSA is particularly concerned, given the amount of classified information we share with your group. If your organization has been compromised, we believe the EOG should stand down completely from all operations until thoroughly vetted by an outside agency."

Paul completed her thought for her. "By the NSA, I suppose?"

She sat even more upright on the couch. "One of my security teams will be sent to do the job early tomorrow."

"You will cooperate with Pamela's inspection team, of course."

Paul paused, considering carefully before he finally replied, "Let me see if I understand what you are suggesting. The Extreme Operations Group is to stand down all operations until this 'inspection' is completed on your authority?"

"That is correct," Pamela replied, a small smile tugging at the corners of her thin mouth.

Paul stood, making a show of smoothing the crease in his slacks. He glanced at both Emmerson and Thorensen before turning and stepping across the room, not stopping to face them again until he reached the doors leading from the room. "There will be no inspection of the Extreme Operations Group by the NSA or any other group unless the Secretary of State directs it. My organization works under a special charter and reports directly to the Secretary. That charter is counter-signed by the President. I am certain she did not direct your actions tonight, and I doubt she knows you called me. I am not sure how you acquired the information you just presented, but I intend to find out. When I do, I will speak with the Secretary, and we will resolve this matter directly. Good evening."

Paul had barely entered the reception area before he had Phil on the line.

"Yes, sir," Phil said, his voice groggy.

Paul knew it had been a long couple of days for his young assistant and that he had gone home early for some much-needed sleep.

"Get back to the office," Paul said. "Bring in anyone you might need but pull all of our communications offline and reboot them with all the additional security you can find. I want everything checked for leaks and taps and anything out of the ordinary."

"Sir?" Phil replied. "We've been compromised?"

Paul paused to consider that question, then replied, "I'm not sure, but I just spoke to two people who had information they should not have gotten on their own. There's a leak, and no one goes home until we find it."

"On it, sir," Phil replied.

Emmerson and Thorensen remained seated long after Paul had left. Thorensen gave Emmerson a sour look. "Do you suppose he's going to take the bait?"

"I don't know. Frankly, I'm not sure I care one way or the other. The only important thing is that he continues to keep his people out of Mexico until we finish our business down there. With what we told him this evening, he will be so busy trying to find out how we knew about his operations that we'll be done long before he can get his teams back into place. We'll have what we want and we can both retire in comfort and luxury."

CHAPTER 34

Sam sat at the tiny café table that served as the cottage's dining room, idly poking at a microwave dinner as he watched the sun drop behind the hills across the water. So much had happened over the past month or so.

He and his team had completed several difficult missions. During one of those missions, he'd rescued Connie in the jungles of Mexico and then run into her several more times in Mexico and now in Olympia. Now he was dating her. The experience was new for him and a little confusing. On one hand, he'd never felt as comfortable with anyone as when he walked hand-in-hand with Connie or when he spent time with her and Tony. Did that mean he was in love with her? Now, there was a tough question. He did not have a lot of experience in that department.

On the other hand, people were threatening Connie over what appeared, at first blush, to be a land deal in Olympia but then felt like something much larger than that. Hired muscle is expensive, and the people facing Connie seemed willing to go as far as they needed to get what they wanted. There had to be more to it than a real estate deal.

And now, the director had him searching for a traitor in the group. Was that related to the bomb he'd just found in the cottage or was it related to the threats against Connie? Without more information, he found it difficult to know which way the issue went, including the inept private investigator hired by a known cartel boss to follow him around.

He dumped his half-eaten microwave dinner in the trash, moved into the small living area, and plopped down at the end of the couch that faced the water. Through the wide patio doors, he gazed at a bright, silver line of light that streaked across the inlet's waters toward the cottage's beach.

His thoughts drifted back to the strange dream. Jim felt the dream was a message from God. Was Jesus reaching out to him just as He had reached out to Paul to open his eyes?

Faith had never been on his front burner but was beginning to feel more important as the days passed. He needed some breathing space to sort this out.

What he'd experienced at church felt tangible and real. The sermon appeared directed at him. He'd been trained to rely on gut feeling to keep him alive—something extra beyond sight, hearing, touch, and taste when danger was nearby or when an opportunity lay ahead. That same extra sense was telling him that Someone he couldn't see was trying to reach him to tell him something important.

You're not alone. The thought echoed in his mind. Who'd said that? Hadn't both the director and Pastor Jim mentioned that? That it was their faith in God that got them through so many of their tough times?

And what was it that Pastor Carson had said? Pray? Maybe he should do that. *But if there is a God and I pray, will He hear me? I'm just one guy, flailing around in unfamiliar territory in a big world. Then again, if I try and nothing happens, could I be any worse off?* As the questions rolled around in his mind, the now-familiar warm sensation of peace flowed through him again.

He felt a calm sense of well-being settle in. That's when the thought came to him. If there were ever a time to reach out, it was now.

He'd seen people pray on television and at the church. He folded his hands in his lap and bowed his head, silent and waiting for some cue to begin. At first, there was nothing, so he just sat there for several minutes in the quiet. Impatient for something to happen, he recalled that Pastor Jim had said to talk to God as if talking to a friend. *Why not?* he thought. So, he started.

"God . . . Jesus. . . this the first time I've ever prayed. I feel a little awkward doing this, so I hope I don't screw things up. It's just that the dream the other day felt so real. And there was Pastor Jim's sermon and how it sounded like he was talking about my dream and talking right to me. He thinks that maybe You are trying to tell me something, and I'm beginning to feel the same way."

He paused, lingering in the silence that followed and feeling an increasing sense that he was not alone in the room, that Someone was in the room with him.

"I'm new to religion, Lord, but I know Connie and Pastor Jim are big fans. Some of my teammates are believers, too, and they are some of the best people I know. Even the director. I'm not sure where to go next."

Like a wave, the memory of his sister's death washed through his mind. She was so young. Then, he thought of how his father and mother followed her in death soon after. Scenes from the time when his brother and he were torn apart and sent to live in separate houses and all the pain that followed. All that was followed by the death of the little girl on the mission. He had held her lifeless body just as he'd held his sister when she'd passed.

As those emotions threatened to take him down, when he felt he couldn't take any more, a sense of comfort and warmth consumed him, and he felt his eyes tear up. He knew he was not alone.

He hadn't dug through these memories in a decade, but now he'd walked through them all in minutes. Or perhaps he'd been led through them. Either way, he felt a sense of reconciliation replace the previous agony he had felt. His sister's death and the accidental death of the little girl on the mission were not his fault. His parents dying did not shape him, and his separation from Carter when they were so young was not only in the past but could be remedied in the future. All he had to do was reach out, as he'd done to Jesus.

This is what Pastor Jim had talked about. This was what the director meant when he said it was his faith that got him through so many hard times. Sam raised his head, opened his eyes, and said, "Thank You, Lord. I believe in You."

He was interrupted by a knocking at the back door. Sam sighed, stood, wiped his face with his sleeve, and made his way to the back door. Pastor Carson and Connie greeted him. "This is weird timing," he said.

As Sam closed the door behind them, Connie wrapped her arms around him from behind. "Nice to see you, too," she said with a grin. "But I'm here because you stole my phone." She paused, then added, "Are you okay?"

Sam reached into his back pocket and pulled out her phone. "On the first count, here's your phone," he said as he handed it to her. "On the second point, I've never felt better."

Connie slid an arm around Sam's waist and nestled her head against his shoulder. "Then what's with the tears?" she asked.

"That might take some explaining," Sam replied.

"I'm just here to relieve you of that little *gift* someone left for you earlier today," Jim said. "I have good relations with the State Patrol, and I've been asked to have it disposed of for you. If you two would like to be alone, I can do that and get out of the way."

Connie spun and faced Sam, her dark eyes flashing. "What package? Were you in danger?"

Sam placed his hands on her arms. "Someone planted a small explosive device in the cottage. Nothing to worry about. I found it and disarmed it."

Connie faced Jim. "You, a pastor, and you dispose of bombs?"

"Before I became a pastor, I did the same sort of work Sam does. Now, my world is Jesus and my church, but I remain supportive of those who put their lives on the line so the rest of us can sleep at night."

Sam stepped over to the kitchen counter and picked up the box with the explosives. He tilted it so Connie could see. She took several long steps back. "That is a bomb," she said. "I saw one of those when I was a kid and my father was still around."

"No worries," Sam said, handing the device to Pastor Carson.

"I have the State Patrol standing by to take this off my hands. I also stopped by to give you this." He handed Sam a thick book he'd been holding in his other hand. "It's a Bible. If you look in Acts, you'll find the story about Paul, the apostle that I mentioned at the service. After praying about it, I believe Jesus was reaching out to you through that dream."

"Dream?" Connie asked.

"Maybe I should explain." Sam waved them both to the living room.

"Let me, if that's all right," Pastor Carson said.

Sam nodded, so Pastor Carson began, "Sam informed me that he'd had a dream, a waking experience if you will. Two operators from his group showed up . . . " Jim outlined the dream for her and how it resembled the story of the apostle Paul.

"The operator who went blind seems to represent Saul. Sam placed a cool cloth across the man's eyes, which brought back the man's eyesight. I think the dream suggests Sam is like Ananias, the believer who guided Saul to accepting Jesus as his Savior. I think God gave Sam the story to let him know warriors like him have a purpose that pleases God."

Connie glanced at Sam, who met her gaze with a confused look. "He is a good man," she said as she tucked several long strands of ebony hair behind her ear.

Pastor Carson scooted the wingback chair closer to Sam and Connie and reached out his huge hand to Sam.

"The truth is, I was praying when you two showed up," Sam said. "When I finished, I felt reconciled to my memories in a way I never had before. I want to be a Christian."

"I think this is your moment, Pastor," Connie said.

After praying and telling God he believed in Him, Sam said, "I do feel different. Like my vision has cleared."

Pastor Jim nodded. "The scales have been removed from your eyes."

Sam felt Connie's hand settle on his shoulder. She gave him a soft kiss and said, "I love you."

Sam felt something flutter in his gut. "I don't have a lot of experience with love or relationships, but I think I love you, too."

"Normally, I'd say this calls for a celebration," Jim said, "but that will have to wait for another day. It's late, and I have an early day tomorrow."

Connie glanced at the time on her phone. "It sure is," she said. "I need to get back home and check on Antonio."

As Sam walked to the door, his cell phone went off. It was a text from Jessica. "Identified the possible sources for our troubles. Traveling south to investigate. The jet will pick you up at eight tomorrow morning at the Oly airport."

Sam raised the phone in their direction. "Guess I'd better call it a night and get some sleep. I'm on the road again."

"Be careful," Connie said in a quiet voice.

Sam glanced at his cell phone as another text came through, this time from Leah. "The director is missing. We need you at the HQ."

CHAPTER 35

Sam rose early the next day, threw his clothes in a duffle bag, cleaned and checked his Sig 226, and headed out the door. As he clutched his duffle in one hand and turned from locking the cottage door, he was knocked sideways by a crushing blow low on his right side. Ignoring the agony of what he knew must be several broken ribs, he dropped into a crouch and spun to his right, one hand clutching at his side.

In the same moment, he raised his eyes to see a huge man with a two-by-four, cocking his arm for another swing. Sam heaved his duffle at the man's legs. The bag slipped between the man's feet, the weight of it knocking his attacker off balance and back a step from the little porch. The big man regained his balance in a moment, sneered, and drew the two-by-four back over his right shoulder like a major league batter at the plate.

Sam lashed out with his right leg, using his higher position on the stoop to drive the heel of his foot into the man's sternum. Sam heard and felt a sharp crack as it shattered. The man let out a gasp and dropped the two-by-four.

Sam slid sideways down the stairs off the stoop and onto the gravel drive. Ignoring the pain lancing across his side, he dropped his right shoulder and looped a long right uppercut to the big man's chin, throwing all his weight behind the punch. The force of it lifted the big thug, leaned him back over his heels, and laid him out, unconscious.

Before the big man struck the ground, two other men attacked, moving in concert. Their body positions—one foot in front of the other, hands in a mixed chest-high and temple guard position, chins tucked—told Sam they were experienced fighters.

Sam stepped around their fallen associate. "We don't need to do this, boys. Why don't you both leave now and take your friend with you before this gets even worse?"

The man on the left took another step. At least six feet tall with hair hanging to shoulders too wide and muscular for the rest of his slender body, Sam registered him as a skilled martial artist but with chicken legs that might be his best target.

The other attacker was short and stocky like a power lifter. He had thick legs, arms like tree trunks, and a shaved head that phased into bulging shoulders without the apparent benefit of a neck. Sam knew from experience not to consider this man as less of a threat in a world where half of the male population had some sort of mixed martial arts training.

Sam spread his feet to shoulder width, flexed his knees to settle his weight, and held his hands low and forward off his thighs. The mixed Chinese-Korean stance offered, he hoped, his best chance for tackling two experienced fighters in simultaneous attacks.

The Sig remained in its holster at his back, but if he could avoid pulling it, he would. Taking a shot at these guys in a residential area would call attention to himself that he did not need.

The plane! Sam remembered it would be landing any minute. He needed to be done with this and get on his way, but with two cracked ribs, he was not at his best. Sam knew from experience that it was unwise to ever underestimate any adversary, especially when you were in less-than-peak condition. In martial arts and combat, there is always someone better than you are. And if there were two of them in this instance, things could get deadly fast.

"Sorry. We have a job to do," the skinny, big-shouldered man replied. "And you're it."

Sam nodded to the unconscious man on the ground. "Who is that guy? It feels like I should know him."

Mr. Skinny frowned at the unconscious man. "Some sort of ex-army guy. Said he knew you from a Ranger test where he'd washed out. Said you were one of the ones who got accepted into the Rangers while he got sent back to his unit in disgrace. I think he held a grudge about that. He was supposed to be some hot shot fighter. So much for that."

"Yeah. So much for that," Sam replied, now recalling the unconscious man. He'd been caught smuggling extra rations into the swamp phase of Ranger trials when living off the land was a part of the test. "Honor above all" had been his Ranger group's motto. The man had shown no honor at all by cheating.

Sam couldn't worry about that now. The key to survival was to be in the present—be sharp and stay focused. Trust your training and take things one step at a time.

The skinny guy shuffled forward and snapped out a front kick at Sam's head. It was a wicked, fast, and powerful blow. In the same moment, Powerlifter slid to his right in an attempt to flank Sam on his wounded side.

Sam knew the first strike in any confrontation between trained adversaries was generally a feint to gauge the other man's abilities. He shuffled his feet back and swatted the kick away with a hand, then shifted right and snapped out a left side kick at Powerlifter, flanking him on his right. Sam's heel connected with the man's jaw and was rewarded with the sound of crunching bone and teeth.

Powerlifter stepped back and raised a hand to his sore jaw. Seeing the opportunity but keeping his eyes on Mr. Skinny, Sam closed on the squat giant, stepped around with his right foot, and spun to his left—pivoting full circle and lashing out with his left heel in a spinning hook-kick to Powerlifter's head.

As he launched his kick, Sam saw Powerlifter grin. He realized he'd fallen into the Powerlifter's trap. Powerlifter reached out and caught Sam's left foot with both hands as it flashed toward his head, stopping Sam's rotation halfway around and pulling Sam off balance and toward him.

Sam recognized the move as one Allen had used whenever they sparred in training. He'd fallen for it once with Allen, but never again. His counter to the man catching his leg and foot was instinctive—all reflex and athletic memory. Sam shuffled his right foot, still under him, toward Powerlifter, shifting his weight onto the man's hands that held Sam's leg. Continuing in one fluid motion, Sam flexed his right knee and launched into the air, rolling over his left leg and snapping out with his right foot as he came over the top. The arch of his right foot smashed into Powerlifter's left temple.

As Sam landed, he continued to turn until he faced Powerlifter. He saw the man's eyes rolled up into his head. The man's grip on Sam's left foot relaxed as the man sagged to the ground. The broken jaw and the sudden impact to his temple had been too much.

The fight with the unconscious powerlifter lasted only a few seconds. When the big man went down, Sam shifted to a relaxed walking stance, right foot forward, left foot back, shoulders angled toward Mr. Skinny, who stood motionless, apparently hoping his stalky friend would carry the day.

As their eyes met, Mr. Skinny lunged forward with a low, right punch. The punch slipped past Sam's guard and connected with his cracked ribs. Sam gasped and stepped back, attempting to put distance between them. But the man pressed forward with a snarl, throwing a wide looping left hook that caught Sam on the cheek. The impact split his skin and sprayed them both with blood.

Mr. Skinny smiled through clenched teeth and lashed out with a left jab to Sam's head to finish him off, but Sam slipped to the side and dropped under the lightning-fast punch.

Sam reached up with both hands as Mr. Skinny's fist passed over him. Catching the man's fist, he jerked him forward and off-balance, exposing the man's stomach, side, and neck. Still gripping the man's fist in his hands, Sam chambered his right foot to his side, then shot a sidekick straight up, smashing the side of his foot into his opponent's left armpit. The combined force of the kick and Sam's pull popped the man's shoulder from its joint. He screamed.

Sam pushed him away. The man staggered, retaining his balance on shaky legs. The blood drained from his face as he raised his one functioning hand in a clenched fist, ready to move on Sam again.

Sam knew he was no longer a threat but needed to finish this. He had a plane to catch. Sam took one step toward the wounded man and shot out a right roundhouse punch that connected with the left side of his chin in the place known in boxing circles as the knockout point. The strike laid him out on the gravel drive. He then slipped his cell phone from his front jeans pocket and dialed 911.

After the call, Sam pulled out his car keys and tossed his duffle onto the back seat of his rental SUV. He fired up the car's engine and backed out of the drive, careful to avoid the three bodies.

Sam rubbed his sore ribs as he headed for the Olympia airport. As he drove, he retrieved his cell phone and punched in the number for the jet's pilot. When she answered, he said, "I'm on my way."

"It's about time. You're wheezing a bit. Do you need medical attention?"

As the group's pilot, Sybil Anderson also carried a level three emergency medical technician's credentials. More than once on his team's missions, she'd been first on the scene during an exfil as team medic.

"I doubt it would help," Sam replied. "I've had worse; and I'm pretty sure by the end of the next couple of days, it will be the least of my worries. See you in twenty."

"Sounds like business as usual for you and Home Team," she replied.

CHAPTER 36

Sybil met Sam at the short stairway leading up to the Gulfstream G500 with a package of frozen peas and a smile. She looked fresh and trim at the top of the boarding stairs in form-fitting jeans; a loose-fitting Denver Broncos football jersey; and a long, blonde ponytail. Sam was sure that the Denver Broncos jersey concealed a long-barreled Remington .44 magnum on her hip. Beautiful and a consummate professional, Sybil was one tough nut when it came to defending her charges and her aircraft.

"Welcome aboard, Empty," she said as Sam trudged up the steps to the plane, dragging his duffle in one hand.

"Thanks," he replied, pressing the package of frozen peas against his cheek. "You got anything more powerful for some broken ribs?"

"You're still on duty, so booze is out of the question. The frozen peas will have to do."

Sam dropped his duffle in the small hold at the back of the jet's passenger compartment. The craft's standard configuration would seat six, with two more on a couch near the back of the plane.

Sybil leaned through the open door of the cockpit and called to Sam. "You need anything before we head out? It's going to be a bit rough, given the weather, so you're probably on your own for the duration. The food locker and fridge are well-stocked if you need anything."

Sam settled into a lounger at the center of the passenger compartment. He knew from experience that the center of the plane felt the bumps and falls the least.

Sam's cell phone indicated a text. "Take the next call."

He slipped the seatbelt around his waist as the cell phone beeped again, this time with a call from a number he didn't recognize. He accepted the call as the whine of the jet's engines hit their peak.

"Are you alone?"

Sam recognized the director's voice at once. "Are you all right, sir? I heard you might be in some trouble."

"Are you alone?" the director repeated.

"Just a minute," Sam replied. He unbuckled his seatbelt and stepped up to the cockpit door. He waved the cell so Sybil could see it.

Sam returned to his seat. "I'm alone now, sir."

"I'll make this quick," the director continued. "I am not in any danger. I staged the kidnapping. I'm at an old CIA safe house on the outskirts of Falls Church, Virginia."

"What's going on, sir?" Sam asked.

"I met with several persons located high in the intelligence community yesterday. My meeting with them was reportedly requested by the Secretary of State, but it wasn't. What the two individuals discussed with me suggests they may be involved in the threats against the group. I have Jessica and Phil digging for information. Jessica believes that Allen may be working with these two people."

"I don't buy the part about Allen, sir. He's one of the most dedicated operators I know. I would not be talking to you today if not for his actions in the field."

"According to what Jessica found, it looks like Allen got himself assigned to the last mission with Team Two on his own. When that team was ambushed, the team leader, Alpha Dog, was badly beaten up, and his remaining team members were killed. Allen walked away without a scratch. It's too suspicious to discount."

Sam and the rest of the Home Team should have known about Allen's assignment.

"I didn't know about the assignment either," the director said as though reading Sam's mind. "The tasking was posted in his secure file. It appeared to come from the Secretary of State's office, which makes it highly suspicious. The Secretary and I have an agreement about such things."

"But it is not unheard of," Sam said. "A few years ago, I was tasked by the Secretary to support the Bureau of Alcohol, Tobacco, Firearms, and Explosives."

"Correct," the director replied. "When I am not available, the Secretary does reach out to specific operators. I just need to be sure in this case. The Secretary is on a tour of the nation. Pharaoh, call sign Fox Romeo, was working in the area near where she landed yesterday. He contacted the Secretary directly to confirm Allen's assignment to Team Two's mission."

"Pharaoh's a solid operator," Sam replied.

"The Secretary confirmed with Pharaoh that she never approved any order for Allen to accompany Team Two."

"It's not looking good for Allen," Sam said.

"No, it's not," the director agreed. "But I want to be sure. I intend to put him to the test. See if we can lure him into his own trap. I have a plan, and I'll need your help to pull it off. Only you and Phil will know what we are doing, and I want to keep it that way."

After ten minutes of explaining his plan, the director ended the call, leaving Sam wondering who he'd been working with for the past two years.

CHAPTER 37

Connie dropped Tony at school the next morning and headed to the community center to meet with her new boss. Questions formed in her mind as she drove through the streets of downtown Olympia.

Making her way west on State Street at a snail's pace, she noticed a public works van parked in the street ahead. A man in dark overalls and a bright orange vest stepped in front of her car and waved her to a stop. She rolled down her window as the man approached.

"Sorry for the inconvenience, ma'am," he said. His breath smelled like stale cigarettes and garlic, and she felt herself recoil from its impact. "There's a short detour here while we do some work on the sewer line crossing under the road." He waved a hand to an alley a few yards ahead and to the right. "You can take that alley for one block, then turn left, and you'll be back on your way without much delay."

The city workman touched the front of his hardhat in salute and stepped back, waving her into the alley. Following his directions, she noticed a small, gray sedan follow her through the turn. The alley was narrow and littered with broken boxes and crumpled paper. Halfway down the narrow passage, two men stepped from the shadows and stopped in front of her vehicle.

Connie slammed on the brakes. One of the men—a short, stocky man with heavy bruising on the side of his face—stepped around her car and gestured for her to get out. A taller man with his arm in a sling and a pistol in the other hand raised the gun and pointed it at her. He waved it to the side, motioning for her to get out of her car.

She rolled down the window and called to the nearest man. "I am not getting out of my vehicle. Please let me pass."

Connie felt a slight jar as the gray sedan bumped her rear bumper. The stocky man, now at her window, raised a hand in the gray car's direction. "You're trapped. You might as well get out," he called.

Connie heard two car doors open and slam shut. Looking in her rearview mirror, she recognized one of the men as Wayne Parsons.

The stocky man kicked the side of her SUV with a loud bang. "Get out now, or we will remove you forcibly," he growled.

Connie glanced at the man in front of the car, still pointing the gun at her, and then eased her driver-side door open. Parsons grabbed her by her arms, spun her around, and slammed her back against the alley's dirty brick wall. Parsons glared at her through bloodshot eyes, inches from her own. "I had hoped to recruit you to be part of a simple business transaction, and now, look what you've done. You have become a major thorn in my side—one that needs to be removed."

He jerked her away from the wall and slammed her back up against it again. "I need to give you a clear message, Ms. Zamora. If in the next twenty-four hours, I do not hear that you have convinced the director of the community to support the sale of that property, I am going to see that word of Paloma Blanca's unusual funding sources in Mexico is made public. Do you understand me? It will ruin you."

So, they did know about the money, Connie thought.

Parsons slammed her against the wall a third time, this time bumping her head hard against the brick. "I understand you," she said.

"Good," Parsons continued. "If you fail me, in addition to me telling the world about your cozy relationship with a cartel boss in Mexico, I will also see to it that your precious 'almost son' is ripped from your custody by the authorities because of your illicit and illegal behavior. Who knows what will happen to the boy if he's put into foster care? Anything can happen. Am I clear, Ms. Zamora?"

Until this point, Parsons' rough tactics had succeeded, raising real fear of her past coming to haunt her and ruin her career. But once Parsons mentioned Antonio, Connie felt that fear being replaced by something else, something stronger. Memories of the training her father had given her and her siblings before his death flashed through her mind. She shot her knee up and into Parsons' groin.

Parsons squealed as Connie swung her head forward and down, head-butting Parsons and smashing the bridge of his nose. Blood gushed from his nose, and she shoved the groaning, injured man away. She dove back into the driver seat of the SUV and shot forward, knocking the man in front of the vehicle to the side as he tried to dive out of the way.

In another second, she was through the end of the alleyway and into the light. She punched the button on her car's steering wheel to activate her hands-off cell phone. "Call Pastor Jim Carson."

Jim answered on the second ring as she made a left out of the alley, followed by a series of right turns, and then around a corner and a left onto Fourth Avenue.

"This is Pastor Carson."

"With Sam gone, you're the only one I could think of to call," Connie said between gasps for breath as she explained what happened in the alley.

"Thank goodness for your father's training. Meet me at the church."

"But what about Antonio?" she asked.

"I'll call Antonio's school," Pastor Carson replied. "I know the principal. She'll make sure Antonio is safe until we can pick him up. I'll get in touch with a few people I know who may be able to lend us a hand."

Connie headed for the church, careful not to speed and draw attention to herself in case Parsons' group might be looking for her. She took unexpected turns through neighborhoods, zig-zagging her way, hoping to elude or spot anyone who might be following her.

"Sam, I wish you were here," she whispered.

CHAPTER 38

Sam sat in a rental car at the edge of the group's private airfield, listening to the croak of frogs in the distance as the sun began to rise over the eastern horizon. The humidity hung at one hundred percent, and the heat was sweltering, even at this early hour.

Three ancient hangars lined the runway, making the place look more abandoned than functional. The metal walls of the hangars were covered with rust and chipped paint, and the roofs were worn and broken. If someone looked closely, the immaculate shape of the extra-long runway would have been the give-away. The group invested a lot in the airfield once it was abandoned by a local flying club, and now it served as the organization's transportation hub for international operations.

Sam watched as a pilot he didn't know and his three teammates lifted off in the group's larger Gulfstream, headed for Mexico and Don Estevez's compound. They'd met with Phil the previous evening at the group's headquarters regarding today's assignment. While the State Department had put out a cease-and-desist order for all missions into Mexico and Central America, intelligence suggested that the drugs-to-ag deal the team made with Don Estevez during the last mission might be going south.

The old don was being pressured by the other cartel bosses and was having second thoughts. Turning Don Estevez away from drugs and redirecting him to agriculture was extremely important to the State Department's long-term strategy for Mexico, so this mission would be an exception.

Citing his authority to act for Samuelson in the director's absence and showing everyone the written order for the Mexico mission from the Secretary, Phil directed Allen, Jessica, and Leah to make the trip to Don Estevez's compound and confirm Estevez's commitment to the plan. Sam would remain behind because of his injuries. Phil emphasized that time was of the essence for success.

During the briefing, Sam kept his concerns to himself. The director had related the Secretary's concerns about the Estevez deal and, from that, had developed the plan for flushing out Allen as a conspirator and traitor. Only Sam, the director, and Sybil knew the details of the old man's plan.

The team had gathered at their usual pub after the briefing with Allen showing up last, and it didn't take Leah long to confront him, her dark eyes flashing anger. "And exactly where have you been?" Leah demanded as soon as Allen slid into his chair.

Allen rocked back in his chair, the fair skin of his face darkening, his eyes becoming slits. "What are you talking about? You all know where I've been."

Leah's balled fist smacked the tabletop as she spit out her next words. "We certainly do not. None of us knew. You just up and disappeared, and that's a clear violation of the rules we operate under."

Jessica gave Allen a scathing look. "You left. You went AWOL. If we'd needed you, we would have been out of luck. If a mission had come up, we would have gone short-handed."

Allen's teeth locked. "I filled out my leave form. I gave it to Phil. He approved it, and I left. I had my vacation. I came back. Case closed!"

"Likely story." Leah threw a thick braid over her shoulder. "If you'd submitted your paperwork, we would have all gotten the message. It's automatic. It's built into the group's system. On top of that, you didn't check in with any of us while you were gone. We always stay in touch. We're a team."

"It was personal," Allen interrupted. "I did fill out the stupid leave forms, and I did give them to Phil. What is this, an inquisition? I had my reasons for being out of touch for a day or so, and you should trust me enough to know that." He slammed his half-empty water glass on the table, splashing water across its surface. "I don't need this," he growled and stormed out of the bar.

"Bingo," Leah said, breaking the silence after a long minute. "Did you hear how he reacted? That boy is hiding something."

Sam remained calm, hoping his demeanor would rub off on Leah and Jessica. "I'm not so sure about that. We've been through too much together not to know if one of us is going off the rails, and I certainly didn't see anything like that with Allen. I can't bring myself to think of Fox as the one who's betraying the group."

"All the data points to him," Jessica said.

"Then the data must be wrong," Sam said. "I don't think we have anything to worry about, but you all be careful on that mission tomorrow. Allen or not, there's something about it that stinks, especially with it coming up when the other missions to the area have been scrubbed."

Sam stood. "Do me one favor, if you will. Keep the team's primary channel open, no matter what. I have a feeling something's going to happen in short order, and we may need to reach each other over the next few days."

As he took his first step toward the exit, Leah called out, "Hey, wait a sec. I saw how you climbed out of your chair and how you walked into this place a while ago. You move pretty well for a man too injured to go on the mission with us. What's going on?"

Sam wondered how much he should reveal. She was one of the three or four people in the world he trusted, but too much was on the line to get this wrong. "The ribs hurt a lot," he replied. "But I'll be fine, little tiger. I just need a little time to heal. Trust me."

Now, as the Home Team's Gulfstream lifted into the horizon without him, Sam wondered how the day would work out, hoping for Allen's exoneration. Sam's mission was to observe the Home Team from a distance without their knowledge and determine whether Allen was working with the cartels. If needed, he would also provide backup for his three teammates.

As Sam heard the soft whine of a smaller jet winding up, he locked the rental car and met the group's Gulfstream four-seater as it pulled through the open hangar doors. Sybil waved at him from the cockpit window and pulled the jet to a halt. She lowered the boarding ladder with the engines still whining.

"We have got to stop meeting like this," Sybil said as he climbed the steps. She wiggled her narrow, blonde eyebrows for emphasis. "All secretive and on the sly, I mean."

"Right," Sam said. "You been briefed?"

"Yep. The director contacted me yesterday evening and read me in. I'm glad you both trust me that much. I'll get you where you need to go, low and slow in whisper mode. You'll go out the back hatch as I slick my way out of there unnoticed. If all goes well, you'll come down a few miles from the Estevez compound and the rest of your team."

"Sounds about right," Sam said.

An hour and a half later, Sam felt Sybil power down the jet's engines and begin her descent. Sam glanced out the window and saw the tops of the trees rising as the jet's engines quieted to a whisper. Here and there, he noticed places where the trees thinned, marking cartel grow fields and processing facilities and the rare animal pasture. He configured his tactical watch as an altimeter.

Sybil glanced back through the cockpit door, holding a can of Dr. Pepper in one hand and piloting the jet with the other, as if flying a falling rock of fiberglass and metal was an everyday occurrence. "Three minutes to the drop. You'll be near a road that should give you easy access to the compound without being seen. You ready?"

Sam had geared up during the flight and ran his hands down his parachute's extra-thick, flat-strapped harness, which covered a good percentage of his dirty green tactical pants, shirt, and vest. The chute was custom-built so it could deploy in seconds from a low height and pull to a quick stop above the tree tops. The landing would be hard, but if he could avoid the trees and find an open patch of ground, he'd be golden.

He pulled his half-cap helmet into place and triggered his cochlear transceiver. He pointed a finger at his right ear. Sybil got the message and activated her own. "I asked if you are set," she repeated.

Sam gave her a thumbs-up. She slapped a large red button on the cockpit dash. The plane bucked as a small hatch at the rear of the jet lowered. The hatch door was small and painted dark so that anyone viewing the jet from the ground would not notice it at all.

Unfortunately, that same stealthy configuration required Sam to crawl through a tiny opening below the door to the jet's single bathroom, barely wide enough for a person, their gear, and chute.

"Two minutes to drop, Empty. Godspeed."

Sam crawled to the edge of the chute's small opening and eased his legs over the edge and into the open air, gritting his teeth against the blast of cold air pushing against him from outside. Sliding off the edge of the ramp, he felt the hard jerk of the chute almost immediately as it opened above him.

Sam slapped his thigh with one hand, glad to confirm that his Sig 226 .40 caliber pistol was still in place. Against his chest, he felt the bump and nudge of his M4A1 carbine as the wind buffeted it against his harness. He may not have used the two weapons much in the past few months, but he felt comforted by their familiar presence.

He glanced down in time to adjust his glide to a small clearing next to a narrow road leading through the forest, just missing the tops of several old-growth pine trees. Thirty feet above the ground, he jerked hard on a blue cord on either side of his head, opening several of the chute's vents and dumping air. The ground rushed at him as the chute lost purchase and gravity took over. He tucked his legs and drew his hands to his chest, pulling the remaining parachute cords in tight. He touched down lightly on his feet, taking several quick steps back to orient the chute in front of him and lay it on the ground.

Sam smacked the harness' release lever to free himself from the chute's semi-rigid pack and harness. He dropped the pack to the ground and braced it between his legs. He pulled a toggle on the back of the chute's pack and watched as a mechanism located inside the pack reeled the chute in, coiling the wide canvass of light-weight cloth into the pack with only a few errant yards of chute hanging outside. He tucked the leftovers inside and closed the pack with Velcro straps. An innovation by the group's logistics team, the Automatic Parachute Retrieval System saved operators in the field precious time with what used to be a tedious task.

Sam stashed the parachute pack in a thick stand of small trees at the edge of the clearing. He triggered a tracking beacon on the top of the pack so it could be relocated following the mission if he wasn't there to do it himself.

He heard voices coming from the road, north of his position. He ducked into the trees and pulled his Sig as four men came around a tree-lined bend. They appeared to be headed south, toward the Estevez compound.

Sam strained to hear their voices and interpret their heavily accented Spanish. "I do not like this one bit, jefe," a burly man in dirty jeans and sleeveless t-shirt said to his boss. He and two others, dressed much like the speaker, accompanied an older man with thick, black hair and a creased, ruddy complexion. The elder man wore new chinos and a tan safari shirt and walked with the air of a man in charge. All but the boss carried AK47s slung over their shoulders. The leader carried what looked from a distance to be a Colt .45 Peacemaker pistol in a fancy shoulder holster.

"We could have driven our new four-by-fours," the burly man continued. "The new trucks would have made a big impression."

"Shut up, Pablo," the elder man said. "We need to come in quietly, humbly, if we are to have the appropriate impact. The shiny, new trucks would not set the correct tone. Now, hold your tongue, or I may forget that you are my wife's nephew and put you out of my misery."

Sam pointed the face of his tactical watch and its tiny, powerful camera at the men. He captured an image of each man's face as they continued along the narrow dirt road and passed his position. He sent the images back to the computers at the Florida headquarters. On this off-the-books mission, overwatch was not an option, so the director arranged direct access for him to the group's extensive database. A response came a few seconds later on a narrow tablet computer strapped to his left arm. He touched the icon on the tablet's small screen, and a picture of the elder man popped up: Manuel Cruz, a noted cartel boss with large marijuana and poppy grows in the area and a reputation as a large-scale exporter of illicit goods.

Now, I wonder what Cruz wants with Estevez and his gang? Sam thought.

Sam let the men get well ahead of him before moving into the road and following. He tagged the four men on his tablet computer using the group's "eyes in the sky" satellite, which would lock onto each man's heat signature and provide a real-time update on their locations to within a few feet. Barring sudden cloud cover, unlikely with today's clear skies, Sam could know where they were at any minute as they moved along the road.

Sam covered the two miles to the Estevez compound in three-quarters of an hour, a few minutes after Cruz and his men arrived. Pausing inside the thick brush of the forest, he noticed that repairs were still under way on the gate that he and his team had broken down in the earlier mission. Don Cruz and his men stood at the base of that entry gate, one tall gate door still leaning askew against its hinges. Cruz and his men stood at rigid attention with arms out to their sides as members of Estevez's crew frisked them for weapons. Their AKs were already laying in the dust at the side of the gate.

Sam saw Estevez approach Cruz from the front door of his mansion—Jessica, Leah, and Allen in tow and walking casually. Sam's teammates still carried their weapons, which was a positive sign, and their casual posture was a good sign. Estevez stopped a few yards from Cruz. Sam keyed in the activation codes for the team's cochlear frequency onto his tactical watch to listen in on what was being said between the men, hoping Jessica, Leah, and Allen had their frequencies open and their mics activated.

"Don Cruz," Carlos Estevez started in Spanish, empty hands held palm-up before him to indicate a cautious welcome. "This is, shall I say, an unexpected pleasure."

Cruz started to respond in rapid Spanish, but Estevez cut him off with a raised hand. "Please, let us talk in English for the sake of my good friends here." Estevez waved a hand to include Jessica, Leah, and Allen and switched to heavily accented English. "They are not native speakers like you and me. It may be important that they clearly understand all that is said between us."

"That is good by me," Cruz replied in English. "I've come here to talk business."

Estevez reached for a nine-millimeter pistol holstered at his side. As he did, the sound of many rifle bolts sliding forward and locking into place echoed across the compound's dusty courtyard. Estevez smiled at the sound of his men's action. "I cannot imagine what business we might have to discuss," he said, hefting the pistol and bouncing it lightly in his hand.

"I am here for peace between us," Cruz replied.

Estevez dropped his pistol back into its holster. "I am glad to hear that, amigo, although it is difficult for me to imagine this to be true, given the long history of complications between us. So, what is this peaceful proposition that you wish to make?" he asked.

"It is a business proposition," Cruz replied.

"I am listening," Estevez said.

"I have learned from mutual friends that you plan to leave the trade that has supported us for so long and convert your fields to farm crops. In truth, I can barely stand the thought. All those potatoes, corn, and so many other things that the poor people of our country raise. The thought of it is degrading. I think I can offer you a much better alternative."

Estevez cast a glance toward Jessica, Leah, and Allen and then gave Cruz a stern look. "How do you know this thing? It is not supposed to be common knowledge."

Cruz shrugged. "You have friends in the U.S. and Mexican governments. I have friends in the U.S. and Mexican governments. I invest in the welfare of several people well-positioned in the U.S. State Department and other agencies. In return, I get information that often serves my business interests."

Estevez turned to Jessica, Leah, and Allen. "No one was to know about this until all was ready. I need more time to prepare my defenses against people who will think as this man does. For all I know, they are planning to attack us right now. I may need to rethink our deal."

Cruz reached a hand out to Estevez. "If your agreement is off with them, better yet! I would like for us to join forces. You and I, together, would own the largest drug operation in Mexico. Just think of the power that goes with that. The country and all its riches would be ours for the taking. We would be partners, and you would no longer need to deal with the Americans."

Estevez turned back to face Cruz and his men. He waved a hand in a circular motion over his head, and a dozen men emerged from behind buildings and vehicles scattered around the plaza. "Why would I need you to help me, even if I did end my agreement with the Americans? I did fine without you in the past, and I have been around many years longer than you have. Do you see my men around you? I need no one to protect my business interests except myself. I snap my fingers now, and you're just a bad memory."

This time, it was Cruz who held up both hands, palms facing forward. "I do not doubt any of that. On the other hand, I do have access to special people in the U.S. government. With them in our combined pockets, we would have increased access to U.S. markets for our products." Cruz paused to gesture to the three men accompanying him. "We could combine forces in the event there was a need to enforce our rule. I have many men, and they are highly trained by the same people who help me in the U.S. government."

"You think that your men, combined with mine, can protect us from the Americans? You overstate your position, amigo, no matter the training you and your men have received. I have seen what these Americans can do, and I am not confident we can stand against them."

Sam felt a certain amount of pride in what he and his team had accomplished.

"That is laughable," Cruz continued.

Sam dropped the standard magazine of .716 rounds from his M4A1 carbine and retrieved a short magazine loaded with tiny, bullet-shaped syringes of high-potency, fast-acting narcotics. He inserted the magazine, racked the first round into the chamber of his carbine and took a careful sight on each of Cruz's men. In three rapid suppressed shots, he landed a round at the base of each of Cruz's men's necks. They crumpled to the dusty ground.

Sam stepped from his hiding place and walked slowly across the clear space separating the forest from the gate to the Estevez compound, his carbine held across his chest.

"Well, well. Look who showed up for the party," Allen said.

"Couldn't let you three have all the fun," Sam replied.

"See what I mean," Estevez said to Cruz. "These people are insidious. They are everywhere and seem to have an answer for anything I plan. I believe it would be much better and safer for me to partner with them. And I wonder just how safe you might be if you do not join forces with them, as well?"

Cruz glanced down at the barrel of Sam's carbine. "You may have a point. What now, amigo?"

Sam shot the old dealer what he hoped was his best steely-eyed stare. "First, I want your word that you will leave Don Estevez and his operation alone as he makes the necessary changes to his business."

"I don't know . . . " Cruz started.

Sam lifted the barrel of his carbine to emphasize his point.

Cruz raised his hands in surrender. "I will give you your assurance that I will not interfere, but I cannot speak for my brethren in the other cartels."

Sam nodded. "I am not interested in the other cartels, but I would like you to answer a question for me before you go. Are you aware of a person who often worked in this area, known in Mexico as the Paloma Blanca?"

"Of course, Señor. She is a legend in this country, and I have had the honor to meet her," Cruz replied.

Sam turned his attention to Don Estevez. "That is all I need to know at this point. Do we still have an agreement?"

"Of course, Señor," Estevez replied.

"Then please have your men stand down and allow Don Cruz to depart as soon as his men are able."

Estevez waved a hand, and his men melted back into the depths of the Estevez compound.

Sam returned his attention to Don Cruz. "If you have an extra moment, I think we may have something to discuss that is of mutual interest."

"I am not willing to give my business to the Americans, if that is what you mean," Cruz replied.

Sam's brow furrowed. "Maybe another time, but that is not what I wish to discuss. It deals with the welfare of Paloma Blanca."

"I am all ears, as you say in English," Cruz replied. "As long as my men and I are free to leave when we are done, I will hear what you have to say."

"Perhaps Don Estevez will allow you the use of his estate," Sam said. "The rest of my team will remain here to watch over your men, to ensure their good health."

Cruz gave Sam a wry smile. "Yes, of course, for their good health."

CHAPTER 39

Parsons sat with his feet propped on a small desk in the corner of his studio apartment's living area. Cheap by any standard, the apartment was less a reflection of his poverty than his reluctance to spend the illicit funds he'd accumulated over the past few years. As a rule, he funneled that money to an offshore account that no one knew of. When this last job was done, when the site for the new low-cost housing was on its way to construction, he would collect his generous finder's fee and leave this dreary, rain-soaked city for warmer climates.

His chirping cell phone interrupted his ruminations about a warm, tropical isle. He glanced at the name and cursed. It was her again—his supposed boss from the city council. He didn't even know her name, only that she gave the orders and paid him the money. She'd made it clear in the beginning that if he tried to identify her beyond her voice, his participation in the land deal would be terminated in the harshest of terms.

"What have you done?" Her voice blasted. "I told you not to confront that woman. What about that order did you not understand?"

"She has become a roadblock," he replied. "When I encounter a roadblock, I remove it. Besides, I intended only to scare her."

"You don't understand. She is famous and much beloved by some of our most important business partners. You can't just ambush her in a dark alley and expect it to go unnoticed."

Their business partners? As far as he knew, she and he were it. Who else was involved in the land scheme? Was there a way he could get in touch with them and steer more of their business his way—cut her out of the deal?

"I apologize for my men," he said. "The two involved have been reprimanded."

"You dolt!" she replied. "I think all three of you were punished by the woman you assaulted. I have access to all the city's security assets, including the security cameras in that alley."

"What would you like me to do now?"

"I want you to sit in that tiny, little apartment of yours and do nothing."

"What about my work on the community center deal?" he asked, feeling he was being cut out of the action. "The woman needs to be dealt with. If she goes to the police, she could start something that would seriously jeopardize our plans."

"You mean *my* plans, don't you?" she replied, her voice noticeably calmer. "This is my deal. You know only a part of what's going down. There is much more at stake and more parties involved than you can imagine."

Parsons scooted forward in his chair.

"In the next day, a shipment of street-ready cocaine and meth will arrive at the Port of Olympia in a narcosub. This may be one of the largest drug deals ever landed in this area. The land deal you are working on will be used to launder the money generated by the drug shipment and enable us to set up a base of operations in the Northwest."

Parsons felt a surge of acid in his stomach. He worked with drug-running operations in the past and the last time had barely gotten out alive.

"Wait a minute!" he said. "You brought me into your land acquisition and construction deal to facilitate the process. I did not sign up to smuggle drugs."

"Put on your big boy pants, Wayne. You are in this up to your chin, and there is no way out for you now."

"But the drugs . . . "

"No buts. You do your job, and you will collect a generous fee for your assistance."

"Okay," Parsons replied. "But why don't we just eliminate the Zamora woman? She knows me and my men."

"That's not a bad idea, but what about her boyfriend? He seems to be everywhere."

"We make the threat good enough, and he'll back off, too."

"Okay. You set things up, but I want to be there to sew this up."

When she hung up, Parsons checked the application on his phone that automatically recorded all of his calls. He couldn't be too careful in his business.

CHAPTER 40

As Sam, Jessica, Cruz, and Estevez headed out the front door of the mansion, Sam felt Estevez's hand on his arm, pulling him aside.

"I have important information for you," Estevez said. "Call it a gesture of goodwill for your country providing the Covid-19 vaccines for my family and men."

Estevez snapped his fingers. A man appeared and handed him a thick manila envelope, which he handed to Sam. "In there you will find evidence, including photographs and bank account information, that my team stumbled across while checking our accounts. The information concerns several of the local dons. One, in particular, has, shall we say, leveraged a relationship inside your government."

"He has had direct dealings with U.S. officials?" Sam asked.

"What I have provided should be sufficient to answer that question," Estevez said.

CHAPTER 41

Sam and his team exited the Estevez compound. It was time to confront Allen and confirm whether he was the traitor.

The four team members headed back up the dusty road toward Sam's chute. Allen took point, with Sam and Leah following. Jessica pulled rear guard. As they walked, Leah called ahead for exfiltration and was given a forty-five-minute window for extraction.

They reached the clearing without mishap, and Sam recovered the parachute. Using it as a seat, Sam hunkered down at the edge of the trees and invited the other three to join him.

Sam looked at the ground as he said in a soft voice, "The director sent me on this mission for a couple of reasons."

Jessica drew a small circle in the dust at her feet with the point of a long-bladed tactical knife. "I can guess. You were to act as a backup in case our mission had been leaked. He also wanted you to confirm if the leak is one of us."

Sam pulled his Sig from its holster, laying it on his leg with the barrel in Allen's direction. "Exactly," he replied.

Allen nodded over his shoulder toward where Leah stood behind him. "And you guys think I am the leak because I dropped off the radar during my vacation."

Jessica gave Sam a hard glare, tacitly ignoring Allen's words. "Someone else leaked the agreement information to Cruz and his men. Considering what Estevez said to you about the contents of the envelope he passed to you, it has to be someone in the U.S. government. Leah and I can account for all our time and communications during the last few weeks. There's only one person on the team who can't do that."

"Yep," Sam replied, his hand firmly on the grip of his pistol as he shifted his gaze to where Allen sat on his heels, his empty hands resting on his knees. "That and a few other facts seem to point at you, Allen. There's the mission with Team Two that none of us knew about, you doing solo training on your own time and dime down here in Mexico, and then you dropping off the map without any word until a few days ago."

"How can you say that," Allen asked and then waved a hand toward Sam's pistol. "You've already tried and convicted me and after all we've been through together?"

"Maybe not the traitor," Leah offered. "Maybe you're just with whomever that person is."

Allen let out a choked laugh. "You have got to be kidding! You guys know me way better than that."

Leah faced him, her carbine now held loosely at her side, barrel down, finger on the trigger guard. It was a nuance not missed by any of them. "Look at the situation from our perspective," she said. "You went silent for almost a week. You did that at the same time someone tried to blow up Sam's house. You know the rules against going off-grid. Add to that, you were on an off-the-books mission with Alpha Dog when his team got taken out, and you walked away without a scratch. That's a lot."

Allen unslung his carbine from where it rested across his chest and set it on the ground at his feet. He drew his pistol and set it beside the carbine. He kept both hands in front of him, empty and in plain sight. "First," he started. "Because the three of you are my best friends in this world—"

"Otherwise," Jessica said, interrupting him, still crouched on her heels but now with her .9 mm Glock in her hand, "you'd shoot us, right?" Her expression was grim as she spoke.

"That thought was never in my mind and never will be. We are a team, and I would never harm any of you or let you down," Allen replied. He pointed to the carbine and pistol on the ground before him. "If you don't believe that, there are my weapons. The truth is I went home to Vermont to propose to my girlfriend. I filled out the leave forms in triplicate as usual and gave them to Phil before I left. He said he'd file them for me, per reg."

Jessica turned to Sam, eyebrows raised, then glanced back to Allen. "If we accept that, what about the mission with Team Two where Dog and his team were ambushed and the chopper destroyed?"

"I was ordered, in writing, by the Secretary of State's office to go with Dog and Team Two on that mission. We were ordered to check out a cartel compound that turned out to be abandoned. The chopper landed for exfiltration, and three members of Team Two climbed in ahead of us with Alpha Dog and me providing rear guard. When we both ran for the chopper, Dog was in front of me. We were about twenty yards from the bird when it was hit by a missile. I got off easy with Dog shielding me like that. I can tell you for sure that I was on that mission on orders. I have copies stashed in my safe at home."

Sam pulled out his cell phone, called up the photo gallery, and selected the picture of the bomb left in his cottage. He tossed the cell phone to Allen, the team's expert for explosive ordinance. "Tell me what you think of that."

Allen caught the phone one-handed and glanced at the picture. "It's an EOG configuration, generally speaking, if you're a first-timer who hasn't actually built one before and knows almost nothing about making a bomb. For one thing, it's sloppy with the excess wire stuffed in the package. Who knows what could have shorted with all that wire in there? Secondly, the firing pins are positioned at the bottom of the two bricks of plastique. They should have been positioned midway up each block. The explosives might not have detonated cleanly. That's not my work. Way too sloppy."

Allen tossed the phone back to Sam. "I think you have your answer. You can confirm the leave form with Phil, and I can show you the orders for the mission with Team Two. Besides, if I was going to blow you up, I'd do a much better job of it."

"Good to know," Sam said with a wry grin. Sam sent his gaze first to Leah and then to Jessica. The two operators each gave him a slight nod in response to the unspoken question.

"Fair enough," Sam said. "Pending Phil's confirmation of your leave status and seeing those orders, you are off the hook."

"That's a relief, but you all owe me for putting me through this," Allen replied.

"I'll admit that if Phil confirms your leave papers," Leah replied. "But then you'll be buying us all a lot of meals out for not telling us about you getting engaged."

Sam looked up as a Blackhawk came in low over the trees and prepared to set down in the road before them, then said, "We still need to figure out who leaked the information to Cruz." He hefted the thick envelope Estevez had provided in one hand as he returned his Sig to its holster at his thigh. "We should be able to get some of that from this information once the guys in the lab confirm its authenticity."

"I have an idea who it might be, but you're not going to like it," Leah started.

CHAPTER 42

The team arrived at the Florida headquarters three hours later, dumped their gear in their cages, and headed for the main office. Phil greeted them with little enthusiasm, not happy with his current administrative role and the postponed training.

"Any messages?" Sam asked as they gathered at Phil's desk in the building's reception area.

"Nothing except a constant stream of message traffic from the FBI, looking for the director. A lot of talk and no one's getting anywhere. There was a message from your brother, Carter," Phil said. He handed Sam a folded note.

At other times, Sam might have flinched at the mention of his estranged brother's name. Then it occurred to him that someone used the reference as a covert heads-up.

Sam took the note from Phil, his expression studied and casual. "Probably wants to borrow money again."

Allen patted the top of Phil's desk to draw Phil's attention. "What happened to the leave form I gave you last week? Everyone thought I'd gone AWOL."

Phil shook his head. "Didn't get to it. Sorry. Things have been crazy with the boss missing and all." Phil dug through a pile of paperwork and pulled out Allen's leave request. He waved it over his head and slapped it down on his desktop. "I'll take care of it now."

The team headed out through the building's front doors. Sam pulled up near the small compound's logistics building, stopping under the cover of a tall oak tree.

"I thought you weren't on speaking terms with your brother," Leah said.

"He wouldn't know how to reach me," Sam replied. "This note is definitely not from Carter."

Sam unfolded the paper and read it to the others. "How about grabbing a bite tonight? We can meet where we first had dinner and catch up. Send a text to confirm. Bring your friends."

"If that's not Carter, who is it?" Allen asked.

It had to be the director. Sam smiled at the reference to where he and the director had met when Sam was recruited into the Extreme Operations Group. "It's the director, and I know the place he refers to. I'll text you the address. We'll take separate cars. Make sure you're not followed. When we get there, we will park at the opposing points of the compass to make sure we have the place adequately surveyed before we meet inside: Allen to the north, Jessica south, Leah east. I'll take the west. Make sure you're armed. I'm not sure what to expect."

When the others had gone, Sam texted the director. "Will comply for this evening. All will attend. Allen is in the clear. Certain of it. Have additional information."

CHAPTER 43

Sam entered the restaurant first, followed at five-to-six-minute intervals by Leah and then Allen. Jessica followed another twenty minutes later, providing final oversight before they settled in for the meeting. As Jess approached the table, she gave a nod to indicate the place was clear. As was SOP for the team, she had arrived a full hour before the meeting time, taking a position on a nearby rooftop and observing the people who entered and left the place, as well as the surrounding area.

Leah smiled as Jess joined them, waving a menu with a pig holding a bell on the front. "There's a restaurant actually called Corky Bell's? When you sent the directions, I thought you were joking."

Sam made a show of sucking in the aroma of fresh seafood and fry-cookers. "This place has some of the best seafood in the area. It's where the director and I met for my interview when he recruited me. The crab fingers and gator tail are worth the drive, but be sure to try the onion straws. They are amazing."

Jessica raised her head from her menu and nodded toward the restaurant's front door. They all watched as Director Samuelson entered the restaurant.

"And there he is," Allen announced in a soft voice. "His Highness himself."

The director wound his way through the crowded restaurant to their table, taking the one remaining chair. Dressed in cargo shorts, a bright Hawaiian shirt, and flip-flops, he looked every bit the tourist looking for a meal after a long day on the beach.

The waitress arrived as the director took his seat. They ordered their food, the silence at the table lingering as they waited for her to leave. When she'd gone, the director leaned forward in his chair, keeping his voice low. "As you all have figured out by now, I was not kidnapped. I fabricated that story. I've been staying out of sight, living on a friend's boat docked not far from here."

"What's going on?" Allen asked. "Phil is ready to hang it up with all the fuss about your abduction and the FBI looking for you, and then we find out you faked it?"

"I'll explain, but first fill me in on what you found out in Mexico."

Sam briefed him on the mission in Mexico, their discussion with Allen, the orders from the secretary's office, and Phil not processing Allen's paperwork.

Samuelson nodded toward Allen. "It's good news that you're cleared. I need people I can trust right now. First, I have been in contact with a friend at the FBI. The official story is that they are looking for me, which is being communicated within the intelligence community. In fact, there is little going on besides message traffic between the FBI and the State Department headquarters, NSA, ATF, CIA, military intelligence, and our group."

"Poor Phil," Jessica replied.

"As much as I value Phil, I frankly do not know who I can trust beyond your team."

"At least that's somewhat reassuring," Leah said with a pointed glance in Allen's direction.

"That includes Allen," the director said with a return glare in Leah's direction. "I've checked his alibi, and it's solid. He's a trusted member of Home Team."

"Sam knows part of this," the director continued. "But I am now one hundred percent sure that we have a traitor in the group. That person is working with several high-placed government officials in the State Department and the National Security Agency."

Samuelson described his meeting with Deputy Secretary of State Emmerson and Deputy NSA Director Thorensen. "I believe they are working for their own interests with one or more of the cartels. That they are linked to someone inside the Extreme Operations Group is certain. They had information about the bomb in Sam's place well before I'd released that information to anyone."

Leah tapped her fork against the table's surface several times. "You sanctioned that last mission to Mexico and used us as bait to draw them out in that last mission, didn't you?" Her expression was cold, icy.

Samuelson met Leah's glare eye-to-eye. "I needed to confirm that someone was passing information to the cartels. With Cruz showing up at the Estevez compound with information about the drugs-to-ag agreement, I have my proof."

"Why the disappearing act?" Allen asked.

Samuelson leaned back in his chair. "A message was left on my secure cell phone, the number that no one has except for the Secretary."

"Sorry, sir," Leah replied. "We all have that number. I got it from Phil when I needed to reach you one night. I never made that call, but

I got the number just the same. When Jess needed it, I gave it to her, then to Sam and Allen in case we needed it in the future."

Samuelson glanced around the table, and everyone nodded. "I can't keep one single secret around you folks," he moaned. "I should never have approved him asking you out on that date, Leah."

Leah grinned. "You trained us well. We eat secrets for breakfast."

Samuelson continued. "The message said that I was to meet the sender at a warehouse in Olympia tomorrow afternoon. I believe whoever shows up for that meeting may have the information we need to bring this situation to a close."

"More likely, it'll be a trap," Jessica said. "You said they threatened to eliminate group operators if we made any wrong moves, and we did. We made the trip to Mexico."

"You're probably right," the director agreed, "but we need to end this situation. I don't think we can afford to pass up meeting them head-on. I want all four of you there with me."

"Armed, I hope," Sam said.

"To the teeth," Samuelson replied. "One way or another, this ends tomorrow."

CHAPTER 44

As the group's jet closed in on the Olympia airport, Sam's cell phone roused him from a deep sleep. He glanced at the screen and saw Jim Carson's name.

Sam glanced around the plane. Allen, Jessica, Leah, and the director were all asleep in their chairs. He keyed the phone and whispered, "Pastor Carson. What can I do for you?"

"We have an issue here, Sam, and we need your help." The pastor described what had happened to Connie. "Consuelo gave as good as she got, but she was pretty shaken up."

"Thanks for taking her in," Sam said.

"I think things are under control for the moment, but that attack suggests these people are upping the ante."

"You have any weapons?" Sam asked.

"There's nothing in the Bible about not defending yourself and those you hold dear. With God on our side, we'll be fine, but I plan to be ready. Several cars just pulled into the church parking lot in front of the church. I don't like it. There's also a tall, old man hanging out down the street in a little, gray car."

Sam smiled. "Don't worry about the old guy. He's your ace in the hole if you need one. He is deeply vested in Connie's welfare." Sam checked the time on his tactical watch. "We'll land in another twenty minutes. I can be at your location within the hour. I'll have my team with me. We'll handle whoever is there."

"Don't leave me out of this, youngster," Carson replied. "These men accosted a member of my flock. I definitely have a stake in this."

Sybil stuck her head through the cockpit door and announced, "Fifteen minutes to wheels down. Wakey, wakey, children."

"I would never think of excluding an old wolf like you from any fight, although I hope it doesn't come to that," Sam whispered into the phone.

"The defense of others is an honorable and righteous cause; and as you once said, with Jesus on our side, how can we lose?"

"Totally," Sam replied. "But please do me one favor: do not, under any circumstances call the police in on this."

"But—" Carson began, but Sam cut him off.

"Just trust me," Sam said and ended the call.

Sam punched another number. "Are you in-country?" Sam asked.

"Yes, Señor. We are in your fair city now. We have settled into a nice hotel that is well off the beaten path. I believe you stayed here not too long ago."

"The people we discussed earlier assaulted Paloma Blanca today. They have her, her pastor, his wife, and her soon-to-be-adopted son cornered in the pastor's house next to a church. My team and I will be there within the hour."

"We can be there sooner. My traveling companions and I will resolve the issue before you can arrive."

"You need to wait for me and my team," Sam said.

"These people attacked Paloma Blanca," Cruz replied. "Those who threaten Paloma Blanca abuse one of Mexico's great treasures and a person to whom I owe a great debt."

Jessica leaned forward in her seat, pulling on her tactical boots. "What was that all about?"

Sam explained the situation.

"Sheesh," Leah exclaimed. "How many times are you going to have to save that girl before you two get down to business?"

"I think she's the one who's saved me," Sam replied. "She helped me find my faith."

"I've been praying you'd find someone like her for over a year," Jessica replied.

Allen shook his head. "God and His mysterious ways, I suppose. Whoever thought someone like you would connect with such a beautiful woman?"

Leah cast Sam a serious glance as she stood and holstered her pistol. "Seriously, I can't imagine anything better happening to you."

Aside from their handguns and carbines, no one carried any more than what they had on their backs.

Sybil taxied up to a black Suburban parked near a small, private hangar. "Everyone out," she said as she emerged from the cockpit, opened the exit door, and dropped the boarding ramp. "I'll arrange for fuel and our flight plan home and await orders."

Just past noon, they parked the Suburban three blocks south of the church. They walked the rest of the way silently.

"Everything is so quiet," Jessica said.

"It's a working day for most people," Allen replied.

They rounded a corner, and the white clapboard church came into view. The bell tower of the old church stood tall against the midday sun. Next to the church stood the bright yellow, single-story parsonage. A small, manicured lawn fronted the house with bright flowers along the sidewalk and driveway. Tall evergreen trees backed the parsonage and the church with the large gravel parking lot out front.

They grouped up next to a large oak tree. He pointed out the three minivans parked in the lot in front of the parsonage. Several tough-looking men stood next to each van with several more standing guard at the front edge of the parsonage's lawn.

Carson stood on the front step, a large pistol visible in his right hand. He appeared to be in a serious conversation with another man, who, when the man turned, Sam recognized as Cruz.

Sam chuckled. "I believe it's safe to approach. It looks like we missed the party."

The director grunted. "Parsons always did like to steal the limelight. Hasn't changed a bit."

Cruz stepped forward as Sam approached. "Amigo! It is so good to see you."

"And you as well," Sam replied. "Your trip went well?"

Cruz nodded. "Yes, and we made some new friends along the way." He waved a hand toward the three minivans. "The people you were concerned about will no longer be a problem for Paloma Blanca. The man named Parsons has learned that Paloma Blanca has many friends. There was a woman with him whom I recognize from her visits to Mexico over the past year. She also sits in the minivan. I believe she is someone important in this city as she tells my traveling companions again and again."

Cruz continued, "Although the woman and Parsons and I never met before this day, I do believe they were employed by some of my more misguided underlings to handle a few investments for me in this area. Since they threatened Paloma Blanca, I find I no longer require their services. It seems they have taken on other business partners, unbeknownst to me. It was a very unprofessional action on their part."

"Ah," Sam replied, placing one foot on the parsonage's front porch and folding his arms across his chest. "What exactly do you plan to do with Mr. Parsons and the woman?"

"There are certain implied conditions in our contract that require them to accompany me back to Mexico where we will discuss this matter further," Cruz replied.

At that moment, Connie stepped through the front door of the parsonage. As she met Sam's eyes, she smiled and silently mouthed the words, "I'm fine."

Cruz laid a hand on Sam's arm to draw back his attention. "One more thing, Mr. Empty."

Sam shrugged off the man's hand and stepped onto the porch. He wrapped his arms around Connie as she stood up on her toes to give him a warm, lingering kiss. After a long moment, she gently pushed Sam away and faced the Mexican cartel boss. "Señor Cruz, it has been a long time."

"Si, Señorita, it has been too long."

"And your family? They are well?" she asked.

"In very good health, thanks to your gracious assistance," Cruz replied.

A half-smile crept across her lips. "As I recall, you gave me little choice."

Sam cleared his throat softly. "Is there anything else?" he asked, drawing Cruz's attention back to their previous discussion.

Cruz raised a hand as if considering his next words carefully, then said, "I have some information you may be interested in. Tomorrow at about this time, a large cargo ship will dock in the Port of Olympia. Towed behind that ship, if one were to examine things closely, a person might identify a submersible vessel carrying approximately ten tons of interesting cargo."

"And in exchange for this information, you want what?" Sam asked, his tone droll.

"You see through me too easily," Cruz replied. "But yes, I was hoping for a quid pro quo. In return, perhaps you can visit me at my compound in Mexico soon. I would like to talk about the agreement you made with Don Estevez about this drugs-to-agriculture program. I have discussed it with my family, and we, like many of my peers, grow weary of the lives lost and the expensive legal battles and bribes that go with our current enterprise."

Sam glanced at the director, who stepped forward and said, "I think we can arrange that visit for you."

The director beckoned to Cruz. "Perhaps we can talk as we walk to your vehicle."

"I would be delighted," Cruz said as the two turned and headed away.

As they left, Sam got a glimpse of another person lingering in the shadows of the tall pine trees that flanked the left side of the parsonage's yard. With swift, smooth movements, the man faded deeper into the shadows. Sam bent close to Connie and whispered, "I think there's someone else here who you need to talk to."

"And exactly who would that be?" she asked.

Sam nodded to the shadows, waved a hand in that direction, and beckoned the man forward.

"Not him. Not again. I don't need—" Connie started, but Sam cut her off.

"We have confirmed it. That man is Fernando Zamora. He is your father."

"But it can't be. He's been dead for years. My mother—"

"Your mother has been keeping the secret for that long. He staged his death a long time ago to protect you and your family from the enemies he has fought for all those years. I think he wants to come in from the cold and back into your life."

"I don't know . . . " Connie started, but Fernando had already made it to where they stood, stopping on the grass a few steps from the porch.

Sam took Connie by the shoulders and turned her to face her father. "Maybe you two should talk. I haven't talked with my brother for over a decade, and I wish things were different. You shouldn't miss this opportunity to pick up your relationship when you have the chance."

Zamora took a step closer as Connie at first stood her ground, then melted as he took her by her shoulders and said, "Daughter."

The group watched as Cruz's three vans disappeared around a corner and into the distance. Sam glanced over to where Pastor Carson remained on the parsonage's front porch. Carson raised a hand and called across the yard, "I've got this covered. You all go take care of the rest of your business."

"I owe you," Sam replied.

"You owe me nothing, brother. God be with you in what you have yet to do."

CHAPTER 45

They checked into a nearby hotel an hour later, interrupting a receptionist who at first appeared less than pleased at someone disturbing her late lunch. As she reviewed their reservation for three of the hotel's large suites and noticed the tactical gear and weapons, she replaced her strained, put-out expression with a wide, white-toothed smile.

In short order, they were in their rooms—Allen and Sam in one suite, Jessica and Leah in another, and the director in a room by himself. All were geared up thirty minutes later and met in a small conference room the director had booked on the hotel's ground floor. As they entered the room, Sybil met them with several cases of ammunition and additional weapons. She remained dressed in the same olive-green tactical jumpsuit she'd worn on the flight from Florida, but with her perfect hair, bright eyes, and energy, somehow managed to look fresh while Sam and the team clung to their Styrofoam coffee cups.

"There's enough ammo and weapons here to refresh all your kits," Sybil said.

Leah yawned and set her coffee aside, pulled open the crates, and hefted several of the magazines. "Feels right," she said and popped a 7.76 round from one of the clips. She inspected the round. "This looks right, too."

"The director had me pull the load personally before we left," Sybil said. "He told me about the defective loads you and some of the other teams received for their missions and wanted it done by someone he trusts. I guess that's me. I'll be back at the plane if you need me."

"Good afternoon, I'm sure," Samuelson declared as he entered the room.

"There's nothing good about it," Jessica replied, uncharacteristically cynical in her tone. "It has been a long week and a long day, and we have a long way to go before we're done today. Let's take these people down and be done with this."

"My sentiments, exactly," the director replied. "Let's do the mission brief now so we can get into position early."

The director moved over to a whiteboard hanging on a conference room wall and pulled a marker from a pocket. As he talked, he listed the important points the team needed to know for the afternoon's mission.

"When I went off-grid, I did it because I was not sure whom I could trust. Working from my remote location and leveraging a back-channel virtual private network back into the group's systems, I dug into the issues facing us today without whoever-the-traitor-is-in-our-organization watching over my shoulder."

His words got several nods from the team.

"The second reason I went dark was to throw a joker into the hand of whomever was in charge for the opposition. Criminals like those we are up against tend to be paranoid. I'd hoped the wildcard I put into play by faking my abduction might stimulate some additional uncertainty, suggesting someone else might be on the field beside us and them and throw them off their game. I'm not sure how successful I was, but I do believe that the combined effect of your mission to Mexico and my faked abduction created enough uncertainty to force them to reveal their hand. I also believe they may be operating on a timeline that we've put at risk through our recent agreement with the Estevez cartel."

"You don't say that with a lot of certainties," Allen said.

"You all recall what I told you all about my meeting in D.C. with Deputy Secretary of State Emmerson and NSA Deputy Director Thorensen," Samuelson said.

"I know that woman from the NSA," Jessica said. "Ms. Prune-Face, herself. She keeps her operations so tightly closed to outsiders it is impossible to work with her group."

The director smiled grimly at Jessica's comment. "I think she affects a lot of people that way. But when I had a moment to review the information in the envelope Estevez provided Sam, I found multiple photos of the two of them, individually and together, meeting with and being entertained by Cruz and other known cartel leaders. The package also included copies of financial statements for Emmerson, Thorensen, and several other unnamed persons, showing large deposits in offshore bank accounts. If half of this is true, we will have enough to turn Emmerson and Thorensen over to the officials for a long list of crimes."

"Why don't you let me take a shot at those bank statements while we're talking?" Jessica asked, retrieving her laptop from a nearby table and flipping open the lid.

"You think you can gain access to their bank accounts?" Samuelson asked.

"Let's just say I have tools at my disposal that have been invaluable to our team," Jessica replied, not taking her eyes off her laptop's screen.

"For the present, I believe we should operate from the assumption that these people saw an opportunity to profit from our government's work with the cartels and took it," the director said. "We also must conclude that someone in our group has been helping them in several profound ways—sending some sort of drone into the capitol building to film and expose your actions and sabotage the faulty ammo loads for you and the other teams."

"What's the play today?" Sam asked.

"Jessica, you, and I will meet with them this afternoon at the warehouse," the director replied, glancing at his watch as he spoke. "I expect we'll find out who we're dealing with at that point and whether this is a trap or not. We have another two hours before the meet, so I want Allen and Leah to head for the warehouse now to set up our internal overwatch. Leah will take her sniper rifle and find a position high in the warehouse. Buildings of that kind generally have plenty of catwalks high in the rafters. Allen will find a spot on the ground in the shadows for direct interdiction should things go south."

"Just the five of us? That sounds a little light, sir," Allen said. "The opposition could show up with a dozen guns or more if they are working with the cartels."

"My thought, exactly, so I've called in a few favors in the area. There's no guarantee any of them will be there for us, so it may well be just the five of us against long odds. On the other hand, there are no other operators I trust."

"Eureka!" Jessica shouted, lifting her eyes from her laptop's screen as she pushed back long strands of night-black hair from her eyes. "I have it!" She held up the papers Samuelson had handed her. "I couldn't identify the owners of the accounts directly since they routed their deposits through a secure intermediary government system."

"From inside the NSA, no doubt," Samuelson added.

"You guessed it, boss. Every transaction was highly encrypted, but I still have the encryption algorithm you gave me for the research I was doing over the past week or so. I used that program to do a high-level scan of outgoing NSA message traffic, looking for atypical data streams. There were more than one, as you'd suspect with the NSA being in the intelligence business, but even those data streams tended to come from a handful of sources. When I excluded those data streams from my search, there were only two remaining message logs to consider. One originated from Deputy Director Thorensen's office computer. Working from her computer's address, I reversed my search and followed the data stream to their destinations in a variety of banks located offshore and in Mexico."

"You ID'd the banks?" Allen asked.

"Correct," Jessica replied. "Thorensen must have coded the tools into the NSA's system herself. Some of that message traffic had to be money from the cartels, originating from account files she'd hidden in the NSA's massive database. It is so big, anyone would have to be looking for the files specifically to find them. And who would suspect her?"

"We've still got a couple of hours before we leave for the meet. Do you think you can work with Homeland Security and get a handle on the funds in those accounts?" the director asked.

"I'm certain of it, if you have someone in mind for me to work with. Homeland is bound to have way more access to banking systems than I do," Jessica replied.

“I’ll text you the name and number for a person who will help you with that,” the director said, pulling out his cell phone and tapping in the information. “I’ll make a call to the Secretary of State and alert her to what you’ve found. She and the director of the NSA are tight, so I’m sure she’ll get someone into Thorensen’s office computer and her home right away. There’s one more piece of direction that I need you all to be sensitive to.”

CHAPTER 46

Sam and Jessica met the director at the Suburban at three p.m. in full tactical gear with sidearms and their M4A1s. Director Samuelson wore a two-piece suit, white shirt, and tie as if he was ready for a meeting on the hill in D.C.

Jessica drove. They exchanged no words as they mentally prepared for the afternoon's events. It was the director who finally broke the silence. "I could get used to this," he said. "Being chauffeured by you two."

"Don't get used to it," Jessica and Sam replied in unison.

Samuelson let out a loud laugh. "Do you guys know just how often the four of you do that, speaking in unison and finishing each other's sentences?"

Twenty minutes later, they arrived at the warehouse where the meet was scheduled. Jessica drove a circuitous route through a maze of warehouses several miles long and equally as wide, Sam checking for tail vehicles as she drove. Another twenty minutes of winding their way through the buildings left Sam satisfied they were not being followed. Jessica made their final approach to a huge warehouse that spanned the equivalent of three long city blocks. She pulled up to a long loading dock with a dozen tall garage doors running the length of the white and blue metal building.

The three exited the Suburban on tactical alert, carbines out and ready, Sam covering right and Jessica left, and Samuelson positioned between them. The silence of the area made the place feel abandoned, but Sam knew they could not let down their guard.

Mounting the steps to the loading dock, Sam located an access door for the building. It opened easily. He stepped in, eyes scanning the warehouse in all directions. Once his eyes adjusted to the dimmer light inside, he saw that the warehouse did appear to be in use. Pallets lifted stacks of boxes and equipment fifteen feet into the air on metal stands that ran the length of the warehouse.

Near the center of the building, they emerged into a broad, open space littered with silent forklifts and stacks of unused, flattened boxes. With the garage doors at their backs, Sam noticed a dark well of shadow on the opposite side of the area and heard two clicks from his cochlear implant.

"Romeo, two. I'm at your nine o'clock in the rafters," Leah whispered.

"Fox, two. I'm at your three o'clock, behind a pile of boxes in a pallet stand," Allen added. "The opposition arrived forty-five minutes ago and are positioned throughout the warehouse with two people located in those shadows across from your position."

They were there only a minute before they heard a voice from the shadows. "Glad you could make it, Director." Sam turned his gaze just enough to see Deputy Secretary of State Emmerson step into the light from the shadows on the opposite side of the central area. "We have a great deal to discuss."

Deputy NSA Director Thorensen also stepped from the shadows. Samuelson walked ahead, but Sam and Jessica remained in position, keeping their eyes on the long rows of shadowed pallet stands surrounding the area.

"I'm not sure we have anything to talk about," Samuelson said. "From what I can tell, you two are responsible for the death of a number of group operators. I'd be within my rights to take action here and now to end all this."

Emmerson smiled, although there was no humor in his expression. "You don't think we'd be that dumb, do you? We have people here with us, scattered throughout the building. That includes some of your own folks. We were not going to underestimate you or your beloved Home Team operators with you today. On the other hand, I'd hoped you and your people might be willing to discuss the situation rationally and perhaps come to an agreement, avoiding any nastiness."

Sam noticed a cruel smile moving across Deputy Director Thorensen's face as she listened to Emmerson. "Regardless of what you choose to do, in a few days, we will have completed all we need to do," she added. "We will retire from government service with no one the wiser. On the other hand, if you will be reasonable and we can reach an agreement, we are prepared to share a portion of the proceeds from our operations with you and your team. After that, for all I care, you and your people can go back to saving the world, and you will not hear from us again."

"About your money . . . " the director started. "Jessica?"

Jessica's carbine did not waver from its position, pointed down a long row of pallet stands as she replied, "We hacked into your computer, Thorensen. With a little help from some of our friends in Mexico, we identified your off-shore accounts. A couple of hours ago, we removed the funds in those accounts and transferred them to a Homeland

Security account set up for that sort of thing. You have no money in your accounts to share with us or anyone else."

Emmerson's face furrowed. "I don't believe you!"

"That's impossible," Thorensen demanded. "I set up that system myself. There's no way someone like you could crack it."

"Oh, but I did. Check for yourself," Jessica replied, the pleasant smile on her face belied by the cold steel in her eyes.

Thorensen pulled out a cell phone, tapped some keys, and let out a shriek as she raised her eyes from its screen. "The money is gone. All of it except what's in the local accounts. It is just as she said. I don't—"

Emmerson cut her off. "Let it go, Pamela. What's in the local accounts and what we receive tonight will be more than enough."

Emmerson took a step closer to Samuelson. "That was a lot of money to lose, and I applaud you for your initiative, but not all is lost. To think, you could have shared our profits, but now . . . "

He snapped his fingers, and Phil and Alpha Dog stepped from the shadows behind Emmerson and Thorensen. Both carried MP5 fully automatic machine guns. Four heavily armed men emerged from deeper in the warehouse, AKs and M16s at the ready. Sam glanced behind him at the sound of soft footfalls to see two men and a woman step around the tall pallet stands, equally well-armed, M16s leveled at him, Samuelson, and Jessica.

Three clicks sounded through Sam's cochlear implant, followed by three more—Leah and Allen letting him, Jessica, and Samuelson know they were aware of the situation and ready to respond.

"I always thought you two were a little pompous, a little full of yourself, Emmerson, but I never took you to be stupid," Samuelson said. "Do you think we would come unprepared for something like this?"

"You're bluffing," Emmerson replied. "I have people watching the outside the building, so I know you and your two operators are here alone. And since there is no reason to consider working with you, the only thing left is to get rid of you. And that will be a real pleasure."

Emmerson shifted his gaze toward Sam. "They call you Empty, right? You're the one who's afraid to use a gun. Well, in another few minutes the only thing that will be empty will be your lifeless body."

Sam returned the man's glare but remained stoic, feeling every muscle in his body relax as he eased his finger onto the trigger of his carbine.

Jessica—with her perfect posture and her hair pulled back from her deeply tanned face and fanning out through the back of her tactical baseball hat—seemed to grow an inch taller, but she otherwise remained silent.

Samuelson seemed not to change at all, standing casually between them, hands at his sides, eyes fixed on Emmerson. If there were any operator left in their aged director, Sam knew Samuelson could have his pistol out and into action in the blink of an eye.

Emmerson laughed, pulled out a small pistol, and aimed it directly at Samuelson. Thorensen took several steps back, raising the back of her hand to cover her mouth, eyes wide. "Do we really need to . . . " she began.

"We need to wrap this up and be on our way. We have somewhere important to be this evening," Deputy Secretary Emmerson said. "Dog, Phil, it's time you earn your pay. Kill them."

Alpha Dog and Phil stepped around Emmerson and faced the trio. Sam met Alpha Dog's smile. Sam shifted slightly, bringing the barrel of his carbine ever so slightly in their direction.

"Why are you doing this, Dog?" Sam asked.

"A fair question with a simple answer," Dog replied. "For the money. I pull an army chief warrant officer's pay as an operator. The pension from that won't cover the house payment for the sort of place I want. I need more, and when you all started those ridiculous missions with paintballs and rubber slugs, that sealed it for me. They offered; I accepted."

"You led your team into an ambush. Operators died," Sam continued.

"Honestly, I am a bit sad about that," Dog replied. "I liked those guys. We had some good times together. But in the end . . . " He shrugged. "They were just collateral damage."

Sam's gut tightened, his thoughts turning cold as he heard Jessica repeat the question to Phil. "What about you, Phil. Why you? You had so much promise."

Sam cut off Phil's response. "Phil wanted to move faster than the director would let him. He's jealous of the rest of us and saw the money and the leverage the situation would give him to raise his standing in the world."

"Exactly," Phil replied, shifting his MP5's barrel from Jessica toward the director. "Why should my talents be wasted in some moronic administrative duties or training program when I can use the skills I already have for my own profit?"

"Then we do, in fact, have nothing further to discuss," Samuelson said. "Home Team: status three."

Dog recognized the director's last words and reacted fast, dropping to the ground and yelling a warning to Phil and Emmerson. "Take cover! Sniper!"

Phil dove for the ground and landed atop his MP5 machine gun. He let go of the weapon and pulled his Glock, rolled onto his back, and snapped off several wild shots into the rafters.

Sam heard a soft, "Shoot!" over the cochlear mic. "Almost nailed me."

"Take out their backup," Sam said into his tactical watch as he lunged across the distance to where Emmerson now crouched. He lashed out with a powerful sidekick and connected with Emmerson's face. The deputy director teetered over backward.

Jessica dropped into a crouch, her carbine tight to her shoulder. She pivoted 180 degrees and sent three shots into the two men and the woman positioned behind them. Each shot landed center of mass, knocking all three down.

Sam dropped to the floor and snapped off two shots from his carbine at the two men to the right of where Emmerson now lay crumpled. His rounds took one man in the right shoulder and spun him around. He rattled off a half dozen shots on fully automatic as his hand spasmed from the pain. One of those shots ricocheted off the concrete floor and took Deputy Director Thorensen in the throat.

Two more muted gunshots sounded from Sam's right as Allen opened up with his carbine. A man to Sam's right slumped to the ground. A shot from the rafters took out the last of Emmerson's men.

"Hold your fire and drop your weapon, now!" Phil yelled from behind Sam.

Sam turned to find Phil with the barrel of his .9 mm pistol against the back of Jessica's head. A few feet to Phil's right, Dog held his pistol to Samuelson's head.

Alpha Dog said, "I'm surprised we weren't the first to be taken out by your team."

"You can thank me for that," Samuelson replied. "The team was ordered to take you alive if possible. We didn't exactly know who the traitors were, but we wanted you for questioning either way."

Sam heard a single click over his cochlear implant. Leah signaled that she did not have a clear shot at either Phil or Alpha Dog.

"The bottom line," Samuelson continued, "is that we wanted whomever the traitor or traitors were alive. Right now, I'm reconsidering that directive."

"Tell your people to stand down or we will kill you both right now. Am I clear?" Alpha Dog demanded.

Just then, Emmerson managed to sit up and grinned through the massive bruise spreading across his face from Sam's side kick. "Nice job," the deputy secretary of state said, spitting out a globule of blood. "We can still get out of this alive. I still have plenty of money stashed away in the local accounts if you can get me out of here alive."

Dog shot an angry glance at Emmerson. "Shut up, you moron! The money is the least of our worries right now. If we get out of this, they will be on our trail before you can blink."

"You," Dog said, pointing to Sam. "Drop the carbine. You, too, Fox and Cap."

Allen stepped out of the shadows as all three operators let their carbines drop to the ground.

Alpha Dog nodded toward where Jessica and Sam stood. "Unholster your sidearms and drop them and get Leah down from the rafters. I don't want to have to worry about her."

The director paused as he appeared to consider Dog's demand, then sighed deeply and said in a resigned voice, "All right. Leah, Allen, Sam, at the count of three, we drop them. I'll count, so Dog can watch, and we can avoid any casualties, but at three, we're on the ground. One, two, three!"

At the count of three, Jessica and the director dropped to the floor, their sudden move leaving Phil and Dog exposed.

Sam's hand flew to his Sig Saur .40 caliber pistol in his thigh holster. He drew it and, in one fluid motion, drew down on Alpha Dog. As Sam pulled the trigger, he saw Phil shift his aim, and then he felt the punch of a .9 mm slug slam into his right side.

Sam gasped as the shot barreled into his bulletproof vest directly over his broken ribs. The impact spun him to the right. His right leg folded beneath him as he spun around to face Phil. He watched as Phil dropped his pistol to where Jessica lay sprawled at his feet.

Sam's vision wavered as several more gun blasts echoed through the warehouse. Raising his Sig, he whispered, "Lord, guide me," and pulled off two rapid shots. The first exploded through Phil's right arm, causing him to drop the pistol. Sam's second shot took Phil low and on the right side. Phil shook once like a rag doll in the teeth of a dog, then slumped to the floor.

In that same instant, a suppressed round buzzed down from Leah's perch in the warehouse's rafters. The shot took Dog in the left temple, and he crumpled to the floor.

Seconds of total silence followed Leah's shot. Sam climbed to his feet and scanned the warehouse's interior. The only persons still moving beside themselves were Emmerson and Phil. The remainder of the warehouse's central area, so full of danger and threat only minutes earlier, now lay littered with corpses.

Samuelson climbed slowly to his feet, retrieved his .45 pistol, holstered it, and said, "I suppose that's it, then."

The director's words were cut off as two loud shots split the air. Sam spun toward the sound but stopped as he saw Emmerson jerk and go still.

"I heard that same gun at the capitol building, just as Connie and the kids showed up. It's distinctive. I never did figure out who . . . " Sam said.

A heavily accented Spanish voice sounded from the darkness between two tall rows of pallet stands at the edge of the open area. "There's no mystery in that, my friend." Connie's father stepped into the light, hands held high and a long-barreled .45 dangling from one index finger. "I am guilty on both accounts, then and now."

"Holster your weapon, you old dog," Samuelson said.

"Gracias," Zamora said. "I have been working on a drug smuggling case of great significance for a very long time. For some time, I suspected someone like your government's Deputy Secretary of State must be at the heart of it all. I believe you have confirmed my suspicion. It is good to know he is no longer a problem for your country or mine."

Zamora walked over to the deputy secretary's corpse, toed it onto one side with a highly polished shoe, and revealed a short-barreled .38 pistol in the man's hand. "I believe he was about to shoot Director Samuelson when I fired."

Sam glanced at the director, who wore a grim smile. "You do know you are supposed to be dead, Fernando. I saw the file, myself."

The corner of the old spy's thin-lipped mouth quirked up at one corner. "You know what they say about death announcements being exaggerated. I have been undercover for so very long."

The director and Zamora clasped hands. "This man saved my life one time when it was him I was hunting," the director said. "We could tell some stories, couldn't we, you old dog?"

"Yes, we could," the old spy replied.

Everyone turned as a shout echoed throughout the warehouse. "Police! Lay down your weapons!"

A dozen heavily armed SWAT members entered in their signature black coveralls, walking crouched in tight formation. It did not help that Leah found that moment to descend from the building's rafters, carrying a sniper rifle nearly as tall as she was.

Samuelson called over the team sergeant, whispered a few words, and showed him a credentials folder he produced from the pocket of his suit jacket. The sergeant called out a command, and his team lowered their weapons.

Sam stepped over to where Phil lay. He pulled a gauze pad from a first aid kit in his tactical pants' pocket, tore off the plastic cover, and pressed it against the entry and exit wounds on Phil's side. "We need a medic over here!" he called.

Phil blinked several times, grimacing as he forced his words. "Everyone said you wouldn't shoot."

Sam felt something akin to sadness overtaking him as he gazed at Phil's face. "Everyone was wrong. I've never been afraid to use a gun, Phil. It's just that sometimes there are other ways to do things."

"At least you missed," Phil added with a painful half-chuckle. "If you were any good with that Sig of yours, I'd be dead now."

The medic cut off Phil's shirt to better reveal the arm and side wounds. "I've seen a lot of wounds in my day, and I'd say you got shot exactly where this man intended to shoot you. You are alive because of this man's skill with a gun."

The medic wrapped a long elastic bandage around Phil's torso to hold the gauze pads in place and gave it a tug that might have been a little harder than necessary.

Phil winced and said, "You should have killed me."

"We need your testimony. And if you're willing to stand up and accept the consequences, even you can find redemption," Sam responded.

A moment later, all attention shifted to the State Patrol's chief as he stepped into the area. The tall dark law enforcement commander reached out a huge hand that engulfed the director's small paw. "Good to see you, Trick Shot," the chief said.

"Good to see you, too, Chief. It's been a long time," Samuelson replied.

"Ranger school was a lifetime ago," the chief replied. "And it looks like you didn't need our help after all."

Sam turned to Allen. "This is starting to feel like old-home week. First, the director knows Zamora and now the chief . . . "

The chief turned at the sound of Sam's voice. "You, again. Seems like wherever you go, bullets fly."

After glancing at his watch, the chief turned back to Samuelson. "I have a meeting with the governor in twenty minutes. Maybe we can catch up later and you can tell me all about this."

Samuelson replied, "Yes to getting together, but I'm afraid it's no to explaining everything. It's all highly classified. I would appreciate your help in getting the wounded man into custody."

"Always the spook," the chief said, shaking his head. "And the charges you want him held under?"

"Take your pick," Samuelson replied. "Treason, for starters. Assaulting a federal agent."

"Treason?" the chief asked.

Samuelson nodded. "We'll handle that end of things once we take custody. I'll have a team here shortly to help with the bodies."

"Nothing ever changes, does it, Trick Shot?"

"Not in any way that I can see," Samuelson replied.

Samuelson turned back to the Home Team members. "Time for us to leave."

They all nodded, except for Leah. "Trick Shot?" she asked.

Samuelson groaned. "Back in the day, my call sign was Tango Sierra. I made a ridiculous bet on a shot at twelve hundred meters one time that involved the chief and an apple on his head. I won the money and the nickname stuck."

"You were a sniper, too?" Leah asked.

Sam clapped Leah on the shoulder before she could drag the conversation out further. "Let's get out of here. I'm sure that there is someplace we'd all rather be about now."

Jessica grinned at Sam. "And someone you'd rather be with."

EPILOGUE

After cleaning and securing weapons and showering and changing clothes, the director and the Home Team gathered in the front of the hotel where Sybil met them for the ride to Tugboat Annie's.

When they arrived, one of the servers waved them to a corner table under wide windows overlooking Puget Sound. Evening approached, and house and boat lights across the inlet winked in the distance. Sam noticed both Pastor Carson and Connie already seated. Sam sat beside Connie as the others took their seats around the table.

"What we have to talk about impacts you all," the director started. "One housekeeping matter before I get to the reason I invited you. You recall the videos taken of the Home Team handling the situation at the capitol building in Olympia and broadcast across regional media. Earnie in Logistics confirmed Phil had four of our new mosquito drones delivered to his associates in D.C., who in turn had them delivered to Wayne Parsons in Olympia. It was Parsons who launched them at the capitol, recorded the video, and provided it to the media to expose the group's undercover operatives and negate our effectiveness."

"Here, here," Allen replied.

Samuelson continued. "Home Team has come through for us numerous times over the past few weeks. We now have two drug lords in Mexico who have agreed to convert their narcotic fields to legitimate agricultural enterprises. This bodes well for the State

Department's Drugs-to-Ag program. The Secretary sends her sincere thanks. She has asked that Home Team spearhead the program's expansion into other areas."

Sam felt his heart sink. It wasn't until that moment that it dawned on him that he might have to leave the area and Connie when his business in Olympia was concluded.

Connie sensed his mood and squeezed his hand under the table. He met her eyes and saw the same sadness.

"Sir," Sam started. "About all that. I can't go back. I want to stay here in Olympia. I've found a home here, a relationship that's important to me, and my faith."

The director raised both of his hands. "I think I can help with all of this. I have been authorized to take several actions to move the Drug-to-Ag program forward into the Pacific Rim area and the rest of the Western Hemisphere. The first is to relocate Home Team's base of operations to the Joint Base Lewis McCord, located just north of Olympia. This will provide an excellent stepping-off point for access to the Pacific Rim areas, as well as keep us within striking distance of Mexico and Central and South America. It will also allow Sam to remain in Olympia if he is willing to remain on the team and the rest of you are willing to relocate to the Northwest."

Sam felt an involuntary smile creep across his face.

Leah was the first to break through Sam's thoughts. "I've got nothing holding me in Florida. I'm in."

Jessica chimed in on Leah's heels. "Me, too. The eastern seaboard has no hold on me. It's about time I saw some new country."

The two women directed two intense stares at Allen. "Okay, fine," he said.

Director Samuelson directed his gaze at Connie. Sam knew that look. Difficult news was coming. "I have one more piece of this puzzle to put into place, and it involves you, Ms. Zamora."

"Me?" Connie asked.

"Connie, the Secretary wants you to become a part of our program. We have contacted your previous employer about the prospect of establishing, equipping, and staffing permanent medical clinics in each of the converted cartel areas included in the Drugs-to-Ag program."

"That's a nice-sounding program, but I have my new job here at the community center!" Connie said.

"No one at the State Department feels that the medical clinic initiative will be a fulltime engagement, so in exchange for your commitment to head that portion of the program, a grant has been authorized to expand the community center's medical clinic and integrate it with the City of Olympia's homeless remediation program."

Sam watched the expression on Connie's face shift to wonder. "I will call the shots on each piece of this? No political interference, no politicians grandstanding, or tactical missions that might jeopardize my efforts at the clinics?"

"You will enjoy relative autonomy."

Sam slipped an arm around Connie's shoulders and hugged her close. "What do you say?" he asked. "We could work together."

Connie nodded and slipped her arm around his waist, hugging him back. "What can I say? I'm in!"

Sam ended the meeting with a toast. "To the One Who carries us through. May we all be worthy of His love and direction."

COMING SOON . . .

HOME TEAM 2

Washington State Trooper Ellen Evander is a woman on a mission. Five years ago, her niece was kidnapped by human traffickers. Now Officer Evander's primary mission is to thwart a human trafficking network, even if she must attempt it single-handedly. However, without back-up, Evander finds herself in need of rescue. Enter Alex Anthem, an Army Ranger with his own mission, and the Home Team, a group of covert operatives under the jurisdiction of the U.S. government.

Together, the Home Team battles the insidious human trafficking ring, and Evander is pushed to the limits of her personal, military, and law enforcement training.

Will the Home Team's unrelenting faith in God and dedication to a righteous cause allow them to prevail against a dangerous ring of criminals?

For more information about
Dave Pratt
and
The Home Team
please visit:

www.daveprattbooks.com
www.facebook.com/DavidPrattBooks

When a prominent city official dies in a car wreck, Scott and Angela find themselves tangled in intrigue and deception. Together they search for the truth and discover that not all is what it seems.

Charlotte Hallaway needs to come to terms with her father's death. He had been her only family, and she wasn't handling her grief well. It was just supposed to be a few weeks of peace and quiet to process it all, but then she saw them—a drug deal and a murder within seconds of each other. And they saw her. Now running for her life, Charlotte boards a bus to escape her pursuers and wakes up the next morning in the woods without a memory of how she got there or of who she is.

After two and a half years of deep depression, anger at God, and guilt over the death of her husband and twin girls, all bestselling romance writer Jessica Lynn Morgan wants is to buy a house, get back to writing, and live out her life alone in peace, but once she moves in, the threat against her life becomes real. Clearly, someone or something wants her out. Now. Will her stubbornness cost Jessica her life?